The Long Way Home

Tara Brown

THANKS SO MUCH ANDREA BURNS FOR EVERYTHING.
THANK YOU, COVER ME DARLING FOR THE GREAT
COVER. IT'S EXACTLY HOW I IMAGINE THE ROAD TRIP!

This is my first hockey romance.
Hope you like it, thanks for picking it up.

Sunday

June, 2012

His hand slid down my back as we listened to the speech from the headmistress. I swallowed slowly, keeping my look calm.

"I meant what I said last week about me and you," Frank whispered into my ear. The room erupted in applause as the speech ended with a toast. I maintained my smile, clapping and looking supportive of the proposed playground being installed at the local elementary school. Honestly, it was a waste of funding, but I didn't have children yet so I wasn't allowed an opinion. Being on the committee for the school my unborn children would attend was dry as hell, but it was what women in my circle did.

Frank chuckled. "Only a few more weeks, and you'll be married and having kids. Then it'll be you whispering into my ear."

I laughed and took the chance to step away from him, hoping no one had noticed his advances on me, not that I was the only one he would have hit on that afternoon. I was certain he had worked the room at least twice already. The problem with being part of the committee was that I had to remain amiable or he wouldn't donate to the school. His kids had long since left it so he had no immediate reason to help out.

The room was filled with prying eyes and sneaky whispers of course, as we were amongst our closest friends and neighbors. I finally started breathing as I made it away from Frank and his octopus hands. I stepped up to the bar, glancing around for my fiancé, Phil. He hadn't brought me a fresh drink. I'd waited for ten minutes, but he never came back. I couldn't see him anywhere. In the sea of well-dressed people, he blended perfectly.

The young bartender smiled at me. "White wine?"

"No." I shook my head. "I had red."

"Really?" He brought the bottle over. "You look like more of a white wine girl to me, than a red."

"Do I? What makes you think that?"

His eyes roamed my face in a way that I could almost feel, as if they were his hands lightly brushing each spot he gazed at. He licked his lips and nodded. "Pink full lips, fresh makeup—not overdone, slight curl to your hair but the frizz is in total control. You're put together enough that I'd say you're organized and maybe a slight ball buster. Red wine drinkers are artistic, messy, and free. You look too confined in your life."

I met his blue eyes with a hard look. "Do you always sweet-talk the ladies this way?"

He leaned across the bar, speaking softly, "I have a sneaky suspicion that you may not qualify for that classification."

My lips lifted into a grin. "I like honesty in a stranger." I also liked the way his black dress shirt fit his body. He looked fit. In my early twenties, he would have been the exact sort of person I would have snuck off with. I missed that carefree time in my past even more when he gave me a cocky grin with dimples and muttered, "I know you'll like me. I get off in two hours, then we can see about getting you off."

I winked, hoping it covered up the blush spreading everywhere. "If I happen back this way for a napkin, you be sure to have a number on it." It was a joke. I had no intention of taking his number. But I did like the way he looked at me and talked dirty to me.

I turned, scanning the room for my next stop. I smiled at Frank, giving me a death glare from across the room. I walked back over to him, feeling recharged and safe from his advances. I stayed at a careful distance from him as I spoke softly, "Did you speak to the school to see what type of donations they're looking for this year? I know it's not just money."

He leaned against the wall, clutching his drink. "You never answered me about not returning my call last week. I was serious about what I offered you a week ago."

I scoffed. "I never returned it because I wasn't interested in what you had to offer. I'm still not. So don't touch me or hit on me. I'm not like that. Phil and I are happy." I hated forcing sentences. I sipped my wine and nodded. "But be sure to find out about the donations."

He shook his head, laughing. "You like acting like a hard bitch, but I bet you enjoy being told what to do."

I leaned in. "Only in the bedroom and only in a certain bedroom. I am a nearly married woman for God's sake. Keep it in your pants." I rested a hand on his forearm, in the exact spot a lady should, and squeezed. "It was nice seeing you, Frank. Say hello to Ruth for me."

He sipped his drink, still chuckling. "Of course. You know she hates you."

I shrugged. "What can I do? Tell her to wait; Phil and I are planning on kids next year after the wedding. By then I'll be needing plastic surgery and extra elastic in my undergarments as well."

"Ha!" His face split into a smile. "I think you'll always be one of those naturally beautiful women, even with a few extra pounds. When you get tired of the kids and Phil, you know my number."

I narrowed my gaze. "Ohhhh, Frank. That was a good one. I may call you this week, after all."

"Right." He scoffed. "I won't hold my breath."

"But you will open your checkbook."

He nodded. "Yes, ma'am."

"There's a good man."

I turned and walked to the group of ladies gossiping in the corner. Angela gave me a sly grin. "Flirting with Frank for donations is almost prostitution. You know that, right? You are working the room hard, considering you don't have any kids yet."

I sipped my wine. "I'd sell my soul to beat Doreen out in donations and investors. She is such a bitch. Besides, we need to keep the loyal investors we have."

Diane winked. "Pretty sure none of them want a hot piece of soul."

"Well, I'd sell that too for the right price."

Helena laughed. "Oh, me too. Lord, at least then I'd be getting some."

We chuckled amongst our group. We were best friends. I didn't trust a single one, but I loved them more than anything. It was the world we lived in.

Diane looked around. "Where is your sister? She should be here. She and Shawn must be ready to start having kids."

"Brandi bailed on this at the last minute. Said she was doing something with Shawn's parents."

Helena gave me a sarcastic smile. "Lucky bitch. Hey, did you girls hear about Rebecca Solez?"

I gave Helena a confused look. "That Rebecca girl we graduated with?" I didn't want to think back that far. We were getting close to ten years. It made me cringe.

She nodded, giving us all a grievous look. "She's pregnant."

"Oh, good for her."

Helena shook her head, and I could tell by Diane's face it was bad news. "Why?"

"Mark is sterile. Has been since eleventh grade."

"What?" My jaw dropped. "Oh wow. Well then," I held my wine glass in the air, "good for her."

We all laughed.

My eyes finally caught a glimpse of Phil. I hadn't noticed he was in the corner talking to someone. I frowned and looked to the side, but I couldn't see any better. I lifted my head to try to get a better look. It was Eleanor Grey— Eleanor who had slept with my neighbor Daniel the summer before. She beamed at Phil and nodded like the idiot she was. She smiled and sipped her drink, not stepping back from his close conversation. A stabbing feeling like from a knife twisted in my stomach as he leaned in too close and laid his hand on her waist. Whatever he was saying made her blush like a schoolgirl. She nodded and grabbed his hand, pulling him to the far side of the room and out the door.

Helena followed my stare. I saw the disapproval on her face. She looked back at me, but I averted my gaze. I didn't need her sympathy or want to confirm that I too suspected something wasn't right there.

I glanced over at the bartender, but forced my gaze away. It was the wrong choice. I didn't even know if Phil was doing anything, not for sure.

Mentally slapping myself I pondered. *Where else would they be going, holding hands?* Of course they were sneaking off to one of the back rooms at the country club.

My throat was burning. "I need the ladies' room." I passed my wine to Angela. She nodded. I knew she'd seen it too. They all did. We always saw everything, but it wasn't usually one of our own husbands or fiancés. I was the last to be married. I had held out the longest.

I fought the urge to run from the room, forcing myself to walk at a controlled pace. I was fully shaking when I got to the bathroom. Leaning against the counter and fumbling with my clutch, I almost cried when I finally got the snap open. The little blue pill felt massive in my fingers. I hated needing it, but I hated the sweat and nerves that came from my panic attacks. I had been taking them more and more lately. My father's doctor had recommended I up my dosage to deal with the stress, with it being so close to my wedding.

I slipped it between my lips, closing my eyes. I couldn't watch myself slip away in the mirror. I hated what taking the pill did to me. What it looked like.

I opened my eyes as it trailed its way down my esophagus. My strawberry-blonde hair was still glossy and in its place. Everything was perfect. My peachy skin tone looked flawless. At least now I didn't look like he had made me red and embarrassed.

I ran my hands over my cheeks and nodded. The pill would hit any second, and I would be fine. My heart was racing. It wasn't the first time I had suspected him of something, but it was the first time he had thrown it in my face.

When my heart had slowed, I walked from the bathroom and rejoined my group. Angela handed my wine back to me. Phil was gone from the corner he had been hiding in. My eyes naturally roamed the room, looking for him. He was gone. Oh God. He was gone. He was in a deserted room of the old mansion, doing Eleanor. I took a deep breath and waited for the pill to hit.

My husband-to-be was having sex with a friend in the same house I was in.

I had given up everything for him. He was the man in the family we were creating. Our families had traditions that I hated, but I accepted them and followed them. I didn't work, I didn't cook or clean, and I never missed a spa appointment or a gym class. I was my mother, only younger and less botoxed. It was a destination, I had never imagined arriving at.

I didn't know where the free-spirited girl I'd been had gone, but at some point I had become the girl my family expected me to be.

Angela's laugh brought me back around. She shook her head. "Oh God, remember that summer we all swore we would go to Europe together? That trip sounded like such fun. We should do it when the kids are older." Her unintentionally cruel comment hit at just the wrong moment.

Helena twisted the already painful knife in my gut. "I know. I miss us the way we were. We really should do a girls' weekend before you and Phil get married and pregnant. You don't want to go pregnant."

I glanced at the bartender and wondered if I could make my joke with him not be a joke. He would make me young and reckless. He would be like the pill and make all the bad feelings go away. If Phil could do it, so could I. *Couldn't I?*

No. I couldn't. Probably not, anyway.

Diane nodded. "Yeah well, I'm down for whenever and whatever you all are. I need some time away from home. I'm going nuts." She grabbed my hand, and I saw desperation hiding in her gaze. "Don't have kids. I swear, they're such a pain in the ass, and they suck every ounce of energy from you and your breasts."

I laughed, letting it be a joke. "Your breasts are beautiful."

"Right." She cocked an eyebrow. "Twenty thousand later."

"Oh." I snorted, spilling some of my wine. I wiped my lip with my fingers. "I never would have guessed. You look beautiful. Do you guys have a napkin?"

They looked around amongst them. I blushed. "Be right back. I can't believe it's only four in the afternoon, and I've got a hole in my lip already." I rolled my eyes and sauntered over to the bar. "Can I get a bit of help, please?" The pill was hitting.

The bartender grinned and ran his hands through his sandy hair. "Sure thing."

"Not that kind. That one was a joke. I need a napkin to wipe up."

"You bet." He passed me a stack. His number was at the top. "Just in case you change your mind."

"Thanks." I laughed bitterly, fighting the urge to cry. I glanced back, noticing Phil standing outside on the balcony with Eleanor. The sides of their bodies were pressed against each other, too close for a casual stance on a deck with a friend. The huge planter next to them didn't hide them well enough for what they were doing.

My heart slipped out of my chest and landed in my stomach with a thud. I nodded and folded it over. "Two hours?"

"You're in trouble."

"I certainly hope so." I wiped my lip and walked back to my group of friends, stuffing the napkin into my clutch.

Angela nodded. "That young, little fresh piece of meat is looking at your ass."

"Is he?" I glanced back, scowling at the young man. "He's like ten years old."

"He's twenty something. We're only a few years older than him. I'd do him in a heartbeat, and you aren't married yet. And it's half your age plus seven—you're good."

I looked at Helena and giggled. "He is a cutie, but likely not experienced enough."

She gave me a look. "Who gives a shit? You should see if he needs help cleaning up the bar later. You know, volunteer work."

"I'm not like that."

She nodded, knowing what I meant. It was true, I wasn't. I had never strayed from our engagement. Once I had agreed, the other way of life ended. I wasn't ever unfaithful. I flirted and joked and played the game, but I had a thing about being touched by other people. It stemmed from childhood. I had never liked being touched by people I didn't know. The fact I had told him two hours was giving me more anxiety than Phil screwing around.

"I know you're not. But that is a fine young man, JD."

"He's jailbait." I pushed it all away. "Anyway, what are your plans for the summer?"

Helena sighed. "Richard has a huge land deal going through, so I am taking the kids to the South of France and staying with my mother. She doesn't want to do it alone, what with it being the first summer with Dad gone."

I sipped slowly, blinking even slower, starting to feel the pill taking away more of my inhibitions. "Of course. I still can't believe he just left, after forty years together."

She rolled her eyes. "He'd been gone the whole time."

I nodded, wondering how long Phil had been gone. Maybe from the start. "The South of France sounds like fun."

"I'll have all three kids. It sounds more like Richard's going to have a summer similar to my dad's."

"No." I focused hard and met her eyes. "Not Richard."

Her eyes widened for a second and I saw it. She knew something. "You just never know people." I didn't have a response. We had never been that open with each other. We suffered in silence or made jokes, but we never flat out said what we knew.

Diane poked her head into the conversation that had turned into whispers. "Did you see Muriel Lawson? She's tanked."

"No." I glanced over at the older woman. Her wrap dress had started to come apart a bit. Her black slip was showing. I handed my wine to Helena. "Oh dear." I walked over, trying not to look intoxicated or draw attention to either of us.

Her face lit up when she saw me. "JD! How are you?"

"Hi." I wrapped my arms around the drunken woman and steered her to the bathroom. "I'm excellent, Muriel. How are you?"

"Oh, uhm." She swallowed hard as she walked, staggering us both. "I am well also, thank you, dear. How is Philip?"

I hated him in that moment. "He is the same. How is Donald?"

"He is a shit, Jacqueline. A shit! I threw him out last week. I'm done being Mrs. Donald Lawson. It's time to just be Muriel."

"Oh dear. I'm so sorry." I laughed and pushed the door to the bathroom open. "And how is that going for you?"

"Not well." She shook her head, pointing at me with a swaying body as I retied her dress for her. "Don't end up like me. The men here are all the same, and I know you don't want to marry Phil. I know that."

"Yes, well, Father got into the good country clubs, you know?"

"Yes." She nodded. "I know. I approved their application solely based on the fact that Henry Bernard told me to."

I straightened her dress and nodded. "There, all better." I didn't want to talk about my family selling me into marriage to get into the most exclusive cliques on the East Coast. It was more common than people realized. Old money had the connections, but the new money had the fortunes. My parents now had both.

She shook her head. "I think I'm going to be sick."

"Oh no, Muriel." I frowned. I had never seen her that way. She was the lady of the old money. I shook my head. "Let's get you home."

I sat her in a stall and slipped from the bathroom. One of the caterers walked up with a tray of used glasses. I grabbed her arm. "Do you have a car here?"

She nodded.

"If I give you a thousand dollars, will you do something for me and tell no one?"

"Sure." She looked confused. "I guess."

"That bathroom has a woman who is so drunk. She's about to throw up. I need you to get her to her house without anyone seeing her leave. Is that possible?"

She smiled. "Oh man, I thought you were going to ask me to do something really nasty."

"It might get there."

I went back into the bathroom and got Muriel cleaned up. The girl took her out the back door.

As soon as I was alone, I leaned against the wall, taking a deep breath. Philip came around the corner, giving me an odd look. "What are you doing back here? I was looking for you." I could see the look of too much whiskey on his face. It was relaxed and cocky. I used to find it attractive. That had always been the only consolation—he was attractive. Unfortunately for him that was fading away rapidly.

I raised my eyebrows. "Nothing."

He stepped too close to me. "You ready to go home?"

"Sure am."

He ran his finger down my bare arm. "You look nicer than normal. Did you do something different with your hair?"

"I did." Of course I didn't. Did he even know me anymore?

He pointed to the door into the party. "So we'll go then?"

I nodded and let him put his hand on the small of my back, leading me back into the party. I nodded at Angela and Helena. They both wore the same glass face, frozen in fake happiness. What a world we lived in.

Philip walked me out. Our driver was there within seconds, getting the door for me.

I climbed in and looked at the back of the front seat, not making eye contact with Phil as he got in the car. He took my hand in his, kissing the back of it. I almost grimaced, imagining where his lips had been. Had he kissed her? Had he made an arrangement to? Or had he just fucked her in a broom closet somewhere?

There were two types of silence I didn't like to be caught in. The first was the empty air between two people, where one was guilty and the other was aware of the situation.

That air tricked you into believing it was empty, and yet its weight was too great for one person to bear. It was heavy with the guilt and the worry of one person, and loaded with the suspicions and self-doubt of the other.

That was the type of air that filled the car we were in. It stole my heartbeat from me. I had no control over the thoughts or feelings weighing me down. I was stuck in the suspicion and self-doubt and the lingering effect of my antianxiety meds.

There were several sentences that could break that silence, but each one would be its own admission of guilt and betrayal. If he did talk, the darting eyes and telephone voice that was overly friendly would be the first indicators. Whether together or separate, we were not overly friendly people. We were flawed in all the right ways, but we were together because we shared the same cause. His family needed more fortune and mine needed old-money connection. We were both attractive and devoted to our families. We were perfectly matched in our flawed ways.

But there in the car, I sensed that a great crime had been committed, and the stains of the death of our relationship marred his hands.

I wanted to be innocent in it all.

I wanted that, more than anything.

I wanted to wallow in the classiness of a woman scorned and martyred within her own home.

But I would not be innocent. I would just not be caught doing the thing that I was now certain he was doing.

When we got home, I sat on my bed staring at the napkin. The number made me feel worse. I had taken someone's number with the intention of calling and screwing his brains out. I wanted to be the girl I was before I had conformed to the life I was stuck in. I took a breath and dialed my mother's number.

"Hello," she answered with her singsong voice.

"Mom, it's me."

"Darling, how are you?" She had grown more like the old-money families.

"Not good." I swallowed. "I think he's having an affair."

She didn't miss a beat. "Sweetie, that is wedding nerves. Don't be fooled. Philip loves you. He proposed long before your father and his made any arrangements."

"I can't marry him."

She chuckled. "Nonsense. You will, and you will correct whatever you've done to make him stray. Stop taking your pills and get pregnant before he too starts to doubt this. Come for tea tomorrow."

I felt numb. I nodded. "Okay."

"Bye, dear." She hung up, not solving my problem at all but complicating it intensely.

When Phil walked into the room, I sat back on the bed, tucking the napkin under my pillow.

"You all right?" he asked.

"Yeah." I nodded, thinking about what my mother had said. "Just tired." I looked up. "I was thinking, why wait the year to get pregnant? Let's do it now. Our wedding is in two weeks. No one will even know." A baby would make him stop cheating. I didn't believe it, but I whispered it.

His face tensed. "JD, we both agreed. People who have kids in the first five years always strain their relationship. We've been together for three years. In a year if you get pregnant, it'll be five years when the baby is born. Let's just have fun with this for a year, before we complicate it with kids."

Complicate it? That's how he saw us making a family? Why were we getting married? He was never going to stop cheating.

"Phil"—my insides twisted—"why did you spend the entire party with Eleanor?"

"What?" His eyes twitched and avoided mine. "She has got some money she needs invested and wanted some advice."

I watched him not look me in the eyes and felt like I would vomit. "I see."

"Why?" He frowned. "What's that tone for? Am I being accused of something?"

"Nope."

"Are you mad?"

"I'm fine."

He smiled and dropped to his knees in front of me. "Fine is the worst reply, ever." He lifted my face up to his. "JD, I love you."

"Okay." I nodded.

He frowned. "It wasn't anything, I swear. It was just some investments."

"Are you attracted to her?" I had no fury, anger, or pain. I was numb from the pill.

"No. It's not like that." He leaned in, kissing my nose. "I love you." His dark hair, cool-blue eyes, and handsome face had tricked me hundreds of times, but the little blue pill prevented me from buying it that time. I could see him clear as daylight for what he was. Guilt was smeared across his face.

And as far as I was concerned, two could play at that game. I kissed his lips softly. "I have to go out."

He stood between my legs, pushing me back onto the bed. He kissed my neck, but I reached under the pillow, clutched the napkin, and shoved him off. "I can't. I have to go see if Muriel is all right."

"Okay. I'll see you in a couple of hours."

"Yup." I looked back at him, hating the version of him that I was stuck with in my mind. How did my mom and everyone else just look the other way?

I got into the car and drove from the house. I dialed the number on the napkin and hung up right away. I took a deep breath and dialed a different number instead.

"Yeah?"

I swallowed. "Hi, Mike. It's me."

There was silence for a second. "Jack?"

"Yeah."

"You okay?"

"No," I whispered almost silently.

"I can't hear you. You okay?"

"Yup." Tears formed in my eyes, regardless of the fact I felt nothing. "I mean, I'm fine. I just wanted to see what was new with you." I pulled the car over to the side of the road next to a large home. My hand was shaking as I held the phone.

"Not much. I'm hungover as fuck. We came in second in the playoffs a couple of nights ago. I know that's almost like speaking Greek to you, but in hockey lingo that's good, babe. Second place is pretty good."

"Thanks." I smiled. "I know that, asshole. I sent the case of champagne. Didn't you get it? I even handwrote the note congratulating you for being the first loser."

"Oh shit, I did. Sorry, we've been drunk for days."

"I can tell. You have that whiskey-burnt voice." I closed my eyes and missed everything about him.

He yawned. "I haven't seen you in a while. Wanna come over? I can show you the pics and shit from the games."

I shook my head again. "No. I'm busy. I just missed your voice. Is that okay?"

He snickered. "Yeah, of course. Why are you being weird? Come over. I'm home for the day, and then I'm heading to the beach house for a few nights. We're having a massive end-of-year party. If you don't come over, I'm going to abduct you and drag you to the beach house. Me and Phil can fight over you in the front yard."

I snorted. "Be there in ten." I loved the fact that he played NHL hockey. He was so chill and easygoing and still the same person he had been a million years before, when we met in school. I smiled, remembering the face of the scholarship kid who everyone sneered at until they saw him play. Then he was a god.

To me he was just always France. He was never The Mike France, lead scorer for the New York Rangers. The money never changed him the way it did other people.

I put the car back in drive and sped to his place. I sat in the driveway, looking at his modest house. He was funny with his houses. He had bought the one I was in front of because it was homey and reminded him of the house his mom bought when he was a teenager.

Mike opened the front door and pointed at me. "Get out of the car."

I nodded and got out. I knew he could see the stress and worry on my face. He stopped mid step. "What's wrong?"

"What?" I shook my head, climbing the stairs alongside the driveway. "Nothing."

He gave me a look of disbelief. "You're such a bad liar."

"You think so?"

He folded his arms over his chest. "I know so. I've played strip poker with you. You have too many tells to count, which is why I always win strip poker. The way you're bending your left thumbnail is one, the way your lips are white all around the edges because you're pinching them together is another. That one causes wrinkles too." He took a step toward me. "The main one though is that haunted look in your eyes."

"That's the wine and Xanax."

He gave me a look. "Why are you taking that shit?"

"Sometimes I just need to." I pointed at him. "This was a mistake. I better go." I backed up a step, but he was too fast.

"Wait." He lunged and grabbed my hand, pulling me into him. "Tell me what's going on."

"Sometimes I just miss you," I whispered into his huge chest. The feel of his cotton tee shirt was like a blanky I had cherished as a kid. He was my soother.

He wrapped around me. "Stay calm, crazy—no more weird pills. I'll order pizza and we'll chill, okay?"

"I can't." I struggled from his grip and backed up another step. "I need someone to touch me, and it can't be you."

His dark eyes narrowed. "I offer every chance I get. Stay."

I hurried back down and opened the car door with him hot on my heels. "No. I love you. It would hurt us both too much."

He stepped close to me again, spinning and pinning my back against the car. "Stay." His dark eyes were like tools a hypnotist would use. They sucked me in with their thick lashes and intensity.

"I shouldn't stay."

He bent his face close to mine. "Let me be the one who touches you. Please don't let someone else touch you."

The second type of silence I hated to be caught in was the tense awkwardness of longing. The stolen glances at one another's lips and eyes as the act was played out in the minds of both parties. They'd lean into one another, but neither moved the last ten percent, and the air was filled with all the things neither would say. The guilt of the act was already a thing. It had energy and consequences without the actual crime being committed. A forbidden kiss and the desire one built within it, created expectations that could never be met. There was no kiss that was as great as the one you could never have.

We were stuck there, leaning against my car, unable to take that last step closer. I lifted my face but pressed my lips against his cheek. "I love you," I whispered into his rough playoffs beard.

"You love torturing me."

I nodded and laughed. "I do."

He stood up, pulling back from the awkward tension. "I want you to come to South Carolina with me."

"No." I pulled the napkin from my purse and passed it to him. "Destroy this."

He looked at the number and the dirty words drawn next to it. "Are you fucking kidding me? Is this some random guy's number?"

I nodded.

"What are you doing? I didn't get why the fuck you're getting married in the first place. Phil's a douche and now this?"

I passed him my phone. "Delete the calls I made so I can't press redial."

He growled down on me. "What are you—a five-year-old?"

"Something like that." He deleted and tossed the phone into the car. He grabbed my face in his huge hands. "Jack, stop this, okay? You're taking drugs with alcohol and numbers off dudes you don't know. This isn't you anymore. Is Phil hurting you? I'll kill him. I'm cool with prison. I got a lot of fans in there. We won the cup last year and made playoffs this year—I'm golden."

I blinked at him, feeling lost in the buzz from the drugs and wine. "I just need to go shopping. I'll feel better."

He pulled me to the passenger side of the car and shoved me inside. He slammed the door and got in the driver's side. He threw the car in reverse and lit the tires up. I sighed and closed my eyes. I felt his warmth next to me and curled toward him.

When I woke up, he was sleeping too. Both our seats were back. I looked at his messy dark hair and beard, and smiled. He looked homeless. I lifted a hand and ran my fingers through the beard. He moaned and shook his head. "That's sleep assault. It's a sex crime."

I giggled and tried not to sigh when he grinned. He was handsome, but he was more. He was comfortable and sweet and fun and mine. He was always mine.

He opened a dark eye. "Run away with me."

"Okay. One day, I swear."

He pointed. "I'm holding you to this."

I narrowed my gaze. "Would you ever want kids? Like if you got married?"

He smirked. "Are you asking me to impregnate you?"

"Not even close. Just curious. I think I want kids one day, maybe. I don't think Phil does though."

"Yeah, I want kids. I actually thought Denise and me might have kids last year. When we broke up, it hit me that I'm mid twenties and I want that, but I'm running out of time. The older guys on the team who are having kids and whatever, they all seem exhausted and stressed. They keep telling me not to do it—not to settle down—but I want it. I just don't want to be forty when I finally have a kid."

The smile that crossed my lips was fake and hateful. I hated the idea of him with anyone but me, and yet I never chose him. I yawned. "I need to go home."

He put a finger to my lips. "No yawning. I still have to fly to SC tonight."

"Why?"

"Gotta get the summer house ready for summer. The whole family starts arriving at the end of June. They stay the whole damned summer. So I told the boys we'll have an impromptu party there in two nights for end of the season, and then I may head on vacation before summer training."

"It's almost the end of June now."

"I know. I don't have a lot of free time. I have a couple of weeks off and then it's summer training and shit."

"Okay. I still need to go home."

He leaned forward, making the awkward moment again

where we wouldn't kiss and brushed his lips against my cheek. "Thanks for the uncomfortable nap."

I wrapped my arms around his neck, holding him to me. "Thank you for making me feel safe again."

He moaned into my neck. "You can't say shit like that. That's not fair. You're getting married. You gotta keep that locked up or start putting out."

I laughed into his neck. "You're nasty."

He pulled back, shooting me a shit-eating grin. "I'm serious. You and me together are hot. You remember the first time?"

I rolled my eyes. "We were fifteen. I barely remember." That was a lie. I recalled every detail of the first time it happened, as well as the millions of times it had nearly happened, and the few times it had since then. I remembered everything about him. The weight of his muscled body on top of mine was still my go-to fantasy when Phil was on top of me.

He looked hurt. "You remember. What about the time when I came back from Los Angeles, and you were practically engaged? Worst summer of my life."

I winced. "You know the choice I had."

He ran a finger along my jawline. "I know you had a choice, Jack. You picked the wrong one."

"I know, France." I pulled back and smiled. "I still need to go home."

He made a happy sound and smiled wide. "I like it when you accidentally call me France. Makes me remember you before you and the Xanax and Phil the douche."

I swatted him. "I meant to say Mike."

"Sure you did." He brought his seat back up and started the engine. He looked too big to be in my car. He wiggled and shot me a look. "This is a shit car. Next time we take a beach nap, we do it in my truck." When he was sleepy his South Carolina accent was thicker. No matter how long he had been away from it all, he was still a country boy.

"Okay. Your seats are comfier anyway."

His lips curled into a sly grin. "They feel better on your back than bucket seats."

"Not going to happen."

His voice changed to a low tone I took seriously. "You're not the kind of girl I'd fuck in my truck anyway."

"Gross."

He chuckled and drove back to his place. We got out at the same time. He wrapped around me. "Say hi to Phil for me."

"Say hi to the puck fucks for me."

He pulled me back, giving me a stern look. "I don't like it when you swear. It's like my fantasy of you being all classy and shit is ruined. Then you become the tree-climbing little slob you were when we were little."

"I love you."

He nodded. "If you need me, call."

"I won't." I got in the car and drove to Muriel's to check on her.

Her maid answered with a wary look. It was late in the evening, and she no doubt had been caring for Muriel for hours.

"Hi. Is she in?"

She nodded. "She's upstairs. She isn't well."

"I know. I'm the one who paid the server to bring her home a few hours ago." I walked past her and up the grand staircase. I knocked on the huge door. "Muriel. It's Jacqueline."

She didn't respond. I opened the door to the room, squinting in the dim light to find her. The room was massive, but I saw her right away. She was curled in a ball in the corner of the room, tucked in near the large windows with thick curtains drawn.

I closed the door and walked over quietly. "Muriel, are you okay?"

She didn't move.

I dropped to my knees next to her, taking her hand in mine.

She sniffled. "I always suspected something was going on. I never imagined anyone else did though. I thought he was careful and that was why I couldn't prove it. I didn't know everyone knew. I didn't know my children knew."

My heart hurt for her. I squeezed her hand.

She continued, "My daughter came to me two weeks ago and told me her best friend's husband was cheating on her. She looked me in the eyes and said, 'Don't worry, Mom. I told her to keep her chin up and act like she didn't know. That's what you do and everyone still respects you.'" She sobbed.

I bent forward, wrapping around her.

"That is the example I gave my child. I taught her to turn a blind eye to the fact people cheat and that the appearance of happiness was what was important. I never taught her that her self-worth was larger than a man." She looked up at me. "I had none, so why would she think she deserved any?"

Tears streamed down my cheeks. "Muriel, you are worth a million of him. She sees the loving person you are."

She shook her head. "I kicked him out. I need my children to see that no one deserves that kind of life and disrespect. I just wish I had chosen love. Back then, you just didn't choose love like that. It was frowned upon. And now I see it all, but I am too late. My kids will never understand real love because no one has showed it to them."

"Of course. They see it. I'm sure they do. I do."

She shook her head. "I am tired of this world. I am tired of being the Muriel everyone expects me to be. I am tired, Jacqueline. Do you know that feeling?"

"I do."

She looked down. "If I died today there is no one who would care, not truly. There is no one whose heart would be smashed and broken into a thousand pieces. I have no love, Jacqueline. No one loves me. Do people even matter if no one loves them? I feel like a tree falling in the forest and no one is around to hear it."

I hugged her tight. "I am here. I would be devastated. This will pass. Trust me. He is a shit and not worth the pain you are feeling."

"It isn't just him. He is the icing on the cake. It is everything. Every minute of my life has been a lie."

She hugged me back and sobbed into me. I held her until she fell asleep. I left the room with her unconscious on the plush carpet and found the maid in the kitchen. "You can't leave her alone. I'm scared she might hurt herself."

She nodded. "I know, me too. She is distraught. Has been for days."

"I have to go home, but if you need me to come back here, I'm in her cell phone under Jacqueline Croix and Phil Bernard."

She nodded. "I know, Ms. Croix."

"Thank you."

"Have a good night."

I winced. "You too. I hope she's okay." I left with a sick feeling in my stomach and a hole in my heart.

Monday

The car door slipped from my fingers, slamming. I winced and looked up at the huge brick house, hoping Phil hadn't heard it. He hated it when I slammed the door.

A smile slipped across my lips, thinking about the way his dark eyebrows would knit together and he would keep talking, even though the slam had annoyed him. He refused to allow anything to stop him from talking. The disapproving look was funny, most of the time. But not when he gave it to strangers. Then it was just a matter of his being uppity. It was unattractive on him.

My eyes scanned the windows as I slipped the bags from the trunk. I needed to start keeping those green reusable bags in the trunk to make it look like I was bringing in groceries from the markets that didn't deliver. Not that I ever went to them. I hoped he would miss the large white letters saying CHANEL on the black bag as I hurried across the courtyard and up the stairs. He deserved whatever therapy shopping I did.

We had spent the entire night avoiding each other. He had been adamant I was imagining things between him and Eleanor, and I was positive he had already done something to destroy the love I had worked hard to force myself to have for him. It wasn't a strong love; it was obligatory. Unnatural love couldn't be saved if the marriage was tested. We would become roommates like our parents.

I could sense us already on that road and our wedding was two weeks away. I had done my duties with the caterers and florists. The wedding planner had everything under control. My bridal shower was over with and the bachelor and bachelorette parties were completely planned.

For all of that I deserved some real shopping. Shopping where I got something I desperately wanted. When I had touched the dress in the bag I was carrying, I knew—she was special. I called her CHANEL, like Coco herself was in the bag, and adored every thread and seam.

I opened the front door and paused.

Nothing.

He must have spent his entire day in his office again. I rolled my eyes and crept up the stairs. Half the fun of buying too much was getting it into the closet, where I could state with a bold face, "I bought that ages ago."

His version of ages and mine differed, a lot.

The third-to-last stair made its usual creak. I'd forgotten to step to the side again. I stayed frozen and a little bit scared. This was my excitement for the day.

He didn't call out.

Whew, I'd made it.

That deserved an extra glass of pinot later. I turned the handle and slipped into the bedroom.

The rest was choppy—not a fluid memory but flashes of bad things.

Long slim fingers grabbing the headboard.

The pounding of his hips into her rounded ass.

A cape.

What the fuck—a cape? Was he in costume?

His hand was woven into her long blonde hair, yanking it back a bit as he grunted and rutted. Yes, rutted. It was the only word I could use for what he was doing to the poor girl. He rutted in a cape.

Why a cape?

He was not the only one in costume though. She had some kind of garter and bustier situation going on. It was like walking into someone else's house. Only it wasn't. It was mine. The blue pill stopped me from truly feeling it. I knew I was upset, but I couldn't find it in my sinking chest.

Of course, she seemed to be enjoying it. In the mirror above the bed, I could see she was making those ridiculous lips—duck lips—and looking back at him like a porn star would. Who actually made that face whilst someone rutted with them? Who actually wore that amount of makeup in the early evening?

Why a fucking cape?

CHANEL almost slipped from my fingers, but I gripped her. I would need her later. I knew that.

Long red nails, face like a porn star, lets a man take her from behind and pull her hair without buying her diamonds—she was a pro. Oh God, she was on my sheets, in my goddamned shoes. *Oh God. MY JIMMY CHOOS!*

I backed out of the room, amazed she hadn't seen me when she was looking back at him. She maintained her duck lips as she faked her orgasm. "Fuck me, Mr. Bernard!" she cried out and immediately I recognized her. Gripping CHANEL like she was my lifeline, I lifted my fingers to my lips as I stepped farther back into the hallway where I became frozen.

"Oh God." She pushed back into him.

My entire life I only ever had one thing in the whole world I feared. It was quicksand. Now it was quicksand and whores wearing my fucking Jimmy Choos.

I had spent my life believing I would never come upon quicksand. However, there I was, frozen. My feet wouldn't budge. They made me watch the whole performance. They refused to walk away until it was over. He collapsed onto our much younger neighbor. Much, much younger.

Somewhere in that frozen moment, his eyes lazily looked back to see me. He didn't seem to comprehend what he was seeing. His face and the recognition of me in his eyes made the quicksand disappear, and I turned and fled from the house. I ran across the courtyard and threw the bags into the backseat, slamming the car door so hard I was scared I'd damaged the damned thing.

"JACQUELINE! STOP! JACQUELINE!"

I didn't turn back to see his naked body out the open window. I had a pretty good idea how it looked.

Why couldn't it have been Eleanor? She was his age at least.

I backed up like I was driving to a fire. The tires skidded the entire way back and forward until I was nearly to the end of our huge driveway.

My hands shook as I left our neighborhood. I didn't think

a single thought until I turned onto the parkway. I merged and let my frozen mind start to work.

Was the girl even eighteen? Was she a minor? Was he a pedophile? *Oh God.* I racked my brain to recall if we'd been invited to her eighteenth birthday or nineteenth.

I pressed the Bluetooth button and spoke softly, "Brandi."

The phone rang.

My sister answered right away, "Hey you, I just called your house a couple of hours ago, and Phil said you were with the wedding planner."

My heart was beating a mile a minute. "Right, yes. I was. Did you happen to recall what birthday party we went to for Ashley Andrews? Like how old she was?"

She was silent for a moment. "The neighbor girl whose party you dragged me to? Her mother had that annoying laugh?"

I swallowed all the bad things I wanted to tell her and nodded. "Yes."

"Are you all right? You sound funny."

I could see the look in my eyes when I glanced in the rearview. It was a funny look to go with a funny sound. "I'm just picking out a gift card. I forgot to give her one."

"Oh, uhmm yeah—she was nineteen because she said she was going to Canada with friends to party legally. Quebec, I think."

"Quebec is eighteen." I recalled that perfectly because I had taken advantage of the fact.

"Oh, then she's eighteen. She graduated this year."

I gagged.

She was a child compared to us, especially since he was nearly thirty.

"Well, I should go. I'm at the checkout counter, and I hate it when people talk on the phone and ignore the cashier. It's uncivilized." I could hear the tension and disbelief in her silence. "You sure you're all right? You sound like you're in the car." Being my older sister, she was like France—she could read me like a book.

"Yes, it's the air conditioning unit I'm next to." I shook my head. "Anyway, I'll call you later when I get home." I hung up and took deep breaths. Air conditioning unit? What store has an air conditioning unit? I sighed as my lower lip started to protrude. Eighteen? She was a kid, and he was a pervert and I hadn't even known.

A flash of something hit my memory. I pressed the Bluetooth button again. "Home."

The phone rang only once.

"Jacqueline, I can explain—"

I cut off his pathetic attempt at lying, "Phil, can you check the closet and see if I have red satin Jimmy Choos? I'm heading back to the shops, and I was thinking about getting some for the bachelorette party, but you know how I am. I may already have them."

"What?" He had that after-sex voice. I almost screamed at him, but I stopped myself. I wanted him to misunderstand everything that was happening. I wanted him to panic and not know what I was going to do.

"Shopping now? Can we just talk about this please? I know you're probably very angry but—"

"The shoe closet—can you have a peek and see if I own red satin Jimmy Choos?"

"Y-yes. You do."

Fucker.

He should have told me no. He should have lied and said I didn't have them. He was fucking a girl in my shoes and was planning on putting them back in the closet? After she'd worn them and him at the same time? Even after he was caught red-handed and caped.

I was breathing so heavily, I was certain I was going to have a heart attack. "Excellent. Thank you."

He sounded annoyed, "Are you coming home? I need to explain. I have a sickness. I never wanted you to see that side of me."

I looked around, shaking my head. "I know about the world we live in, Phil. I understand how we all are expected to live. I need to adjust. I have never been unfaithful to you, so I just need to get used to the idea we will be stepping outside our marriage for sex and other things."

He sounded furious, "Jacqueline, it doesn't have to be this way. This is nothing. I swear. I fucked up. We don't have to be like our parents or anyone else. I love you. Come home."

"I'm taking a drive after I get some new shoes, and then when I get wherever I am going I'll call you." I hung up the phone and felt the first tear threaten my eyes. I forbade it. My reaction needed to be far more dramatic than a single tear on the parkway in a BMW. It needed to be Casablanca theatrical or have a Love Affair type of intensity. I drove until I came up with a plan. I filled up twice, driving in some crazy circle, hopping states before I saw my destination clearly.

I stopped next in Virginia Beach. I had drunk far more coffee than I imagined people capable of, and at the last stop I started to realize I wasn't anywhere near Manhattan any longer. My heels clicking against the cold white linoleum had been the only sound in the gas station. Everyone else had stopped, staring at me like I was a circus freak.

I sped away, eating my pastry that tasted far more like freezer food one would eat in desperation or an apocalypse maybe, and pulled back onto the highway.

My next stop was a little place called Hampstead in North Carolina. I started to notice the air was warmer, more loving and understanding.

I couldn't remember exactly where I was going. I knew there was a tiki bar, a beach, and it was in South Carolina. Why had I not paid more attention when he spoke of the damned beach house?

I looked at the water, and I swore I saw the things that were my fault. The things I might have done better. I should have listened to my mother.

No, screw that. I should've let the bartender have me, even if it was only for an hour.

I got gas and more food from packets. Everything was salty and dry, like the moisture had been sucked away in the heat of sealing the plastic wrappers.

The sugar and coffee were mixing in my stomach. It wasn't happy.

Tuesday

I bypassed Charleston and continued heading south. She was a beautiful old city that deserved my first visit under better tidings. Seeing her through the cloud I was stuck under wasn't fair. She would be tainted by the rage bubbling on simmer inside me. The last blue pill was holding off my hate rage, but I knew eventually it would leak out.

I ended up in a beach resort-looking area that reminded me of Florida, the richer sections. I never liked Florida—too tanned and obvious about plastic surgery.

I had driven all night, getting lost and found, sleeping on the side of the road for a while at one point, and then driving the rest of the way. The trip had been twenty hours, to be exact. Twenty hours of huge circles and getting completely lost before I found myself. My phone had rung twenty-eight times. I'd driven some ungodly number of miles and drank a horrendous amount of caffeine. I had one hundred and fourteen text messages and twenty voicemails. My poor phone was nearly dead. Of course, I had forgotten my car charger.

I pulled my car into the market and stepped out. The air was warm, the sea was inviting, and the people looked like a fucking J. Crew catalogue. I shuddered and walked into the store with my phone. I got one last set of directions from Siri before she died as I bought snacks and wine.

I drove to a street called South Forest Beach Drive. There were houses and a Marriott, but I was looking for one place. I parked in the parking lot for the Tiki Hut Bar and walked down to the beach. Rednecks in beach shirts watched me storm down the beach with my bags and fancy shoes.

All I knew was that France was close. These were his people. They wore things like beards and plaid. I needed him. I regretted not letting myself call him when my phone still had a charge.

I stopped and looked at a man sitting at a table. I tilted my head. "Can I steal the wine glass from your table?" He sat in a section that was under the thatched tiki hut roof but looked like he'd gotten a lot of sun. He smiled and passed it to me.

"You wanna have a drink?"

I looked around the touristy pit and shook my head. "Thank you, but no." I clutched the wine glass and walked down the beach, veering left. I walked up until I felt it. It was like following a scent. One minute I had it and then it was gone. I stopped when I was sure I was there. I would drink my wine and go find him. Unless he found me first. I knew his house was somewhere near the Tiki Hut. I remembered the story of the drunken Tiki Hut night.

I cropped the bags and looked at my high-heeled boots. They were scuffed from the sand. I groaned and looked around. Being two in the afternoon, the beach was still packed. I walked to a quieter area, but it was still populated with a few people. I sat in the sand in my Burberry navy plaid short trench coat, Comme des Garçons black pleated skirt, Helmut Lang sheer-sleeved blouse, and Giorgio Armani knee-high leather boots.

I wasn't dressed for the beach or South Carolina.

I unzipped a boot, wiping sweat from my face. I pulled my fun polka dot, knee-high cashmere socks off and stuffed them into my boots. I undid the tie on my jacket and then the buttons. I was pouring sweat. It had to be close to eighty-five degrees out if not hotter. I spread my jacket out and pulled my sunglasses from my pocket. I slipped them on and lay back in the sun. I was certain I looked like a fool in a black pleated skirt with a white blouse unbuttoned as low as I could without being sleazy.

I lay there and contemplated the essence of life. My life. My arranged marriage was a mess. My family and his would still want us to go ahead with it. Could I do it? Could I still marry, ignoring the fact he liked to dirty screw eighteen-year-olds?

No.

I lay there, gripping my dead phone and willing France to find me. The warm sand and comforting breeze made it impossible for me to fight the emotions. They released hard, tearing my insides a bit.

I sobbed.

I bawled until I didn't have anything left. I should have left when France asked me to. I should have come with him. I would have suspected Phil of cheating, but I wouldn't have known about Ashley.

At least, if I was going to have a crisis, I was there close to him.

The sun had started to set. I sat up and watched it. It began with a fire in the sky, slowly changing by brushing color against only the tips and edges of the clouds. The white clouds had layers of colors with dark shadows and bright-orange brush strokes and fluffy pillow-looking bits. It was stunning and a perfectly dramatic end to my day. I imagined it was exactly how Charles Boyer had felt when he realized Irene Dunne wasn't coming. It was the exquisite pain people like he and I never let our hearts feel.

I opened the bottle of wine and poured my first glass. As I sipped I walked down to the water and pulled my marquise-cut diamond engagement ring off. Gripping it tightly, I closed my eyes and took a deep breath.

"Thank you, God, for showing me how wrong I was." I kissed the ring and walked into the cold water. I threw the ring as hard as I could and watched the waves for a moment. Technically, the whole past forty-eight hours had been a sign of how wrong I was. The fundraiser, seeing Muriel in such pain, nearly sleeping with the bartender against my better judgment, and seeing Phil with Eleanor, had all been signs. I had made up excuses for each one. Finally, God decided to show me exactly what I needed to leave. Ashley. That I couldn't stand for. I didn't care if my parents and his were fine with that type of life—I wasn't.

I squished the sand in my toes and drank back the first glass far too quickly. It was poetic and something I'd wanted to do since the minute I'd become engaged. I could admit that, now that it was the end.

I turned and walked back to my spot on the beach. I plunked back down on my jacket and poured the second glass. I looked around, wondering where his house was.

The second glass was dedicated to my broken heart. I placed a hand over it, cupping the swell of my own breast and waited for it to make a snapping noise, but it never did. It was my pride he had broken, not my heart.

The wind picked up, and I started to feel a little bit guilty. Was any of it my fault? Had I driven him to it? Had I been so closed off that I made him—*fuck that.*

If he had depraved fantasies about teenaged girls, I certainly hadn't made him follow through with them. He was as close to a pedophile as I imagined grown men got without crossing over completely. Maybe it was good we hadn't married or had kids yet. Was that why he didn't want them? I shuddered. Maybe he knew about his problem. I almost gagged.

I nodded and drank the second glass back in several gulps. I broke open the bag of snacks. I perused, scanning over each item as if it were my last meal. Finally, I selected a bag of gourmet popcorn. I took a huge handful of it and shoved several servings in at once. I chewed and savored the light aged-cheddar taste. I poured a third glass and swallowed back the last of the popcorn. It was a bad combination, but I didn't care.

I looked at CHANEL and nodded. This was that moment. I lifted the tissue-wrapped garment and sighed when my fingers brushed the mesh fabric. I laid it out and looked down on it. It was perfect. I undid my blouse and pulled the dress on. I slipped my bra strap down to make a half-assed strapless and slid my pleated skirt off. I stuffed everything into the CHANEL bag and let the wind blow through the white mesh fabric of the short dress. The petals of the embroidered 3-D flowers fluttered in the breeze and looked like blue and purple butterflies. I knew it was what the dressmaker had envisioned: someone like me—less broken perhaps—but thin and tall and standing on the beach with the flowers fluttering away. The sun faded and the air cooled, but I didn't care. I drank my third glass and ate my popcorn in my dress worth more than all my other clothes in the bag combined.

It was the freest meal I'd ever eaten.

Having this lightbulb moment immediately brought up a memory that hurt just a little. But I was being honest with myself so I had to let the memory play out.

I looked at the fading light of the day and remembered exactly the moment I had fallen in love while eating the freest meal ever.

It was a hot dog from a vendor after a long walk in Central Park. The backs of two hands had brushed against each other innocently, and yet too frequently. It was perfect in every way. The way France had wiped my cheek with his thumb and licked the mustard off. Or the way I had felt when I went to sleep that night, dying for it to be light out so I could find him again. Only I didn't have to. He had scaled my house and tapped on my window in the dark. I let him in, but he didn't try anything. We snuggled like always. I swore to France then that I'd break it off with Phil and move with him to Los Angeles for him to play hockey. We were young and in love, crazy and free. It was the last free moment in my life.

The next morning, Philip showed up with a ring. I stood on the stairs as my father looked like a gushing bride and accepted the ring for me as Phil proposed from the bottom of the stairs. I knew France had heard it all from upstairs, but I was frozen there on the stairs, watching as my life ended. My heart broke when I got back upstairs and France was gone. He had gone out the window just like he had come in. We never discussed it after that. We just hung out and pretended I wasn't on a speeding train to despair.

I shivered, remembering it and swearing somewhere in the back of my mind I could still taste the hot dog.

Doing the right thing had sealed my fate. A fate I would never escape, beyond this trip into madness.

I had to be strong and stop them from convincing me to take him back.

I looked down, letting my strawberry-blonde hair fall around my face and for the first time in a long time, I felt fear.

It was of the unknown, my father, and the possibility I would be made to try to save my upcoming marriage. I lived in the same world as Muriel. I knew my mother had made the same choices as Muriel had. The blue pills had worn off and were long gone. I was stuck with my own frightening reality and the pain it caused in my chest. A pain I had only ever felt once. That was when I started letting my dad and Dr. Michaels give me the blue pills.

We all made the same sacrifices to be in the life we wanted. My heart started to panic against the aching pain, but I slipped a finger against my lips and shushed myself. I needed to stay calm. The crying wasn't allowed to happen after the wine had been drunk. There were rules.

I needed to find France and there was no crying in that dress. It was a dress of possibilities, summer love, and youth. I would die in that dress before I would allow one tear to be shed.

It was the opposite of every other garment I owned. It was a freedom dress. I knew it when I had first seen it. It would be my morning-after married dress for the gift opening. Later, I would wear it to garden parties. I loved the cut of it, and the fact that I could be slightly risqué and free in it. It was the small things I could still control when everything was planned out and reined in. I imagined I would be showing my shoulders midday while sipping from a champagne glass, not alone on a beach in South Carolina with a bottle of wine as my only friend.

I hadn't foreseen any of it as the way my life would be.

Or the dog knocking me over, and yet there he was. He dove for the bag of popcorn and tore off with it. I screamed and laughed at the same time. I got up and ran after my meal but hands grabbed my arm. "Are you all right, ma'am?"

I looked up, scowling. "Do I look like a ma'am in this dress?"

He chortled. "Oh uhhh, no?" He shook his head. "No, you look beautiful in that dress." He smiled at me.

I smiled back. "Thank you."

"My dog, Jack—sorry about that."

I pointed after the hound still running away. "Jack's going

to get sick from that."

He chuckled, running his hands through his dark hair. "No. No, he won't. He's a labradoodle."

"I don't know what that means."

"It means he has the guts of a lab, the craziness of a standard poodle, and he's never been sick, no matter what he ate."

He was an older man. I would bet he'd lived there for a while. I pressed my lips together. "Do you know which house is Mike France's? He told me to meet him here, and I wrote down the address wrong."

He gave me a funny look and nodded. "Three up the beach."

I smiled. "Thank you." I bent forward, trying not to tip over while filling my bags back up with all my stuff. Everything was sandy and heavy.

"Good evening." I waved.

He nodded. "You also."

The sand in my toes felt amazing as I stumbled along the beach past three houses and walked up to the huge glass doors.

There were people inside the house, crowds of them. I spotted France immediately. He was at the bar, dumping bags of chips into bowls. The glass doors were open. Music was playing. It was the music I had faintly heard when I was down the beach. I had thought it was the Tiki Hut place. A couple of people slipped outside. A handsome but rugged man walked up to me with a smile. He had tanned skin, sexy whiskey-colored eyes, and plump lips. "Hi."

"Hi." I smiled back and dropped my bag behind the chair on the deck, trying desperately to stay upright.

"You a friend of France's?"

"I am."

"I'm Willy." He put a huge hand out.

I took it and let him shake us both. "Nice to meet you. I'm JD."

He nodded. "Sexy. I love girls with names like that. My first love was a girl named AJ. She was hot."

I giggled. He pointed back at the house. "You want a

drink?"

"Yes, please."

He hurried inside and grabbed a drink from the counter. It looked like a slushy drink. He carried it outside. France's eyes followed him out of the house to the deck. They met mine. He frowned, tilted his head, and then pointed at me, shouting, "You real?"

I snickered. "What?"

"You really here?"

I didn't know what the answer was so I looked back at Willy as he handed me my drink. "They're frozen margs from the Tiki Hut. They made them for us." He didn't notice France coming out of the house. He stepped in front of Willy and lifted me up into his arms. "You came? How did you find it?"

I pointed down the beach. "An old man with a dog named Jack."

"Brian. Yeah, he's my neighbor." He looked back at Willy. "Dude, this one is off limits."

"Actually, this one can say for herself, and since he bought me my first drink, I am obligated to drink it with him." I winked at Willy.

He stepped back. "It was nice meeting you, JD."

I gave France a look. "What was that?"

He put me down. "You drunk?"

"I am." I sipped the margarita and smiled. "This is good."

His dark eyes filled with worry. "Baby, you okay?"

"I can't talk about it right now."

I watched his jaw set. He took my hand and pulled me inside to the kitchen. He passed me a sandwich from a tray. "How did you end up here?"

I swallowed a huge bite. "My heart or my pride broke, and I went into survival mode, and all I could think of was finding you."

He looked hurt. "Go lay down upstairs. I'll be up in a bit, okay?"

"Okay." I passed him my margarita and pointed to the deck. "I need my clothes. There, in a bag behind a deck chair."

He waved me off. "I'll get them. Just go lay down."

I walked up the stairs, but like a kid who wanted to be part of the party after bedtime, I stayed at the top couple of steps and watched them have fun.

Seeing Mike France in action was intoxicating. He was funny and loud, always laughing and having fun. He made a series of filthy revenge-sex thoughts rattle their way through my addled brain. His shirt was open, revealing a tight body with a tiny smattering of dark chest hair. He was tall, hugely tall. I'd never considered myself short. I was average, five foot six, but he was tall and thick. I had always liked that about him. He made me feel safe, always. His dark hair was shaggy, as though he was from Greenwich Village. The playoff beard was the part I hated the most, and yet I imagined how it would feel on certain parts of my body.

I leaned against the railing and listened to the laughing and joking. The guys all looked the same—hockey players and managers. The girls didn't look like spouses, but more like puck fucks. Miniskirts and bathing suit tops, bleach-blonde hair, and tanned skin. I was like a sore thumb, even in my freedom dress. It bummed me out that he was having a party like that, even though that's just who he was.

He was a player.

Willy spotted me and came up the stairs. He smiled and passed me another margarita. "Sent upstairs early?"

"No. This just isn't my scene, and he knows it."

He smiled. "It's not a wife party, that's for sure."

"You married?"

"We don't work the kind of job that is conducive to having a wife and kids."

"That's pretty true."

"I don't want to get a divorce. My parents had one when I was eleven and it was hard. I never want to put my kids through that. So I want to wait a bit more before I settle down. I want my wife to be the sole focus in my life. I know hockey isn't forever, and when I fall in love I want it to be forever." His whiskey eyes were killing me.

"Wow, I wish I were marrying you instead."

"You married?" He glanced at my ring finger.

"Not yet. I just threw my engagement ring in the Atlantic though, sooooo maybe I'm not getting married anymore."

"Just phone him up and say I divorce you three times, and it's done spiritually. No more engagement."

I put a hand out. "You have a cell phone?"

He laughed and passed me his iPhone. I dialed home and waited as it rang, plugging my other ear.

"Hello?"

"Phil?"

"Oh, thank God. I was so worried. I called the police. Are you okay?"

"I divorce you, I divorce you, I divorce you." I didn't even hesitate. I wanted the wedding off.

"Jacqueline, are you okay? What are you talking about? We haven't married yet, baby."

I swallowed and felt the world moving slowly around me, like I was the sun. "Please—I just saw you with Ashley, and I saw you with Eleanor. I know you don't love me. Get my things ready. I'll be home in a week or so, and I'm moving out." I hung up the phone and passed it back. "I would turn that off, if I were you. He's going to call back."

His eyes were wide. "Are you okay?"

"I think so. I will be." I watched as a blonde girl stuck her hand in France's back pocket and grabbed his ass cheek.

Willy followed my gaze and cleared his throat. "Wanna take a walk on the beach?"

I gave him a grin. "Not if you think I'm doing anything beyond walking and maybe throwing up."

He nodded. "I think you're safe. I'm sick right now for you."

I linked my arm into his. "I like you, Willy. Not your name though. May I call you Will? I have a couple of friends I would love to introduce you to, and they would never stand for a Willy."

He chuckled. "I get that weekly, the hook up and the name change. My last name is Burettes, not easy like France." I walked behind him, holding his thick arm and following him outside. We walked down the beach and away from the house.

The fresh air made me feel much better. "It's so hot here."

He chuckled. "It's so much nicer than New York. So, what does JD stand for?"

"Jane Doe."

He snickered. "Come on. What is it?"

I rolled my eyes and muttered, "Jacqueline Diana."

He nodded. "Yeah, I'd go with JD too."

"My last name is Croix. My father has informed me that when I get married to Philip, I will be keeping my name. My name will be Jacqueline Diana Croix-Bernard."

He whistled. "Sounds fancy and French." His southern drawl mocked me, but I didn't mind. "So how long have you been together?"

I thought for a minute. "Well, I met him when I was a teenager, and we dated for a few years. We broke up, and then a couple years later he proposed and my father said yes. So we have been engaged for a few years."

He frowned. "Wow. Your dad said yes? Didn't you want to marry Phil? Why would your dad agree for you? Were you planning on having kids?"

I shook my head, laughing. "My father runs everything in my house—people, money, and business transactions. That includes marriages. As far as kids go, Phil didn't want them right away, and then he wanted to make sure we had a stable relationship. None of it made sense though. He was the one who wanted the hugely long engagement, even though I was the one who didn't want to get married. I assumed we would have them just after we married since we've been together for so long now. But the other day, he actually told me that couples who have kids in the first few years of marriage are more likely to divorce. Now I'm not sure I want them. I can't see myself getting married at all now."

"Wow, all that and he has affairs. What a dick. Some people don't know what they have until it's too late."

I nodded and took a huge gulp of my margarita. The old man I had met on the beach earlier walked past us. "Hey, did you find the party?"

"I did. Thank you."

He sat in the sand next to where we were standing. "I don't think I'll ever catch that damned dog. He grabbed that bag of food from you, and he's been crazy since."

I flopped onto the sand next to Brian. "Sorry about that."

Will sat beside me, giving me a weird look. "You guys know each other?"

I shook my head, passing him the massive glass of margarita. "No." I looked at Brian. "I'm JD."

He smiled. "Brian."

Will waved. "I'm Willy."

I nudged Will. "He prefers to be called Will though."

He blushed and looked down.

Jack the labradoodle came running over to me, tackling me into the sand again. I managed to grasp his collar, but he dragged me a little bit.

Brian jumped up and grabbed his collar from me. "Ha, you little bastard. Sorry about that JD. He's a brat."

I chuckled and wiped the sand off my arm. I felt the petals of my poor dress. They were intact.

"Well, I better get him home. Night you two."

"Night." We both waved at him as he left.

Will nudged me. "Are you sure you're going to be okay? I would be dying right now."

I smiled. "I don't know. My heart hurts, but I think my pride hurts more."

"Do you feel lost? You don't seem like you're lost by any means. I think I would be lost."

"I would have to say it's quite the contrary to lost." I glanced at him. "I feel found, newly found, and free." I took the glass back from him and had a huge gulp of it. It was melting fast. I sighed. "I can't believe I'm saying this, but it was an arranged marriage of sorts. Not a love marriage."

"Yeah, I got that. I hear a lot of blue bloods do that." He played with the sand. "How do you know France?"

I laughed and hiccupped at the same time and then drank a large sip. The wine was hitting harder with the addition of the margarita. "We grew up together. He was a badass kid who played sports and did naughty shit. Our hockey team actually paid for him to go to our prep school because he was such an amazing player. I think his mom hoped we would straighten him out. You know, a bunch of snooty brats would keep him in line. But honestly, I think we just helped him learn to be corrupt on the down-low. He was lost and we sort of helped him find himself, and at the same time, somehow helped him avoid becoming one of us. We're broken, always have been. The new money is so desperate to be accepted by the old money, they won't do anything that's frowned upon. The old money is getting dreadfully broke in comparison to the newly rich, so that they fear the end of their empire. They hang on to the reins fiercely. France ignored it all. He's always been real and alive and crazy. Not like the people in our cliques. Most don't have human hearts. Probably all the inbreeding to keep the blood blue."

"You're deep for a drunk on a beach."

I chuckled. "I have a lot of practice at being polite and put together while under the influence."

He grinned, and I realized there was something about him that made me comfortable. It might have been the wine and margaritas that did it, but regardless, I felt compelled to tell him my something horrid. I took a deep breath and muttered, "My fiancé isn't just a regular philanderer. He is a pervert who likes younger girls—you know, the barely legal types. I discovered it today. I suspected he might be having an affair the other day, but today I caught him having sex in my bed with our much younger neighbor, in a cape."

"A cape? That was with the Ashley girl you mentioned on the phone?"

I looked out at the water and answered robotically, "Yes. She just turned eighteen. I hate him."

"Well, JD, he's a damned fool and a pervert."

I held my glass up. "Fuck him."

He choked and laughed as I finished the glass. I looked at him. "Tell me something horrible."

He smiled, making his eyes squint. "My parents' divorce was a hard year. I got arrested a bunch of times for drinking, and then when I got my license, I drank and drove. I crashed the car and hurt my friend. I never got charged because I was a good player, and they didn't want to ruin my career. They made my friend take all the blame, even though he was the one who was hurt. He took the charges, and they told him he would get off. He didn't. He went to juvie for two months. He's a drug addict and a career criminal now. He was the good kid. I was the trouble. I ruined his life and mine is awesome."

"That's awful, but you can't take responsibility for the fact that he got in the car with you, took the blame for you, or turned to drugs afterward. Had he done the time that wasn't fair for him to get, and been a good kid when he got out, he would have been fine. Kids' records are sealed when they're eighteen. No one would have even known it had happened."

"You know a bizarre amount of shit about youth criminal records and that's a creepy way of looking at it."

I grinned. "I volunteer with kids like your friend. We try to get them to stay on the good path so when they're older they can have normal jobs. It's all about making citizens, not coddling them and making criminals." I shook my head. "You can only take responsibility for letting him take the blame."

He nudged me again as if we were old friends. "We should get back."

I gave him a smile. "Okay. Yeah, France is probably looking for me." I looked around at our little spot. "What a weird couple of days." I stood on my wobbly legs and took a second to get my bearings.

He got up fast, grabbing my arm to steady me. "Maybe no more liquor tonight."

I shrugged. "I'm well past the point of return on this. I'm drunk. I can feel it now."

We walked back to the house. I saw my bag was still on the back deck and rolled my eyes. Of course France hadn't grabbed it.

I smiled at Will. "I'm just going to grab my things. I'll meet you inside."

He nodded and walked into the house. I dropped to my knees to shove the things back in that had fallen out of my CHANEL bag.

I heard a noise and looked up. France was behind the barbecue and a couple of chairs on the far side of the patio. I was about to say something to him, but the blonde girl leapt at him, wrapping her arms around his neck. She giggled and I realized I couldn't watch him with someone else either. I grabbed my belongings quickly and jumped up, running down the beach.

"Jack! Wait!" he shouted at me, but I ran harder. My boot dropped out of the bag. I stopped and picked it up, but he was there.

"Where are you going?"

"Coming here was a mistake. I'm going home."

He was breathing heavily. "Maybe you should let me drive you home tomorrow, huh? You're pretty drunk, babe."

"No." I poked his chest. "Don't call me babe. I don't want to get in the way with the blonde girl. And if I stay, I might molest your nice friend. I suspect he's too sweet for me to do that to."

His face tightened. "Jack, I can't let you drive, the blonde is nobody, and if you go near Willy, I might have to kill him."

My stomach rumbled as I was about to argue my point. I held it tightly, feeling the mess. My eyes flew open wide. I panicked as I spoke to him, "Quickly! Get my shirt and blouse from the bag."

He grabbed the bag, dumping it. I pulled my dress off and folded it. I placed it delicately in his hands. "Please wrap it in the tissue and put it back into the bag."

His jaw dropped. He stood there like an idiot, staring at my breasts that had completely fallen out of my bra. I pulled the straps up, shrugged on my blouse, did up one button, and pulled on my skirt. I staggered up the beach to a grassy spot and threw up everywhere. I held on to the piece of broken fence I was beside.

His warmth was behind me, snuggled up against me. He gathered my hair back as I bent forward and heaved into the grass again. "It's okay, Jack. It's okay."

"No, it's not." I started to tremble as I sobbed and heaved again. "I need to lie down, France."

He pulled me back into him. "Come on. My bed is empty,

I swear." He took my hand in his and pulled me back to my stuff. I stood there, swaying in the wind like the beach grass as he packed up all my clothes and food. The warmth of his hand over mine gave me a chill. I stopped myself from walking with him and shook my head. "Uhmmmm, no." I hauled my hand free, shaking my head and backtracking. "This is a bad idea." I knew where it would go. I was too drunk to go back there and suffer through loving him and watching the blonde all over him.

I turned and ran, probably faster than either he or I had anticipated I could. I rounded the corner to the open dining area of the Tiki Hut, pressing the unlock button on the car. I dove into the driver's seat and slammed the door fast. Mike was slamming his hand on the passenger side of the car as I started it. I heard another noise just as the driver's door was ripped open. Out of nowhere, there were lights—flashing bright white ones. Then there was yelling, and I was jerked from the seat. It was too much for me to take in all at once. Things got blurry.

My face was pressed into the cement. Something was holding it there, pressing on my back. In the dim glow of the streetlights and my hazy vision, I saw France. He looked angry.

The voices greeted him. They knew him.

He picked me up. I nodded. "Hi, Mike."

He snarled at me and looked back at the man in the uniform. "We good?"

The man nodded. "Get her outta here."

Wednesday

Light was the enemy. I'd tried opening my eyes a couple of times, but it had ended badly. I felt something touch my arm. I jumped, opening my eyes and groaning as the instant headache started.

I was with Mike.

That was all there was.

I looked up, seeing his light and breezy beach house and everything was back instantly. I closed my eyes. "Oh, this is real. My shoes really are ruined?"

France sat up from the opposite couch. "What?" He rubbed his eyes, giving me a funny look.

"My shoes." I put a hand to my face. "Everything's a bit hazy, but I remember my shoes. My Jimmy Choos. She was wearing them. They're ruined now. He was in a cape."

He cocked an eyebrow. "Jack, you all right?"

"No. I feel like death. I ate so many carbs and sugars and drove—and I had some of those energy drinks, and then that full bottle of wine. My body hates me."

"You're dehydrated as shit." He got up and grabbed a Gatorade. He passed it to me with the drinking spout opened.

I moaned, "We didn't—did we?"

"I have to admit, I was tempted last night when you were undoing my pants. 'Course, I had a bad feeling you wouldn't remember and that's not how I see us reuniting in my bed. Not just that, but you'd thrown up a lot, and I had this horrible thought that it would be wonderful timing for you to get sick again."

My eyes widened. "Oh my God. I tried to take your pants off? I'm so sorry."

He smiled. "Not the first time a drunk girl tried to get my pants off. But it was the first time a girl called me 'sexy-lumberjack France.' Now drink up. I haven't heard that outta your mouth in a while."

I gripped the Gatorade and shook my head. "Oh my God. I'm so sorry. I also hate you for enjoying this so much."

"Can't help it." He knelt beside the couch, smiling. His eyes were so beautiful and dark. His lashes clumped together a bit, making them frame his eyes so much more. I could have gotten lost in them. Until he spoke, "So, you going to thank me for saving you from getting arrested with a DUI? Those cops were pissed."

I closed my eyes, groaning. "Oh my God. I drove drunk?"

He nodded, looking serious. "You tried. They got you out of the car before you were able to. They said even though you didn't drive, you could have been charged under the 'actual physical control' clause, and they were pissed. I took the blame for you. I told them you got scared that I was going to attack you."

I frowned at that. I couldn't make myself believe he would. His eyes were sweet and kind. They were nice, everything about him was sort of nice. He didn't scare me. "You told them you scared me? They believed that?"

"You told them I chased you on the beach. Granted, it was in a muddled form of English. I had to explain I wanted your keys so you wouldn't drive drunk."

I ran my sticky fingers through my nappy hair. "Oh, France. I am so sorry if I embarrassed you."

He sat back, chuckling softly but giving me an odd look with those dark eyes. "Jack, you were trashed and upset, and I am not embarrassed by anything you said or did last night. In fact, the two strip shows made up for your almost drunk driving."

"What?"

He pointed. "On the beach, you ripped all your clothes off and got changed. It was entertainment at its best." He pointed to the door. "Then after you threw up everywhere and we got back here, you did a really nice slow one. It was classy." His grin was also classy.

There wasn't a single spot in or out of me that wasn't completely destroyed. He hit me in the arm lightly. "Mellow out. It was funny. You were drunk and fun. Except the trying to drive. That was less fun." He got up and started doing things in the kitchen. I drank the blue liquid, shuddering at the sweetness.

"Don't you have any coconut water?"

He gave me a look. "What?"

I winced and swallowed more. "It rehydrates much more efficiently and without the chemicals and artificial sweeteners."

He shrugged. "No, and I couldn't find any of that weird green drink you have for breakfast, but I made you medium eggs. You can still eat those, right?"

"How do you remember the green drink?"

"Last Christmas when Phil went to Washington for that two days and you spent them at my place. You drank it then. I remember trying to find it everywhere."

For whatever reason, that memory hurt me. Maybe because I'd hurt him when I left.

He put the plates on the table. I got up, clutching the blue drink, and plopped into a seat.

He smiled. "So what's the plan?" He sat down and ate something I had to give a second look to fully comprehend. It looked like four eggs, a stack of pancakes, a mound of fried potatoes, and several links of sausage.

I pointed. "You can't eat all that—you're too old to eat like a teenager. I assumed at Christmas it was a bit of a holiday indulgence. You don't still eat breakfast like this every day? You'll die."

"I'll work it off later."

"France, you'll die if you eat that."

He winked. "Worry about your breakfast and keeping it down."

I shook my head and sighed.

He cut a corner of egg and picked it up with a piece of sausage. He somehow managed to also get a chunk of potato on the fork and then stuffed the huge bite into his mouth. I didn't realize my fork was down and my eyes were wide. "What?" he asked through the huge mouthful of food.

I shook my head and looked around at the beautiful waterfront home. "You don't suit this place. It isn't how I imagined your beach house. I imagined it more like a log cabin."

He gave me a quizzical look. "No?" He scratched his scruffy dark beard. "If it makes you feel better, I just bought a log house in Boulder."

I rolled my eyes.

The furnishings were stunning. Everything was done with taste and elegance. The whitewashed wood and light blues made the house feel like it was part of the beach. The bright, airy feel and huge windows brought so much light into the place. He looked like a basement dweller who ate chips from the bag in front of a TV. It made me smile. I liked that he had more money than Philip, but it hadn't changed him. No matter what they tried, he never stopped being real.

"So you still think I'm a slob? I should be living like Jeremiah Johnson?"

I closed my mouth and shook my head. "No, you're just—just different and the same, all at once. You haven't changed any of the good things."

His eyes had a twinkle to them, a zest for humor and life. "I've changed. I've changed tons. You just haven't been around much to see it."

I tried to keep the smile on my face, but I couldn't. I felt sick and my life was in the toilet.

I put a hand forward. "I didn't mean that, the way it came out. I don't think you're just a slob. You're just casual and real, and I always liked that."

He still smiled. "I get it. My dad wasn't a cardiologist like yours. I was the scholarship kid at your school. I get it."

"France, I'm sorry. I didn't mean it that way, at all. You've been my best friend for a hundred years."

"It feels that way sometimes. I can't believe it's been so many years."

I ate a bite of breakfast and tried not to gag. I swallowed, shuddering.

He shrugged. "Besides, it would take a heck of a lot more than that to hurt my feelings. I wasn't offended, honestly."

I put down my fork and nodded. I drank the rest of the

liquid and felt like I might be sick again. I pointed. "I know it's impolite to leave during a meal, but do you mind if I take a shower?"

He looked stunned. "Of course not. Why are you asking? You're being weird. You've been weird for days. Why are you here, Jack? What's going on?"

"Headache and need shower first."

He nodded. "Take a shower. You look like shit. There's some girls' clothes in my room. Go pick stuff out. After that, we are talking about this shit."

I waved him off as I sauntered away. "Thank you, but puck-fuck clothing is not my thing." I was an idiot. I hated the way my parents' snobbery had rubbed off on me and sometimes slipped out in the worst way.

I didn't take any of the clothes or go near his bedroom. I was scared of what I would find in there. I went into the bathroom and closed the door, leaning my back against it and trying to catch my breath. It was a beautiful room with a huge window overlooking the beach. I pulled my clothes off and started the shower. I felt miserable. I couldn't believe I'd nearly driven drunk. I'd never done anything like that before in my life.

I climbed in and leaned against the side. The shower was massive. I felt my legs giving out as I slid down the wall.

I was an idiot to have believed Phil ever wanted to be with me, for me. He wanted the right cow from the right farm. He cared about my branding, not me. He was like the rest of the guys in my world. I closed my eyes as tears leaked out. I couldn't hold them back anymore. I was ashamed of trying and forcing myself to be there in that relationship. I was ashamed of what everyone was going to say. I would lose my friends and my family if I walked away. The tears rained down my face, becoming one with the water pouring down on me.

I cradled my head, sobbing into my hands.

I finished the shower and stepped out to find a stack of clothes on the counter. I stood and stared at them.

He had come into the bathroom? Wouldn't be the first time.

The door was closed, but he had come in at some point. Had he heard me crying? After drying off, I pulled on the plain purple tee shirt and black jogging pants. They only came mid calf. I hated them, but it was nice to be in something comfortable.

I gathered my clothes and stuffed them into the bag with CHANEL, making sure the dress was wrapped properly so my other clothes wouldn't touch it. I noticed my boots and pouted. I picked one up and sighed. The sand had scuffed the hell out of the leather.

I pulled them on and picked up my bags, looking like an idiot in capri jogging pants and knee-high leather boots.

I grabbed one of his pieces of mail and copied down the address on a piece of paper. On another I wrote,

> *Mike,*
>
> *Thank you for being you, but I have to go home and face the music. I can't run away from this. I swear we will talk about it.*
>
> *JD XOXO*

I turned and left the house. The warm salty air blew across the driveway at me. I almost smiled at the fresh start and possibilities in it. I had at least a few days before Phil would alert my family. I could find a map, let my phone stay dead, and drive home the long way. I would need at least five days to figure it all out. My sister would know I was missing. She was like a hound when it came to the tone of my voice, or the way I paused.

She might have alerted them already. The look on my father's face would be one of disappointment. He would wonder if I had done enough. He would wonder if I had ignored my fiancé or let myself slip just a little. I looked down at the capri jogging pants and scuffed boots and laughed to myself.

I shuddered from exhaustion and the possibility I would be made to return home.

"Jack!"

I looked back, seeing France running down the beach to me. "What are you doing?"

I pointed toward the Tiki Hut. "My car is down there."

He held up the note. "You owe me more than a note."

"France, we've talked about this a thousand times. Not today, okay? I'm hungover and exhausted, and I have a whole day of driving to get through."

His cheeks blushed. "I love it when you call me France. Now you know I meant a proper goodbye and a game plan. You know if I wanted your sexy ass, I would wait for you to be dressed half decent, at least. Not slumming in my sister's jogging pants."

I laughed weakly. "Shit. I hate you sometimes." I looked at him with sincerity. "I'm really sorry about last night, and I feel like an asshole."

He put a hand up. "Stop saying that damned word. Say it again and you'll be sorry."

"Okay. I have no game plan, and I'm thirsty for something like coffee and a pastry. I think there's addictive chemicals in the gas station food."

"Probably." He nodded. "But you need to come with me. I know where all the good coffee and pastries are. Now what's the plan, after you add carbs and coffee?"

"I don't know. Go home."

He pointed behind us. "Your car is at my house. You actually had to have walked right past it. How are you getting home anyway?"

"Driving." I frowned. Was that even possible? How had I walked past my own car? I was a hot mess. I looked down at the jogging pants and sneered—okay, just a mess.

As we walked back, he took my hand in his. "Now let's get you home."

"What?"

His eyes twinkled. "I have a couple of weeks off. I can get you home and take a flight back."

"I can't ask that of you. I know you have to get this place ready."

He frowned. "You didn't ask it of me. I offered. But that's

not the only reason though. You lost your license for a week last night. It's being mailed to the police station closest to your address. They wouldn't give it to me. The only reason they left you with me was that they're fans, and you never actually drove." He grabbed my bags and started walking toward the car in the driveway.

I slumped onto the ground in the driveway. "I lost my license?"

He ran inside and grabbed a small bag of stuff. I stayed where I was, enjoying my pity party for one. He came back out and offered me his hand. "Come on, baby. I'll take you home, and you can straighten this whole thing out with Phil. We'll get you sorted out. You can stay with me. If Phil comes and grovels, I'll kick the shit out of him. It'll be fun. Willy told me you were upset. He said Phil was cheating. I need to beat his ass now anyway."

"I don't want to talk about it. I can't believe this." I took his hand.

He walked right over to my car. "This is going to be just like old times."

"You can't come with me. That's outrageous. How can I pay for hotels with no license? I have to fly back. This is crazy."

He nodded. "I agree. It's also crazy to drive to South Carolina and get drunk on a beach and lure unsuspecting men to their demise with your striptease, and yet here we are." His eyes turned serious. "Jack, I can't let you leave here without making sure you're safe. You can't board a plane without ID, and you can't drive. I can't let you go home to Phil until I know the story." His eyes sparkled. "I mean, you're welcome to stay if you want to."

"Seriously? Me and you in a small space for the two-day drive is going to be messy. You forget how much we used to fight."

He grinned. "Baby, I remember how annoying you are. Get in the car." He walked over, opened the trunk of my car, and stuffed CHANEL in there with everything else.

"You have my keys?"

He nodded. "Yeah, I had the special task of driving you

home. Are you okay? We talked about this."

I shook my head. He climbed into the driver's seat, looking too big for my car. I sighed and got in. I closed the door, nestling into the warm seat. He pulled out his cell phone and dialed as he started the car.

"Dan, hey. Look, I need you to stay at the house and get it sorted out for Mom and Dad and everyone. I had a party last night. I cleared everyone out, but it's still messy. Yeah, the beach house—about a week—New York. Thanks, man. Yup, I'll let you know." He hung up and looked at me. "My calendar is clear."

I smiled. "I can stay here and help you get everything ready."

He shrugged. "I honestly didn't want to do it. This is good. It'll force my family to participate in the task of running the beach house. I do everything, pay for everything, and they all take. This is going to be a treat for me."

He drove slowly out of the parking lot. I closed my eyes, even though I didn't want to, and drifted off to sleep.

I woke with a start. We were parked near a store. I looked at a strange man standing outside the window. I jumped up, but stopped myself from freaking out when I saw the gas pump.

"Shit." I rubbed my eyes, grabbed my wallet, and ran inside, barefoot. I looked down. He had taken my boots off. I growled and stalked across the store to where he was standing at the microwave with a stick of pepperoni hanging from his lips. He smiled. I scowled.

"What?"

"You took my boots off? Let me pay for the gas."

"That's okay. You can pay me back some other time. If I pay, fucktard Phil can't track you around the countryside."

I stepped back. "Don't swear so loud in here." I glanced around the dingy gas station. No one even batted an eyelash at him cussing. I sighed. "Besides, he doesn't care where I am."

He shrugged. "If you were mine, which you should have been, and I screwed up as bad as he has—which for the record I would never do—I would be scouring the bank accounts to see if you're all right. I would need to know where you were, and I would be on a flight to come and get you."

I flinched at the crazed look in his eyes. "He won't do that."

"Then it's like I always said—he never deserved you in the first place. Fuck him. Let him wonder where you are. Let him die of curiosity and hate himself. You want a man to suffer, don't let him know what you're doing. You women are all the same, you say too much. You let us in on too many things. We're hunters, we need the chase." The microwave beeped. He pulled out two wrapped-up round things. He carried them over to the counter, looking back at me as he paid. "You want anything else?"

I opened my mouth. "No. I'm sor—" I stopped myself when he gave me a look. "No." I blushed and helped him carry the things from the store.

He placed a steamy round thing in my hand. "Gas station cheeseburgers are the best." He opened his and squirted packets of mustard and ketchup on the bun. I opened mine and let him do the same. He closed my bun and nodded. I took a bite, watching him take one as well. It was delicious, and yet somehow I knew I would regret eating it.

I moaned and smiled, covering my mouth with my hand. "It's good." We stood outside, eating off the hood of the car. He opened a root beer and passed it to me. I drank from the can and sighed. The fact I was barefoot was bothering me less and less.

He pointed at a bush across the broken concrete of the small parking lot. "Look."

I glanced over to see a duck with her babies walking alongside the parking lot and vanishing down a hillside. It was quiet, except for the buzzing of flies and things, but that was a peaceful sort of noise.

I finished off the burger and soda with a burp. I covered my mouth, horrified. He winked at me. "You shouldn't hold them back. It's better for you to let it all out."

"I'm barefoot in a filthy parking lot, eating food from a

packet and drinking soda from a can. I probably need a vaccine from all this."

He scowled. "You're such a princess now. Where is the fearless girl I once knew?"

I wrinkled my nose at him. "I never was fearless."

He cocked an eyebrow. "Yeah, you were. You were on fire when we were younger. You let them kill that part of you."

I looked down at my pedicure and scowled at the broken toenail. "You know what it's like there."

"I always hated it there. Let's just get in the car before I drag you into the woods and make you climb a tree and eat a bug."

My eye twitched. I watched his face the entire time I climbed into the car and locked my door. He got in, flinging bags of food and drinks onto the backseat. My other bags were back there. I remembered the shoes I'd bought. I unbuckled, grabbed the bag, and pulled the box out. I looked at the brand-new Prada wedges. They were silver and white and had thick straps crisscrossing the top. I looked down at my filthy feet and decided to wait to put them on. I put them in the backseat.

He gave me a sideways glance. "You need some flip-flops."

"What?"

He nodded. "Yup. Next store we see, I'll get you some."

I shuddered. Wearing the black jogging pants was almost killing all of my pride. I flipped down the visor and flinched. My strawberry-blonde hair was curled and unruly. The glossy sheen of my straightened hairdo was long gone. My dark eyes looked haunted and exhausted. I had a full set of Gucci bags under each one. My skin was lackluster and pale.

"Why are you looking at yourself like that?"

I glanced over at him. "Oh, just checking the damage."

"You look fine. You always do."

"Wow, fine. Thank you for that. All my worries have just instantly dissolved with that word 'fine.' You, my friend, have always been a wordsmith and an ego booster."

He narrowed his gaze. "I did go to college. I'm not a tree trunk."

I smirked. "You played hockey, you're not fooling me. And you told me I looked like shit back at the house."

"That was before you showered. You know what I like about you, Jack? Your attitude is just shitty enough that I feel *fine* saying you look hot or you look fine. You're a sexy woman and you know it. I know you—well, better than anyone. No one talks about the fact your dad runs the household, cheats on your mom, and you're still stuck in that old-boys' club sort of mentality. Your dad's an asshole. He'd still have black servants if Abe Lincoln hadn't told him no. Your mom is a doormat, and I have always hated that they planned your marriage. You got that subservient look in your eyes now. It never was there before. The years aren't aging your face, but they're killing your eyes. Your soul is dying. I'm fucking glad he cheated on you or whatever he did. I'm glad you finally see what a douche Phil is." His grin was bitter looking and a bit crazy. "I'll wager you anything you want that this is the first crazy thing you've done since you and I fell apart. Besides sneaking off to my house on Christmas."

I put my hand up. "You don't know me so well anymore. Don't sum me up like that." I gave him a narrow gaze. "I think things and feel things, but I can't just act them out like you. You're still such a child. Try being engaged, France. It's hard work."

"I did try once, if you will recall." He grabbed my hand, squeezing it. "He never deserved you, and this is your chance to be your own person and run your own life. Fuck them."

I fought my tears, and instead, gave him a deadly stare. "I have done something crazy, and you don't know about it."

He rolled his eyes. "What—you been robbing banks on the side?"

I punched his massive arm. "No."

"You have to tell me what it is now."

"No." I closed my eyes and fell back to sleep instantly.

He'd driven along back roads and through small towns

the whole way. So when he entered Atlanta city limits, I was stunned.

"We're in Georgia?"

He nodded. "You ever been to Georgia?"

"No." I shook my head.

He smiled. "You're in for a treat."

He pulled into the Four Seasons, and I looked down at my clothes. "Oh God. France, I can't stay here, looking like this."

"We'll get a personal shopper to grab you some things. These places always have that included in the concierge services. I've used them before, on away games."

I thought for a second. "Okay. I know what I like. That works." I was excited about getting some things that suited me. I didn't care if Phil saw where my credit cards were being used. I wasn't ready to talk to him.

France parked. I pulled my sunglasses on and gathered my bags from the backseat. He grabbed the rest of my things from the trunk and handed the keys to the valet.

We walked inside. I felt a small bit of relief, seeing something more my style again. The hotel was lovely.

He reserved the rooms while I booked a spa treatment and wrote a list of things I would need from the girl running out to shop for me. She gave me a once-over, but she stopped when she saw France. I looked at the way she smiled at him and rolled my eyes.

He came over to me and put his hand on the small of my back. "Let's go." He led me away before I was even able to thank her. A man's hand at the small of my back was familiar to me. His hand was more than that. The elevator opened and he led me inside, taking my bags from me.

"Presidential Suite, please."

I shot him a look. "You didn't get two rooms?"

"Nope." He led me off the elevator when we got to the nineteenth floor.

I followed him to the door. He opened it and held it open for me. I glared at him.

"What?"

"One room?"

"What? We nap in the same car, and you always come and sleep at my place. Besides, it's a suite. It has two bathrooms. The other suites were booked, and all that was left were those regular rooms." He winked. "I don't know about you, but I haven't stayed in a regular room in a long time."

"You eat from gas stations, but you're picky about your sleeping quarters?"

He walked through the sitting room and into the bedroom. "This is pretty nice." He flopped onto the bed. "You want to sleep on the bed or the pull-out couch?"

I looked at the couches. "Same bed—no sexy time, Mike. I mean it." I took the second key. "I have a spa appointment in ten minutes from now. When the shopper drops my stuff off, can you tip her?"

"Yup."

"Admit you're taking advantage."

He smiled at me, dazzling me with his dark eyes. "Yup."

I stomped off.

Wednesday night

The spa, at least, was amazing. Two hours later, I walked out in a robe with a polished and massaged body, fresh-smelling skin, and a glowing face. The facial had been the nicest part. I felt the years and stress melt off.

I had almost frowned when they refused my credit card, stating it was paid for. But I didn't let him get to me. I took deep breaths and found my Zen.

He was gone when I got back upstairs. I was good with that.

My clothes were laid out on the bed and my makeup and products were placed on the bathroom counter.

I took a shower.

The tears started to leak out again. I closed my eyes, sliding down the marble wall.

"Do you always cry in the shower now? You used to like the shower. What happened to that girl?" he asked from outside the door.

I jumped up. "No. Why are you in here?" The door was glass. I kept my hands over my parts. "Get out!" I couldn't see him.

"I'm not looking. I just heard you crying, and I wanted to make sure you're okay." I slumped back down the wall. His hand slipped inside the shower door. He dropped a pink bikini. "Put it on."

"No. You know I don't wear pink, anyway."

"I'm coming in, so you either put it on, or I come in and see you naked. Not like it would be the first time."

I pulled the bathing suit on with an intense amount of work. Being wet made it harder. He stepped into the shower wearing swimming shorts and stood under the water. I backed up and sat on the floor again.

He smiled. "It's like an adult water park in here."

"Why are you in here?"

He shrugged. "I went and got bathing suits. I figured we could go swimming. The personal shopper was back so I hoped you'd return soon. I wanted to catch you before your shower." He grinned. "You look good in pink."

I snarled at him. "I don't swim in hotel pools. You know that."

"Yeah, well I was counting on some things being different." He sat on the opposite side of the shower, ignoring me. "You okay?"

"No. I feel like an idiot. I don't think I even care that he screwed someone else. I expected that, if I'm being honest with myself. I mean, look at the world we live in. People like us are fucking ridiculous. My parents are insane and his are worse. But I do care that he was living out some sick, twisted fantasy in my bed. I mean come on, get a hotel room and a hooker—just don't let her wear my shoes. MY FUCKING SHOES AND HIM WEARING A FUCKING CAPE! WHAT IS THAT?"

He didn't say anything. I wasn't making sense.

I tilted my head back, letting the water soak me. "I don't get why my bed, my shoes." I was on a roll and the pain in my chest didn't stop me from saying it, "It's like I wasn't enough. He needed more."

I closed my eyes and let my tears fall off my face with the water from the rainfall showerhead.

"You wanna know what I think?"

I nodded. I didn't know why, but I did.

"I think you and him haven't ever been honest with each other. He's probably into porn and other trashy shit. He's probably a borderline sex addict and never had a minute to be comfortable with the man he is. He has to live up to the rules of your blue-blood bullshit too. The cape is weird for me. I know you haven't told me the whole story yet, but the cape is freaking me out."

Was he making excuses for Phil? Had that just happened? I opened my eyes and looked at him with daggers until he opened his mouth again. "And you, you're so much bigger than the tiny box you're supposed to fit in.

You act like you're okay being that prissy girl, but I know if given the chance, the girl I used to know is still in there. She's a little booze-soaked and tired out from the bullshit, but she's there."

"She's not."

He scooted forward, towering over me. He tilted my chin. "What are you doing right now?"

"I don't have a clue."

He smiled. "You're hiding. You need to let that girl out, babe. You think I don't see what this all is? You knew you needed five days to make it home, not because of the drive. You did it to get a little break before you go back." His smile faded and his eyes burned. "You're going back and you know it."

"I have to go back, France. You know my dad."

He lifted me into his arms. "Then let's make it a fun five days."

"I can't. I don't feel fun. I feel sick."

He lowered his face onto mine. "I can." He brushed his lips against mine softly. It felt right, instantly.

I pushed him back. "Fine, but none of that, okay? I wasn't kidding when I said I wasn't complicating this all with you and me. We are confused about what we are. Sex with another man isn't going to fix my engagement to Phil and his cape."

"I tore up some random dude's number like two days ago. You sleep at my house at least a couple of times a year. Don't tell me what you are. I know what you are. It's you that's confused. Not me." His face turned up into a grin. "I need to have a drink when you tell me this cape story."

I snorted and shuddered, exhausted with my own shit. "Just let me process all this and the cape and the being disowned if I leave and everything, and then we can discuss kissing."

He smiled. "I'll wait for you to ask me to kiss you again."

I grinned and slid back against the wall. "You do that."

He looked down on me. "I think you're the prettiest girl I have ever seen."

I laughed out loud. "Liar."

"Laugh all you want, but it's true. There are fireworks inside you that haven't been lit since the last time me and you—"

I laughed and pointed. "You keep that puck-fuck shit to yourself. I don't want to hear the lines."

His eyes sparkled. "You know you like it when I try."

"'Cause I know nothing is going to come of it."

He laughed.

I sat forward. "What do you want to do after the five days?"

He put a hand on my thigh. "Run away and drag you with me."

"Okay, let me confront my family, and if I can't go back, I'll run away with you."

He cocked his head. "I need some kind of guarantee."

"No." I shook my head and wiped away the water. "The most I'll do is shake on it."

"I guess. How about this? You don't run away with me, and you have to tell me that bad thing you did."

My brows knit together. "Deal." He shook my hand, pulling me in, and kissed along the side of my mouth.

He stood up and offered me his hand. I waited a second and then took it. He lifted me up but didn't let go of my hand. We just looked at each other for a minute. The shower got thick with the tense feeling of the forbidden kiss. He flashed me a grin. "You have to say it, or I won't kiss you."

I swatted him with my free hand. "It's not going to happen." I climbed out and dried off. I noticed the changes in his body. He was thick and beefy, but toned. I had to pull my eyes away from the square of his jaw and his soft lips, and the memory of how they felt against mine. His scruffy face made me want him more for some barbaric reason. I had the dirtiest thoughts ever and blushed.

"What are you thinking about?"

"Nothing," I answered too quickly.

It made him smile. "Your face just went a hundred shades of red." He winked. "I can imagine what you were thinking." He scoffed and left the bathroom. I stood there, clutching my towel and trembling. He poked his head back in. "If you want me to kiss you, all you have to do is ask."

I threw a rolled towel at him. We were flirting. This was us half a decade ago.

I dried off and started opening my boxes of stuff. I did my makeup without actually meeting my own gaze. I knew what was in there—the thoughts and feelings that I had been fighting for some time.

I wore the robe out to the room and grabbed the clothes I'd asked for. I carried them into the bedroom and dressed. The bra and underwear made me uncomfortable, but I knew in boutiques they were not tried on. I slipped on the black dress I already owned. It was a classic sleeveless knit dress with pleats sewn into the skirt. It hung perfectly and was the most comfortable dress ever. I took the pearl earrings from my purse and put them on and ran my fingers through my curly hair. The long strawberry-blonde ringlets sat perfectly, thanks to hundreds of dollars' worth of product.

I looked good, like me again.

"I got the hotel dry cleaning the clothes you had in the bags."

"YOU WHAT?"

He stepped back. "What's happening here? Why are you yelling at me?"

I stomped across the floor to the phone.

He grabbed it from my hands. "Are you insane? I did you a favor."

I growled through a clenched jaw. "That coat is my favorite. It's discontinued and there is one Chinese lady I trust with my clothes."

He laughed, actually in my face.

"I don't do dry cleaning." I took a deep breath and turned and walked to the door. "Are you ready?" I was still raging inside, but I wasn't about to show him my fucking fireworks. He was always patronizing me and making derogatory "ginger" remarks about my temper.

He stopped laughing. "Yeah." He opened the door as I reached for it and placed his hand on my lower back. I walked fast to get away from his hand. He grabbed my arm and pulled me back to him, pressing me into his chest. "I was trying to be helpful."

"Don't." I glared, seething. I wasn't a fan of being manhandled.

He locked his gaze on mine. "You're being insane. It's a fucking coat, Jack."

I started to laugh. The sentence was absurd—a coat? I shoved him back and walked to the elevator. He pushed me playfully from behind. I turned. "Screw you."

He grabbed my hand, grinning like an idiot, and pulled me into his arms. "I wanna screw. You keep saying no."

I laughed again, but it wasn't the homicidal one I wanted it to be. It was genuine. "Don't say screw. Sometimes I hate you."

He wrapped his huge arm around my shoulders. "Nothing better than getting a princess to hate you and love you at the same time."

I rolled my eyes as he pushed the button. When we got inside, he nodded. "Don't forget that I'll be swarmed if anyone recognizes me."

"If I end up in pictures again, I'm going to get disowned. My mother and father hate you."

He looked down on me. "Your mom likes me. She grabbed my butt once."

"That doesn't mean she likes you. She doesn't have to like you, to do that."

He scowled. "Your mom is sort of a player."

The restaurant was full when we got down there. I ignored everyone as I sat and glanced at the wine list. The server walked up, smiling at me. He was sexy as hell and probably not much older than the little bartender that could.

"Can I get you a drink to start?"

France shook his head. "I'll just have some water."

I smiled. "Do you have any Lafite?"

He nodded. "The '95 Bordeaux."

"We'll have that."

He winked. "Excellent choice."

A small chuckle slipped from my lips. I glanced at the confused and rigid-looking face of France and started to laugh harder. I shook my head. "Just a coat? I can't even believe you said that. It's a one of a kind and some seventeen-year-old is dry cleaning it now. That's excellent."

He pointed after the server. "I'm not drinking that snooty wine."

"You ruined my jacket." I leaned forward. "You are. Trust me."

He looked like he might growl, but he sat back, relenting. "So where should we go tomorrow?"

"I don't know. You're the captain."

He drummed his fingers on the chair, glancing about the busy dining room. He was avoiding me.

"If you want, I can just hop on a train or a bus." I shuddered as I imagined the feel of it, but I had to be realistic about what was happening. I ordered an entire bottle of wine. He would have half a glass and bitch about it the entire time. I would drink the rest, and then all my choices would be tainted by my undying love for him and delicious Bordeaux.

He shook his head, still averting his eyes. "No. I want you to stay with me." An evil grin crossed his lips. "Besides, we both know you have never set foot on any form of public transit. You would panic and call me to come get you anyway."

I couldn't fight the smile on my lips. "Shut up."

He laughed and my heart pitter-pattered.

The server brought the wine and poured him a small taste of it. He frowned. "Well, fill it up, son. I don't love it, but I can drink more than that."

"Just taste it and see if you like it."

The server looked confused as France lifted the glass and drank the little sip. He shuddered. "Tastes like vinegar."

I nodded at the flushed and upset face of the young man. "It's perfect then. You may fill both glasses."

He hesitated and poured us each a glass.

I sipped. It was bliss. I might have even slipped out a moan. My dream had always been to own a vineyard. My parents always mocked my dream. Owning a vineyard was equivalent to farming.

France took a sip and made a face. "I can't, Jack." He

looked at the young man. "How about a Bud? You got beer here?" That made me chuckle.

He got a nod, and I got another wink as he left our table.

France pointed. "That kid winks at you one more time, I'll close his eye for him."

"You aren't my boyfriend, what do you care?"

His voice still sounded throaty from the sip of wine, "He doesn't know that." His twang was thick suddenly.

I laughed harder. "You are cute jealous."

He laughed sarcastically. "No, I'm not."

The beer and an iced mug were delivered. Of course, he drank from the bottle. He sighed. "That's good." He sat back and nodded. "All right, tell me the story."

I glanced at the menu. "You sure?"

"Yup. We're hundreds of miles away, and I have you here and a beer in my hand. I can take it. I know he cheated. I know there was a cape. I know you're pissed. Spill."

I bit my lip, deciding on both our meals and then nodded. "Okay." I pushed the menu to the side of me and took a massive gulp of the still airing wine. I smacked my lips. "I was at a party on Sunday. He was with this woman who is notorious for her affairs with married men. They were together on the balcony and then they were gone, and she was so close to him—the body language was nuts. They held hands and walked off together, whispering in each other's ears. It was obvious and not just to me." I took another drink.

He made a face. "Jack, I hate Phil. We both know that. But that's not proof, baby. You sounded mad upstairs. Was he wearing the cape at the party? Was it a costume party?"

"No, shut up." I took another breath. "It gets worse."

"Okay, is there a second story? Is this the shoe story?"

I nodded, finishing the glass. "Shhhh." I took a deep breath and looked into his dark eyes. "The next day I walked into the house, and he was having sex, the naughty way, with our eighteen-year-old neighbor. She had a weird outfit on with garters and a bustier and my red Jimmy Choos. She was calling him Mr. Bernard, and he was pulling her hair. I think she's eighteen, but she might be nineteen. We just went to her birthday party, and Brandi and I think she just graduated. He was fucking in a cape and some kind of outfit I couldn't see. Maybe a superhero. He wanted her to call him Mr. Bernard. He wanted that dirty costume sex, and he defiled my shoes, my bed, and my pride by doing it. And he didn't care. I even called him like ten minutes later and asked if I had those shoes, hoping he would lie and tell me I didn't have them. But he didn't. He let me think my shoes were fine, even after he had fucked her in them. I know it's wrong that I care about the shoes, but I feel so dirty that they brought parts of me into their game. Like I am a joke to him. My role as his wife is a joke."

His grip on the bottle was intensifying. He looked like it might break as he lifted it to his lips and sucked the whole thing back. He lowered his trembling hand. "I'm going to kill him."

"No. You aren't. I need you out of jail."

He leaned across the table, fighting his horrid temper. "You aren't marrying him." It wasn't a question. "You are not going back, no matter what. I will drug you and move you to a secluded island. This is some bullshit. The man's a pedo."

I swallowed hard, knowing what the outcome would be if I told him I had to, and shook my head.

"You can honestly say that you chose him over me because his upbringing was better than mine? This is the man your family thinks is good enough for you? He fucks kids?"

"Shhhhh. Don't." I shook my head again.

He got up, tossed a hundred-dollar bill on the table and grabbed my hand. He dragged me from the restaurant. I struggled. "France, that wasn't enough for the bottle of wine."

He was done. He didn't hear me. He dragged me to the elevator doors. I could feel him pulsating with rage as we stood there in the awkward silence of knowing. Knowing what was about to happen.

The doors opened. He stepped into the elevator in a civilized manner, but his grip was so tight, my hand was going numb. He pulled me into him as he hit the floor button. His hand went right for my skirt. His mouth lowered close to mine. He didn't go all the way. I could feel his breath on my lips as his hands ripped the pleats from my skirt, tearing a long slit up the side. He smiled, but I jumped as the fabric tore.

We stood there, ninety-percent in and holding. The elevator dinged for our floor. He lifted me up into his arms, wrapping my legs around him as he carried me to our room. I was about to ask him to kiss me when he asked, "You hungry?"

I nodded, swallowing hard and unsure. I felt the door to our room open and heard it close, but I never broke my stare from him. My hands had slid up into his hair. I was gripping him. His fingers started to roam across my underwear as he carried me to the bed. He laid me back on the comforter and stood up. I could see something changing on his face. He looked confused as he stepped back and pointed at me. "Don't move." He turned and left the room.

I could barely breathe.

I tried to stay there, imagining all the places he could have gone, but the look in his eyes told me everything. He couldn't do it. He couldn't touch me and feel sorry for me in the same breath. Or he had left to murder Phil.

When the door was kicked open thirty minutes later, he came in with a box of pizza and a bag of something else. He laid them on the bed.

"What just happened?"

He shook his head and ran his hands through his dark bushy hair. "I can't eat that highfalutin food and wine and listen to the goddamned hair pulling story. And I can't kiss you until you ask me to. And your eyes are still puffy from crying over that douche Phil, so I can't make love to you. So let's get you good and drunk and eat normal food." He dumped the bag.

I started to laugh. "Pear ciders?"

He nodded. "Remember the summer we started hanging out? I wasn't allowed to leave for South Carolina because coach had too many summer practices I would miss. They billeted me out at Jimmy's house, and his mom kept trying to sleep with me, so I hid at your place all summer. Your sister bought us these to drink. It was what she and all her friends were drinking at the time. You got sick and we slept outside on the patio furniture. You told me you were still a virgin, and I told you I was too. So we had sex under the stars. It was the best and worst sex I ever had." His eyes were burning, but he didn't move.

"It was an amazing way to lose it. Most of my friends were pretty much date-raped or pressured into doing it. No one did it with their best friend poolside and under the stars."

He nodded. "I agree."

I couldn't read his face. I didn't know what he was thinking, but I had a feeling it wasn't rowdy sex.

He cleared his throat. "I just wanted us to try to remember being best friends. And I want you to know I am here for you, jokes aside. I didn't know you saw him doing that. I didn't realize how embarrassed you feel. I can't take advantage of that, as much as I want to." He sat on the bed with his back to me and opened the pizza. He took a piece and passed me the box. I wanted to cry, but I didn't. I took a piece and tried to choke it down. He was saving himself from the tragic affair he knew would end with me going back.

He cracked a cider and passed it to me. I sipped the sickly sweet drink, picking at the label. He looked back. "You want to watch a movie?"

I nodded.

He got the remote and started fiddling with it. I stared at his broad back and thick arms and imagined the weight of him on me. I loved that feeling. It had been years, but I still remembered it. He was the only person I liked touching me. Growing up with no one ever touching you, you'd think I would have worked hard for any affection, but I went the other way. I grew to be like them, my parents. I hated affection from anyone. I never liked being touched or hugged. It felt too foreign to me, unless I was trashed or high. Then I liked drinking and fucking, but that wasn't the same as having someone touch you. France was the only one who could touch me and make me feel safe.

Not even Phil had ever reached the level of comfort that France did.

He picked a movie and crawled up onto the bed. He patted his chest. I abandoned my pizza and cider and crawled over to him. He wrapped around me, kissing my head. I closed my eyes and pretended that was my life. That was my reality.

Thursday morning

The warmth around me was suffocating me. I tried to push it off, but when I opened my eyes, I realized it was France. I smiled and let the weight of him press me into the bed. He moaned and slid between my thighs. We had stripped to our undergarments when we decided it was bedtime. Now, in the light of the morning, it seemed like that had been a bad plan. He was used to waking next to a puck fuck. His erection pressed against me hard as his face dipped into my neck. My breath became a moan as his body woke up. He slid against me, cupping and gripping. I wrapped my legs around his waist, pulling him into me more. His lips started leaving kisses along my collarbone and nape. He lowered more, dragging my bra strap down with his lips. His mouth kissed its way to my nipple. He kissed around it, teasing and licking. Finally, he landed his whole mouth over it, sending chills everywhere. I moaned, wrapping my legs tighter and pressing myself against his rigid cock.

His hands made their way down between my legs, pushing my underwear to the side. I was freeing him from his underwear at the same time.

He rested his tip between my legs but paused. He sat up from my breast. "You going home to him?"

I tried to move my pelvis to force his entry, but he pulled back with my movements. I groaned. "I can't decide now."

He cocked an eyebrow. "You going back?"

"Yeah." I bit my lip and nodded. "I have to break things off. I have to go back and talk to him and get my things."

"No. If you go back there you're gonna let your parents tell you to stay with him."

I pushed him back. "Screw you, Mike." I pushed my underwear back into place and tried to get out from under him, but he didn't budge. He stared me down. I turned my face to the side, feeling the red-hot rage of unsatisfied sexual urges.

"I wanna screw, JD." He saw my face and laughed. "It was a bad joke. Look, I don't want to start this up, if it is just ending with you and him again."

I refused to look at him. "I don't know, okay? I don't have an answer for you. Stop saying screw. It's gross."

He kissed my shoulder. "I want you to be mine. That hasn't ever changed."

I wriggled away and turned my back to him. His cock was still pressed into me. I wanted it so badly. I closed my eyes and tried to think about my grandma. Instead, he kissed my neck and rubbed himself against me and made me think about him playing hockey.

"I love you."

"You love all women. That's sort of always been your problem."

"I know being with you would make me an honest man."

"That's a pretty big risk on both our parts, considering the friendship we have is the only good thing in my life."

"You've always been the best thing in my life." He pushed his cock up against my butt cheek. I turned over, annoyed and impatient. I pushed him on his back and slid down the bed fast. I grabbed his cock and wrapped my lips around it. He jumped, unprepared and completely taken aback. I sucked like I was being paid to do it. I remembered that filthy party I'd been to with Diane. The lady had told us to stroke as we sucked and meet in the middle. I wiggled my tongue as I sucked up and down the shaft.

"Oh shit, Jack. Damn."

I almost smiled, but I remembered not to break the rhythm. He started to push himself into my mouth farther. Since I wasn't being paid and had a gag reflex, I decided to take that as my opportunity to teach him a lesson. I pulled away, wiped my mouth and jumped off the bed. I waved back at him. "Don't start shit with me, France. You won't win. I'm not one of your toys." I slammed the bathroom door and locked it.

I heard him scramble off the bed. "JD, get the hell out here." He pounded on the door. "What the hell was that?"

I smiled. "That was what you get for messing with me. You started this, and then you started talking about Phil."

He pounded on the door. "Guys can die from that, Jack. Open the door."

I started to laugh. "No way. Go finish by yourself. I'm taking a shower." I started the shower and dropped my bra and underwear to the floor. As I was stepping in, he busted through the door. He looked like a bull in a china shop as he seethed. He looked positively malicious as he grabbed my hand and dragged me into the shower. He slammed my back against the tiles, but dropped to his knees.

Gently, he parted my lips and buried his wooly face between my legs. His warm mouth kissed and sucked as his tongue slid up and down my slit. The beard felt incredible against the delicate flesh there. I cried out as he slid one of his thick fingers inside me. The hot water splashed down on us as my knees weakened. I felt the climax building. He must have too. He pumped faster and sucked my clit. I tried to grip the tile, but I couldn't. I was slipping. He wrapped my legs onto his shoulders and pushed them farther apart.

I mumbled something like, "Mike, I'm gonna come." But it was a mess with the water, orgasm, and awkward positioning.

"I know, baby. Come for me. Come on my face." He tickled me with his beard and mustache.

And I did.

I twitched and came, and when he brought me down into his lap, he sat me on his cock. I eased it inside myself. Right away, the orgasm started to come back.

He knelt back a bit on his heels as I rode him. He cupped my ass, working me on him. His huge hands, gripping my ass and moving me in a circular motion under the spray of the water, was hot.

Not as hot as the things he whispered into my ears.

"I love fucking you, JD." He pushed me back and licked my nipple, sucking it, and biting lightly. His beard against my breast tickled. "You feel so good, baby."

He rocked us back and forth. My feet no longer held me. They wrapped around him, clinging to each other. He lifted and lowered my body on his cock, bouncing me on him. I felt the buildup again. He sucked harder, bit harder. I barely registered as I clenched around his cock. He was maintaining the momentum for me. I orgasmed again. He bit down hard, making me cry out but not from the pain of it. When I came out of the haze, he laid me on the tiles, lifted my legs, and placed my feet on his shoulders. He grabbed my hips and fucked me hard. It was everything I remembered, and yet so much better. We hadn't done it since we were young, but it felt the same.

"Goddamn, JD. You love it, don't you? You love my cock."

I tried to nod. I tried to do anything beyond moan and drool on myself, but that wasn't possible.

"My cock loves you. Goddamn, you have a sweet pussy."

My head started bouncing on the tiles, but I barely registered that. He ran his thumb over my clit as he slowed the pace again. I shook my head. "No. Fuck me." I looked up to see the wild look in his eyes and the grin on his lips. He lifted me up farther. I pushed with my feet on his shoulders, and he pounded me until I screamed again.

He came into me, exploding. I felt it fill me. He collapsed on me, kissing my shoulders and muttering things I didn't understand.

I patted his shoulder. "France, you have to get off me. You're squishing me into the tiles. I swear I heard a rib crack." He shook his head and rolled onto his back. We both lay there for a minute with the water spraying down on us.

I glanced at him, aware of the swollen mouth, satisfied look on my face, and blush covering my cheeks. "That was amazing."

He nodded. "No one fucks you like I do. You know you want to stay with me."

"That's not a reason to stay with someone. Almost, but no."

He grabbed my hand and kissed it. "Jack, you're mine.

You always were."

I had no argument for that.

We dried off and made our way to the bed. He was snuggled around me, like he always did and snoring before I even got comfortable.

I watched him sleeping, mesmerized by the size of him and the way his lips curled. I wondered if I would ever be able to just be strong like him, for him, and run away from it all.

Thursday night

We got into the elevator after dinner. He dropped to his knees instantly and lifted my skirt. He pulled my underwear to the side and licked me before I realized what was happening. My eyes shot open. "Again? Not in here."

He ran a finger up and down my slit. "Why not? You're wet."

I shook my head, looking around for a surveillance camera. "It's because you keep kissing my neck. Stop this."

"You haven't asked me to kiss your lips so I have to kiss somewhere." He lowered his face again, brushing his beard against the soft part of my thigh. "You want me again, Jack. Admit it."

I whimpered a little.

He dipped a finger inside my pussy and trailed the moisture up to my clit. His bearded face made its way up between my legs. He dragged his tongue the whole way up to my clit. He sucked and flicked.

When the elevator got to our floor, he tossed me over his shoulder and carried me to the room. He laid me on the bed and buried his face between my legs again.

I moaned, tugging at my dress. When I got the buttons open, exposing my breasts, he sat up on his knees and unbuttoned his pants. He dragged them down, bouncing his huge cock between my legs.

"You ready for me, Jack? 'Cause I can't wait a second longer."

I nodded, pulling at his dress shirt. He yanked it off and bent his face down to my nipple. He sucked as he slowly moved the head of his cock between my legs. He traced it up and down my slit, getting me ready. I held my breath as he entered me. He moaned into my chest as he made a second plunge, getting all the way in.

His beard dragged against my nipple as he breathed into the top of my chest.

"Fuck me. Jack, you see what you do to me?" He pumped into me hard once.

I cried out, "Please kiss me, Mike."

Finally, he put his mouth on mine as he pumped hard. My legs were spread as wide as they would go to accommodate his thick body. They bounced in the air as he thrust wildly. He rolled onto his back, flipping me with him, no doubt too close to finishing. I slid up his cock as he moved my hips the way he wanted them to. His hands moved to my breasts. I leaned forward so he could suck one and roll the other. I worked his cock, sliding up and down it, making it hit the right spot until I felt it. The buildup hit. I moaned as he felt me climaxing and he increased his sucking and flicking. I clenched down on him, riding his cock rapidly as I came.

Sounds escaped my mouth that I didn't know I could make. I felt him get into position to roll again. I finished orgasming, and he rolled on top of me. He sat up, holding my thighs and thrashed hard until he came in a series of groans and ball slapping. He collapsed on me. I couldn't stop smiling or trying to pull him farther into me.

We finished and I grinned into the spattering of hair on his chest. "You have a one-track mind, I swear."

"No, it's just you." We lay there half dressed and panting, until I realized I'd left my purse in the restaurant. "Shit. I have to go downstairs and get my bag."

He sighed. "I'll go."

I kissed his cheek. "That's okay. You go get some water and snacks, and we can watch another movie."

"So much for a road trip. All we've done is stay here and have sex."

I laughed and walked to the bathroom.

By the time I had cleaned up, he was already gone. I hurried down and grabbed my purse from the front desk where it had been turned in. I walked across the foyer, lost in thought and smiles. Under different circumstances and considerably less stress, I might have recognized him sitting across from the elevator, but somehow my brain didn't register Phil being there. I walked right past him as he got up quickly, looking rough. I jumped as he offered a sad stare.

Fuck him.

I frowned when I saw him walking to me. My heart was pounding and my stomach was clenched. I just needed to get away from him. All I saw was the cape and the lies. Devastation and foolishness filled me as he shouted, "Jacqueline, wait."

I pressed the button for the elevator. "No."

He grabbed my wrist, but I stepped into the elevator, forcing him to come with me.

Being in the small space alone was a bad idea. He stepped toward me. "Baby, I'm so sorry."

I shook my head indignantly, almost wishing I could curl into a ball, but I needed Mike. "No you're not. You're sorry you got caught—in a fucking cape, no less. You aren't sorry you fucked the hell out of that child on my sheets and bed in my shoes!" Anger and rage were fueling my hatred.

He winced. "I'm getting counseling. I have a sickness. Please, come home."

I looked at him like he had three heads. "Are you high right now? Because you have to be, to think I would go anywhere with you."

He handed me a bag. "I replaced your shoes."

"You can mail them to me." I snatched the bag. Fuck him, I loved those shoes. The elevator landed, and I stepped off. I walked to the door with him at my heels.

I slid the key in, stepped inside the room, and slammed the door in his face, but he caught it. He stepped in and closed it behind him.

"I know I screwed up, but I love you. Please, give me a second chance."

I tossed the shoe bag onto the bed I had slept in with France and crossed my arms. "I want you gone. I'm going to call security."

"Your father is here with me."

I felt a sickening twist inside of me. My eyes almost watered because I knew what it meant. "How could you? How could you involve him? Did you tell him what you did?"

He looked down, shaking his head slowly. "He just wants you to come home with us on the jet. He wants you downstairs and ready to leave in half an hour."

I looked at him. "I'm here with someone."

He nodded. "I know about Mike. I always have." He fought something when he said it.

"I have never done a thing with him, not since you and I got engaged. I never cheated on you, not once."

"But you loved him from the minute I met you. You think it was easy knowing I was always second to him?"

I felt the rage building. "So you eased your pain with the pussy of a young girl? Did you get her V-card, Phil? She's eighteen years old!"

"Nineteen." He stood taller, meeting my rage. "We are leaving in half an hour. Pack your shit, JD." He stepped into my face, towering over me. "You think your family will let you marry someone like him? Not a chance. Your father has worked too hard to prove himself to the elite families. He isn't going to let you throw away all that hard work." He spit on me as he spoke, "People like him, they're the ones we have affairs with in seedy hotels. You just try to be more elegant about it. I am willing to concede that you will never love me, but I refuse to be left for a hockey player. Why not a janitor or a bartender? You think I didn't know about that young man giving you his number the other day? You think I missed that?"

I shoved him back. "While you were balls deep in Eleanor? Yeah, I do think you missed that."

He slapped me hard. It caught me off guard. I fell back onto the bed. He stopped himself from attacking. I watched the flinch in his body. His chest was rising and falling like he was about to scream. I gripped my face as my lower lip started to tremble. I had never been hit before. Tears of hatred and anger filled my eyes. "Fuck you, Phil." I pointed at the door. "Get out!"

"You think you can humiliate me with a man like that and not expect me to retaliate?"

My whole body was trembling with fear and loathing, and even a little shame. Somehow, he made me feel it. I sniffled, hating that he had made me cry. I hated crying for him. He grabbed my arm and dragged me to the door. I put my feet down, fighting him, but he won out. He threw me over his shoulder and opened the door. I pounded on his back, but he walked as if I were a child having a fit.

He pressed the elevator. I was kicking and screaming, but no one was around. The Presidential Suite was the only room on the floor.

As the door opened, I didn't see what happened, but I flew back off his shoulder, slamming into the wall. I cried out as Phil landed on me. I tried to crawl away as tears were streaming my face and sobs were ripping from me. I heaved and crawled. Someone grabbed my arm, dragging me into the room. I caught a glimpse of Phil on the ground moaning as the door was shut. I collapsed onto the floor as France wrapped around me. I could feel him breathing as he held me.

He carried me to the bed and kissed my forehead. "I'll be right back."

I grabbed him, holding him to me. "No. My father is here too. Stay. They'll press charges if you hurt him." I knew he was capable of killing Phil.

He climbed onto the bed with me.

"Did he hurt you?"

"No."

He lifted my face. Obviously there was a mark. He was up and off the bed and flying out the door. It slammed shut before I could stop him.

I lay there, contemplating leaving the room and witnessing him murdering Phil, but I decided against it. I knew, seeing my bruises and the way I would kowtow to my father, it would only enrage him more.

I waited for a long time, frozen and afraid of the outcome of my actions. France was an innocent bystander, but he would lose the most.

Finally, the door opened, and he came sauntering in. His wooly face was flushed. He looked at me. "Your dad is here." My father walked in behind him. When he saw the state of me, he stopped. I wiped my eyes and sat upright, perfectly.

He looked at my cheek and sighed. "Phil?"

I nodded.

He beckoned and straightened his suit. "Mike, do you mind if I have a moment?"

Mike gave me a look. I nodded and he walked out of the room. I caught a glimpse of Phil in the hallway. I didn't even want to imagine how that was going to go.

My father looked around the huge room, settling on the couches on the other side. He held his hand out toward them. "Shall we?" I got up, straightening my dress and hair and followed him over there. We sat opposite one another. He cleared his throat. "I have spoken with Phil on this matter of infidelity. He is seeking some guidance from his family's doctor. You have to see how awkward this is for us all, you two having troubles right now. With it being so close to the wedding and all."

I felt the look creep across my face. "He had sex with a young girl in our house in a cape, and he hit me."

He nodded. "People make mistakes, Jacqueline. I have made my fair share, and your mother doesn't rub my face in them."

"I know. I know about the affairs you have had on Mom. I know you have hit her. I have seen you do it. You think I want that for my life? Even worse, is that the life you want for me?"

His eyes filled with anger. "The life we have given you has been taxing. Yes, there have been moments that weren't perfect, but we sacrificed a lot for you and your sister. We have had highs and lows like all marriages. One day, you will grow up and make the same kind of choices for your children so they too can school with the best. Marry the best. Live amongst the best."

I shook my head, feeling the tears dripping down my cheeks as empty pain was taking all my strength and will away. "Daddy, I never cared where I went to school. I was never one of them, not really. I can't marry Phil. You can't make me." It was a weak attempt at defiance. Even I heard the pathetic tone in my voice.

His voice never changed from soft and controlled when

he nodded. "I can. I'm friends with some people who will make sure Mike doesn't play anymore. It's quite political, that hockey. Or even worse, what would happen if they found a bunch of drugs in his locker or house or a dead whore? I can make that happen. I can also make sure that you have nothing. No money and no connections. I will cut you off completely, and none of your family or friends will ever speak to you again."

My stomach dropped. Dead whore, no money, no jobs. Was love worth the loss of everything else? Was my self-respect worth Mike losing everything?

He nodded at the empty look on my face. "The jet will be waiting for you for one hour." He knew my answer. He got up and placed a small bottle on the table and left the room. He didn't care about me at all. He would ruin Mike—I would ruin Mike. I would drag him down with me. He had worked so hard to get to where he was. My stomach ached as I came face to face with the brutal truth. I crawled on my knees to the small bottle. Defeated and broken, I opened the pill bottle and slipped the single blue pill into my fingertips. I rolled it back and forth, contemplating not taking it and forcing myself to suffer through the immense pain I was going to feel when I broke Mike's heart. I placed the pill between my lips and tilted my head back, taking the coward's path as always. The pill was sliding down my throat when Mike walked into the room, looking lost and confused. He glanced at the pills in my hand and the tears on my cheeks.

"Are you leaving?"

I nodded slowly.

He tilted his head, like he was begging God for strength to deal with me and the giant failure I was. "Jack, come on. How are you still scared of him? I will protect you from them. Stay with me." He dropped to his knees in front of me.

I ran my hands through his beard, unable to control the tears streaming my cheeks. I couldn't blink. I couldn't do anything beyond breathe and touch him. I couldn't risk dragging him in anymore. I knew goodbye this time meant goodbye.

I leaned forward and pressed my lips against his

forehead and whispered, "I am leaving something very important with you. Keep it safe for me."

He pulled back, gripping my wrists. "No. You are staying." He looked angry and hurt, and I hated myself. The panic attack inside me was holding off, waiting for the blue pill to start.

"I need to grow up and be the girl I was born to be, Mike. Together we are always going to be fifteen years old. I need to be part of the adult world now. Thank you for coming to my rescue."

He looked angry, but he didn't speak. He sat back and watched me get up. Finally, he blew. "ARE YOU FUCKING KIDDING ME RIGHT NOW? HE HITS YOU AND FUCKS SOME KID, AND YOU ARE GOING BACK? JESUS CHRIST, JACK! WHAT DOES IT TAKE? HOW MUCH MORE MONEY DO I HAVE TO MAKE TO MAKE YOU HAPPY? HOW MUCH, JACK? I HAVE ALWAYS BEEN ABOUT ME AND YOU! ALWAYS!" I stepped into his arms, calming him down. He whispered into my hair, "Always."

I nodded blankly. "I know." I couldn't tell him my dad's threats weren't against me, but against him. Mike would have given up his career for me in a heartbeat. I wouldn't ever ask him for that.

"Don't go."

I sniffled, but I barely felt it. The pill was starting to take effect. "I have to. I have to at least go back. I can't let them bring you into this."

"I don't fucking care about them. Walk—I have enough money for us both. Who cares? Let's leave. We'll get that stupid vineyard in Italy you always wanted."

I shuddered with a sob. "You've worked so hard to get where you are. I can't do this."

He grabbed my face roughly and pressed his lips against mine. "You can. You can be brave, I've seen it. Stop being such a baby and trust me. Please."

I looked into his dark eyes and shook my head. "I can't." I lowered my face and just told him the truth. I had never kept a secret from him ever. "France, my dad is threatening your safety and mine. He's going to plant drugs, or get you fired or arrested, or put a dead hooker in one of your houses." The secret spilled out.

He was silent for a moment. "Baby, I don't care. I don't care. I'd go to jail for you."

"I know." I stood on my tiptoes and kissed him. "I can't ask you to though. I would protect you from everything. I love you. Forever."

He nodded slowly. "I will be in New York tomorrow—like that cheesy-ass movie you made me watch a hundred times. If you change your mind, I will be waiting at Grand Central Station. I can't do the fucking Empire State Building. I hate heights. I'll meet you there at 6 p.m. I will wait there tomorrow and the next day. If you don't come then, I'm done—forever."

My heart was breaking. Only he would remember how much I loved that movie. Only he would make a gesture like that. Only I would be stupid enough to not go. I kissed him once more, savoring the feel of the playoffs beard and the softness of his lips. My tears crept into our kiss. I sobbed as I left the room, leaving him for good. I heard him say something, but I didn't wait for the elevator. I pulled my shoes off and ran down the stairs.

When I got to the door to the main floor, I put them back on and wiped my face. I took a deep breath and walked out into the lobby. My father saw me, stood and walked from the hotel. Phil gave me a look of remorse. I walked past him and out of the hotel after my father.

At least at home I had more of the little blue pills.

Friday

"Where is your ring?"

I looked up at my mother. "What?"

"Your engagement ring?"

I looked down at my hand. "The Atlantic Ocean." I almost laughed when I said it, but the blue pill was working. I was almost the woman I had been the week before. The woman my mother was and had been for years.

She smiled the fake fucking smile I detested. "Darling, we can't go throwing forty-thousand-dollar rings into the ocean. What if some poverty-stricken person comes upon it? They'll pawn it or worse—keep it."

I snorted. "I hope they do find it and pawn it and get a lot of drugs, food, or booze. I hope it means something to someone someday."

She maintained the forced smile until Diane stormed in. Mom stood. "Oh thank God, Diane. How are you?"

She gave my mother a look. "Leave us please, Mrs. Croix."

My mother ignored the rude tone coming from Diane and took her chance to leave me with someone else.

Diane did something I couldn't possibly imagine her doing. She walked to me, dropping to her knees, and grabbing my hands. "Run."

I looked down on her face. I saw it. "What?"

She nodded. "You can't marry him. Run away and never come back."

"My dad said he'll end Mike's career. I don't think he has the power, but I bet Phil's dad does. I have to go through with this for him."

"You're an idiot."

"Duly noted."

She sighed. "Trust me, don't do this. You are slowly

going to die inside and end up sleeping with random bartenders like me."

I winced. "Hottie from Sunday?"

She nodded and sniffled.

I grimaced.

She shrugged. "JD, you do what you have to do to get through."

I didn't want that. I didn't want to get through. I didn't want my life to be about surviving it. I didn't want to take another blue pill. I never even thought about them with Mike. There in the house, I was almost chopping them up and snorting them in the bathroom. I grabbed one and slipped it between my lips.

My sister, Brandi, came in with a glass of champagne for the three of us. I took mine and swallowed the jagged little pill that made me "me" again. Not the me I wanted to be, but the me I had to be.

Brandi was beaming. "Did you at least fuck his brains out? Mike France is the hottest piece of ass in the NHL. Tell me you got yourself enough to get you through, with the gift I got you for your bridal shower."

My cheeks blushed before I could say no.

"Of course you did. Good girl." She shot the champagne down her throat and shuddered. "How are we doing this?"

Diane shook her head.

"What?"

She gave Brandi a nervous look. Brandi nodded at her and scowled at me. "We need to get you the fuck out of here. Dad is a tyrant and the fact he sold you into this bullshit wedding is like some Third-World-country craziness. Like did he get cattle for you? No. He got a country club invitation from the blue bloods. Fuck them all." She looked at Diane. "Except you."

Diane snorted. "My family is the worst."

"I can't. They'll get Mike fired or arrested for drugs, or frame him for something. I was warned. I need a bigger fish than Dad to protect Mike." A light came on in my mind. I looked up at my sister. "Can you stall them? I need to go see Muriel."

She cocked an eyebrow. "Are you serious?"

I nodded.

She sighed. "Fine, slip back into the charity bitch and drug ho role."

"No, not for that. Just trust me and cover for me." I got up and ran to the back stairs and across the grass. I ran to our backyard neighbor's house and down the block. I stood on the side of the road and pulled out the new cell phone Phil had given me and dialed.

"Can I get a cab at the corner of Mohawk and Westview in Short Hills?" I hung up and stood there, waiting and wondering if it would work at all.

Later that night when I got back from Muriel's, I had a slight pep in my step when I walked into the house. My plan was playing out. Phil walked out of the office, looking exhausted. He glared at me. "Where were you?"

I sneered. "Why? Are you going to beat me if you don't like the answer?"

He shook his head. I could see the regret all over his face. I didn't care. He could regret all he wanted. He had hit me and that was where I drew the line. I would never let him near me again. He took a step toward me. "I told you, I'm so sorry."

I shook my head and walked past him to the kitchen. I pulled out a bottle of Chianti from the Italian wine tasting I had been to. I poured it into the decanter and swirled it around. Phil sauntered in after me, leaning against the counter. "What's it going to take?"

I looked up. "For what?"

"For you to forgive me? What do you need? I'll do it. I'd do anything to take back the last week."

I shrugged. "It's only been a week. It's still pretty fresh. Check back in a decade and see how I am. Say hi to Ashley too. Tell her to ask her mom if we are still on for yoga and let her keep those other heels. I don't need two pairs."

He clenched his jaw. His blue eyes grew cold. "You will be a good wife. Do you want our life to be like this? Do you want me to force your devotion to me?"

I poured my first glass. "I wanted it from the start. I never knew I was competing against seniors in high school for it."

His hands clenched. I winced, remembering the feel of his hand across my face.

He pointed at me. "Your father has Dr. Michaels coming tomorrow. I think he'll remedy everything for us."

I felt a sickening twist of a knife in my guts. I didn't make a move, beyond lifting the glass to my face and smelling the Chianti. Phil patted his hand on the counter. "See you in bed."

"No, thanks."

He stormed across the kitchen. I put my glass down and backed away. He grabbed my wrist, pushing me against the fridge. "We can make this work, Jacqueline. You just have to try. You have to choose to love me instead of him. Give me a fair chance to win your heart."

I shoved him back. "With this? With anger and rage and cheating and getting my father to drug me? That's what you think wins me over?"

He dropped to his knees. "I don't know how to love you. I know I don't deserve you, but I want to try."

It was a weird moment.

I wrapped my arms around his head and buried his face in my ribs so he couldn't see the face I was making. It had to be part horror and part disbelief.

He looked up at me. "Tell me what to do?"

I shook my head, meeting his blue gaze head on. "I don't know. We pushed it so far, I don't think we can fix it."

"Neither of us comes from failures. We are both bred to be successful and strong. We can do this. Promise me you'll try."

"I will." It was a lie, but I wanted to sleep without the worry of sleep assault. "I think we should spend the next two weeks just figuring ourselves out. Sleep apart."

He stood up and looked down on me, tilting my chin up. "I will do anything to win you back—" he smiled, "—or win you for the first time."

I smiled and let him walk out of the kitchen. I trembled a little when I lifted the wine to my lips.

Tomorrow couldn't come fast enough.

Saturday

I sat at the makeup table and let my mother ramble on as I dressed for the day. She had been coming over and acting like she gave a rat's ass about me since I had come back. Two days of hell, actually.

I dusted the powder over my face and looked at the faded mark on my cheek. Makeup covered it completely, but the fear of him hitting me again was always going to be there.

"So you see why it's important to marry well?"

I looked at her in the mirror and smiled the same fake-ass smile she always gave me.

She nodded and left the room. "Excellent. We'll be downstairs."

I went and sat on the couch on the far side of my bedroom and waited for Dr. Michaels. He was my father's solution to everything, from my sister's morning-after pill to the mental health of the women in our family.

Finally, after a few moments he walked in, looking old and creepy as always.

"How are you, Jacqueline?"

I smiled and pointed to the other couch. "Excellent. How are you?"

He nodded. "Well enough. So let's talk about the issues you've been having."

"I am not having any I am aware of."

He studied my face, scrutinizing. After a moment he smiled, patronizingly. "Are you still taking the medication I prescribed you?"

I nodded.

"Do you still feel the same anxiety you had before or is it helping?"

"It's helping. What has my father told you?"

He chuckled. "Nothing much. Just that you were under

the weather, a little depressed maybe."

I folded my hands in my lap. "My father is forcing me to marry someone I don't want to. My fiancé is having affairs with young girls. And even with all that, I am not depressed. I think that earns me some sort of medal, don't you?"

He laughed harder. "I do. That is a feat. Do you have proof of the affairs?"

I scoffed. "I saw him."

He nodded. "Had you been taking the pills I prescribed for you, when you saw him? He says you take them with liquor, and that's not their intended use. It can lead to hallucinations and mental instability and other things."

I felt my expression grow somber. "What?"

He put his hands up. "Just some food for thought."

I pointed. "If you'll excuse me, I am going to lie down now."

He stood, passing me a bottle of pills. "This is a slightly stronger prescription. Let's give it a whirl for a couple of weeks, and then we will reassess after the wedding. I assure you this is all wedding jitters and completely normal."

He stood and left the room.

I sat, staring at the pills. I wanted to scream and destroy things, but I couldn't. I needed to keep it under wraps until 5:00 that evening. Then I could head for the city. Muriel was coming over then. She had agreed to my evil plan. Feeling like the energy had been sucked out of me, I crawled into my bed.

I just needed a little nap.

The nap turned into a sleep. I woke with a start. My sister was shaking me by the foot and attempting to drag me from the bed. "You have to wake up. JD get up. It's 5:30."

I felt the cotton mouth and knew immediately, my mother had drugged me. I looked at the tea she had made for me, still on the makeup table.

"Mom."

My sister nodded. "She roofied you. You need to get up."

"I'm going to be sick."

She dragged me from the bed. "Get sick out the window of my SUV. I'll pack us a couple of plastic baggies." She wrapped my arm around her neck and helped me from the room. The shrill laugh of Muriel filled the house. I looked at my sister. "She came."

She nodded. "And Father has been ever so silent since she asked to speak to him in private."

I smiled. "Good. Fuck him." My words were weak and exhausted. Brandi carried me down the back stairs and across the lawn. She ran for her SUV as my legs woke up a bit. She started it and drove like a wild woman. The traffic was nuts.

"Shit, I hope we don't miss him."

She passed me her phone. "Call."

I dialed, but his phone went to voice mail. "France, it's me. Wait for me. I'm coming. Please wait." I hung up and looked at her. "What if because I didn't come yesterday, he doesn't come today?"

She gave me a look. "He has loved you since high school. Remember that summer he fawned over you? Oh God, I was so in love with him. All the girls were. No one was brave enough to be around him though, not a dirty scholarship kid."

I snorted and looked out the window. My palms were sweating. She pulled up and I ran, barefoot from the SUV. My pencil skirt made it hard to run, but my stride was strong enough that it ripped the skirt a bit. I pushed my legs hard as I raced into Grand Central Station. My eyes frantically scanned the benches, but he wasn't there. My heart was pounding in my throat as I spun, looking every which way.

Tears were instant. He had gone. I looked at the time: 6:30. He had waited as long as he could and then left, no doubt broken and believing I wasn't coming.

I walked to a seat, looking like a crack addict. After a while someone walked up and placed a five-dollar bill in my hand, but I just sat there until Brandi made me leave.

I shook my head as she dragged me to the SUV. "He might come back. I should stay, in case."

She shook her head. "He isn't coming, babe."

I tried not to heave as I cried. "I just don't get it. I had Muriel come over and threaten Daddy. She was my backup plan. I won and I still lost."

Brandi flung her phone at me. "Try again."

I dialed, but it didn't even go to voice mail. It just rang and rang. I dialed again, but he didn't answer.

"Can you go to his apartment on the Upper East Side?"

She gave me a look. "Honey, he didn't come. There is no way he only waited half an hour. It's Mike France. You think he came to Grand Central Station and got out of there without signing anything in less than an hour? That place was packed. He didn't come. He would have still been surrounded when we arrived. People would have demanded autographs."

I swallowed my pride and my pain, and nodded. She was right. He hadn't been there. He had flaked, typical hockey-star-Mike style. He probably had some puck fuck warming his hurt feelings because I never picked him.

Little did he know, I had picked him.

I looked out the window as she drove us home and tried not to be completely brokenhearted.

Of course as luck would have it, "Beth" by KISS came on. The song, the droplets of rain that fell on the window as the sky got dark, and the tearing of my soul, pretty much made up the worst moment of my life. Brandi sang along. I sniffled and watched the city lights pass me by in a stream of colors.

Saturday night

One week later

"WHO IS READY TO GET THEIR DRINK ON?" Brandi screamed in the limo.

I spaced out as they all grinded against each other to the song "I Love It" by Icona Pop. Some of the girls were hanging out the moon roof and others were just dancing hunched over. The music was so loud I could barely breathe.

A glass was put in my hand. I lifted it to my lips, trying to get out of the haze from whatever they had already made me take or drink. I felt like my entire body was detached.

Helena shook her ass in my face, making me smile. When we pulled up in front of the club, I was dragged out and over to the lineup. The bouncer was shaking hands with the ladies in our group and suddenly we were inside.

The stupid bachelorette banner and lacy hat were annoying me. I tried to pull them off, but Diane hauled me onto the dance floor.

I let the shit they had given me take over. I threw my arms into the air and danced like I was a carefree girl again.

Someone came up behind me, grinding against me. I let them. I tilted my head back as their hands roamed my body.

I laughed and drank whatever was given to me. I shook my ass and dragged my hands through my hair. It was like senior year all over again.

We started to bounce with the crowd, a sea of moving and writhing people. It was fun and free, and I knew in that moment, I would forever be a drug addict. Whatever they had given me was the best. My hair felt amazing. My body felt tight and soft at the same time. The beat of the music made my heart beat at the same time. I could feel the music as I bounced.

The hands behind me were gone suddenly. I turned to

see the angry face of Will. I leapt at him, kissing his cheek. "WILLY!"

He wrapped his arms around me and whispered, "What are you doing here?"

I stepped back and showed him my banner.

He nodded. "Why was that guy grinding on you?"

"What guy?"

He looked annoyed as he grabbed my hand and dragged me to the bathroom. He clutched my face. "Are you high?"

"I don't know. Let's go dance."

He winced and pulled his phone out. He was shouting into it as I was dancing to the music in the boys' bathroom. "SHE'S RIGHT HERE!"

"Who is that?"

"France."

I snatched the phone from him. "France, you fucker. You stood me up. I showed up at the train station, and you never came. So FUCK YOU! Come party, France. It's my bachelorette party. I have to get married in a week, baby. Come save me. I love you. You son of a bitch. No, I take that back. Your mom is nice. She would have been at the train station." I turned the phone off and grabbed Will's face. My lips almost planted themselves on his.

He pushed me away and dragged me to the back of the building, through the storage area, and out into the alley behind the bar.

The music was deafening. I was still bouncing to the beat as he plucked me away from the bar.

"Willy, you aren't very fun. You were more fun in South Carolina."

He looked back. "You're enough fun for us both." He was texting. I knew it was France. I pulled my hand from his. "What are you doing?"

"You need to go to France's place. He wants me to take you there."

I jerked my hand free. "He had his chance. You want yours, Willy?" I pulled at his belt. It seemed like the right choice.

He grabbed my hands. "You are a hot mess." He dragged me down the street, but I was in fabulous but impractical shoes. I shook him off. "I can't walk anymore. These are my two-block shoes."

He stopped, looking exasperated. "What is a two-block shoe?"

I wiggled my pretty foot in the air, waving my Louboutin pump. "I can't walk more than two blocks or my feet get sore. These are fun shoes, not sport shoes."

"You are high maintenance."

"I know."

"I get it though, you're cute and kind of crazy. I get it."

I frowned and he flagged a cab. In the car something terrible happened. I started to feel the motion of the cab in a bad way. My stomach twisted. I opened the window, leaned out, and threw up.

"Come on, dude. Get your girl in the window."

Will sighed. "She isn't my girl. She's a friend's girl."

I gagged and heaved as he pulled up in front of France's apartment. I felt the lace tiara thing slip from my bed. I looked back as it bounced along the pavement. Something about it was troubling and maybe a little sobering. "My friends and sister are going to worry."

He rubbed my back. "You can message them when I get you to France, safe and sound."

"Please, don't touch me. I don't like to be touched." I shook my head. "He doesn't want to see me, Will." I sat down on the seat, looking at my hands. "I'm probably interrupting something."

He sat next to me. "He just screamed at me and told me to bring you to his apartment to sleep it off. I'm guessing that means he wants to see you."

The cab stopped. Will paid and climbed out. He ran around and opened my door, offering me his hand. I hesitated before I took it, letting him close his hand around mine and pull me from the car. The cabbie sped away, screeching the tires. Will lifted me up into his arms as my knees buckled. I shook my head. "I don't like being touched by people. I can walk." He put me down, but I staggered and grabbed onto his arm for support.

"You had that guy at the bar crawling all over you. You didn't seem to mind."

"I don't care when I drink." I shuddered with a threat of more vomit. "I don't feel good anymore."

My face nestled into his chest. He lifted me up again and carried me to the elevator. When the doors opened, France was standing inside, taking up a lot of the space. He looked pissed when he held his arms out for Will to hand me over. The minute I was in his arms, I closed my eyes, letting the room spinning take me. The safety of his chest and the smell of him, told me it was time to sleep.

"Thanks, man," I heard France say to Will.

"Anytime. You get some rest, JD."

I waved weakly at Will, more like flopping my arm about. The elevator moved, but we didn't talk. He held me to him, and I let the comfort of him make me feel better. When we got to his floor, he carried me inside. He was being gentle as he laid me down on his sofa. He forced my eyes open. I winced.

"Fuck, Jack. You're stoned. What did you take?"

"I don't know. A white pill and my blue pills and drinks."

He shoved me back onto the couch. "Did you eat?"

"I had some olives."

He sighed and walked away. The dimly lit room burned my eyes. I closed them but tried to stand. I barely managed to get to my feet and stumble into the kitchen.

I leaned against the metal countertop I always hated. It felt too industrial. He was making eggs or something. He looked different. "You shaved."

He nodded, not meeting my gaze. His handsome face was back. The beard might have hidden the clench of his jaw. Clean-shaven, I could see just how angry he was.

He looked up at me. "Bachelorette party?"

I nodded and slumped onto a barstool.

"Why? Why didn't you just come?"

"I did. You didn't come. I was there."

He looked lost. "When?"

I swallowed and tried not to throw up anymore. "The

second day you were meeting me. I couldn't get there the first day. I had something to do."

He slammed his fist on the counter. "More important than meeting me? Really? You're such a bitch sometimes, Jack. Sometimes you are one of them."

I couldn't get the words out to explain. I stepped off the stool and slumped onto the floor. The room spins were out of control. The last vision I had was his moving mouth, still shouting at me for not meeting him.

Sunday

The bed was the worst I'd slept on in a while. My back was aching. I opened one eye to see bright light and a lady moving in white. She smiled. "You're awake."

I winced, lifting a hand to my face. "Where am I?"

"Presbyterian Hospital."

"What happened?" Was I hit by a cab? I was dying for sure.

"Partied a bit too hard, I'm afraid. Your friend there brought you in last night. You were dehydrated beyond what I have seen in a while."

I glanced over at Mike, passed out on a chair. He looked small there on the chair, curled into himself. I smiled. "He brought me in?"

What the fuck had happened? I had nothing. He had a banner or sash in his hands. It was bright pink. Was I in the Ms. New York contest?

"What's that he's holding?"

The nurse smiled harder. "Your bachelorette party sash. Guess you had fun." She left the room.

It didn't feel like I'd had fun. It felt like I was dying.

"France."

He stirred.

I drank the water in the paper cup she had set next to me, and then tossed it at him. "France!"

He opened his eyes slowly. "Piss off, Jack. I'm sleeping. Damn."

"What happened, France? Why am I here? Where's my sister?"

He nodded. "She came by earlier and went home to sleep. People need sleep."

"Jacqueline, oh you're all right!" I looked over as my

mother came rushing into the room.

God, who had called her?

She grabbed my hand. "Honey, are you feeling better?"

I snatched my hand from her.

She smiled. "Your sister called and said you had not been feeling well."

I watched her face turn cold as her eyes landed on Mike. Her jaw became set and her eyes narrowed. "What are you doing here? You don't think you've done enough? Did you do this to her? They said you brought her in. You and your trailer-trash, drug-addict ways. You get out of here. You've done enough." Mike sat up, rubbing his eyes. I could see the fury starting on his face.

I swatted her arm. "Don't talk to him like that."

She snapped her head back around at me, and I saw a look I had never seen on my mother's face. She pointed. "Your father has worked painstakingly to get you into the engagement you are in. You spoiled little bitch. You will not ruin that for him. Your father and Phil will be here in a few minutes. I expect that gone when they get here." She turned on her heel and stormed from the room.

Mike laughed. "Good to see the Prozac is working on her."

I didn't laugh. I reached for him. "You don't have to leave. I made sure he can't touch you. None of them can."

He got up, taking my hand. "What are you talking about? What did you do?"

"There isn't any time. You shouldn't have called my sister."

I looked over to see two guards come in. "Hey man, we gotta ask you to leave. Her family is making a stink." They looked somber.

Mike nodded. "Yeah, I probably shouldn't cause another scene. Bad for press." He bent and kissed my cheek. "Call me tomorrow." I pressed my face into his. He stood up, taking my sash with him and walked out.

"Can I get an autograph though, when we get downstairs?"

Mike laughed. "Yeah, sure."

I felt trapped. The IV in my arm was cold like a handcuff, pinning me to the bed.

I looked out the window. The light was filtering in softly. It looked like a beautiful day to run away from home. Even in my mid twenties, I had no power over how things were going to play out. I hated that.

His voice interrupted my pity party for one. "Jacqueline, I am so disappointed in you."

"I know." I nodded, not meeting my father's eyes. "Fuck you."

He chuckled. "You always were the difficult one. This little stunt of yours has actually proved to be fruitful though. I have to thank you for that one. I never imagined you would make it easier for me to force your hand."

I looked at him. The hateful look on his face was a sinister smirk. Dr. Michaels walked in after my father, holding a folder. His look matched my father's. "We take suicide attempts very seriously now, Jacqueline."

"What? I went partying. I never tried to kill myself. You two are grasping for that one."

My father folded his arms smugly. "Your blood work has a deadly cocktail of narcotics in it."

"Whatever. That is terrible. You would actually lie for him, Dr. Michaels? I'm an adult."

He nodded. "I am worried for your mental health. Worse comes to worst, you could require a twenty-eight-day dry out at rehab. This is serious."

I swallowed hard. "You gave me the drugs."

"The only prescription you have from me is a one-time prescription for Xanax. The other bottle wasn't prescribed by me." He nodded once. "I'll leave you two to discuss the therapy I am recommending, and a possible two-week stay for observation in the mental ward."

The room spun.

My father walked close, grabbing my hand like a viper. He squeezed. "You dare to threaten me with Muriel? You don't have to worry about that Mike France. I won't be going near him—I don't need to. You fuck up enough that I don't need to threaten his career." He licked his lips. "So

Jacqueline, which is it? The nut house, rehab, or Phil?"

And there it was.

The truth of the matter. I was never going to get away. I was now a danger to myself. I shook my head. "Whatever you have on Dr. Michaels must be impressive."

He smiled. "You would never believe it."

He was right, I probably wouldn't. My father had a flair for finding people's weaknesses.

Tears didn't come.

My heart didn't flutter or break.

I went completely numb.

I smiled at him with the fake, frozen smile my mother always gave him. "Phil it is then." I understood then—she hated him as much as I did.

He squeezed my hand again and kissed the top of it. "There's my good girl." He winked and let my hand drop.

He left the room with a smug saunter. Phil came in after him. He looked exhausted and worn out.

"What happened?"

"Drank too much."

He looked worried. "The blood work showed Ecstasy, speed, and pharmaceuticals. It looks like you tried to kill yourself."

"Phil, when have I ever seemed like I could be strong enough to do that?"

He sat on the bed. "This is because of Ashley, isn't it? I just feel sick. JD, I wish I could take it all back. I have pushed you to this. I hate myself."

I realized then, he was still drunk from his bachelor party.

"I need to get some sleep."

He climbed up onto the bed with me and wrapped himself around me. I lay there, frozen and dead inside as he whispered, "I love you. I will make this up to you. I am so sorry." He slipped a new ring on my thin finger. It was ridiculous in size. "I will make you happy again."

Saturday

One week later
The wedding day

The dress was loose. I had basically stopped eating when Phil's mother insisted on spending every waking moment with me, trying to make up for what her son had driven me to.

My father had relished in the glory of the incident he now held over the Bernard family. Their son's infidelity with a child had driven me to suicide instead of a bachelorette party. As if I was so feeble and fragile.

I had spent the week desperately searching for a moment to escape.

Of course that moment never came.

Brandi spritzed me with perfume. Her eyes were haunted. The room was silent until my mother and Mrs. Bernard finally left. It was more like a funeral than a wedding.

"Oh God, JD, I am so sorry."

I looked at Diane. "We took a little Ecstasy. We used to do that all the time. Stop."

Helena wiped her eyes. "Brandi told us your dad is blackmailing you to marry him, with mental ward and rehab."

Angela crossed her arms. "Take rehab. I went when we were nineteen. It wasn't so bad."

I snorted. "No. I'll be cut off completely—no money. My father has full control over every dime I have. He threatened me with hiding drugs in Mike's house and getting him fired. He threatened me with rehab and the mental ward. He has Dr. Michaels on his side. I don't stand a chance." I looked at myself in my lace wedding dress. "Phil is the best option. At least he thinks he drove me to try to take my life. His whole family is disturbingly grateful I am alive. I'll have them all under my thumb the rest of my life." I saw the cold look in my eyes in the mirror. For a second, I was my father's daughter. Eventually, I would be high 24/7 and become my mother. I wondered if somewhere out there in the world, my mother had a Mike. Someone she loved more than anything but had married my father out of duty.

Brandi started to cry again. She had been a mess all week.

We all drank a fourth mimosa and straightened our gowns.

The wedding planners came bustling in. "Everyone ready?"

I nodded as the lace was placed over my face. Under the veil, I would swear I could see things clearer. I slipped a blue pill into my mouth and nodded at the image in my mind: I would become my father. I would rule the Bernard family with guilt and misery because I hated my life and the choice I had been forced to take.

We walked out into the foyer where the groomsmen and my father waited for us. The dead look in his eyes was enough to force the decision I was about to make. One day I would be dead inside like him. Eventually, the numbness would take over everything.

The music started. I hadn't noticed the church or the decorations or the people there. I didn't give two shits about a single thing, beyond the crack in my heart.

The girls all walked down the aisle before us. As we arrived at the doors, the music changed and the room stood. The faces of the crowd were unsure. They didn't know what to expect or how to act. The ones who knew the truth were devastated, and the ones who assumed I was driven to a suicide attempt were scared. Some judged. I could see that on their faces. The veil hid the fact I was scrutinizing them.

My father passed me over to Phil. No one spoke or kissed or cried, except Brandi.

Everyone else was still, like a calm before a storm.

My heart took that moment to panic. Like it was beating in one last desperate attempt to wake me from the coma I was stuck in.

The brave girl who had driven to South Carolina was dying inside me. She was screaming and clawing and trying to get out, but the cloud of heavy shit smothered her. That, and the blue pills that blocked her out.

Phil took me in his arms and led me to the priest.

We stood there, listening to the man speak, but I heard nothing. Nothing, apart from my beating heart.

Then I heard something unbelievable.

"Jack! Goddamn. Jack, you can't marry him. You love me ard I love you."

I turned to see a hammered Mike France staggering up the aisle. He was in a tee shirt, jeans, and sneakers. He looked like he had been living in them.

I gasped. "France." I blinked my eyes several times and shook my head. He was my kryptonite. I couldn't see him without tears forming. He made me alive again. The haze of the blue pill was starting though.

He pointed. "Baby, I have something I want to show you. Well, I have a few things, but the main one is your dream come true. Come on."

My father stood. "Leave now. She didn't choose you. She won't."

Brandi heaved a loud sob and Phil gripped me tighter, holding me there. My father walked to France. He said things in hushed tones, but Mike ignored him. "Jack, come on."

I almost took a step toward him, but Phil moved before I could. He walked up, throwing a punch.

Mike took the hit and then jumped Phil. Several guys jumped in, making a pile of people in suits thrashing in the middle of the aisle. The rich friends and family sat, frozen still.

My mother never budged. My sister sobbed. My friends whispered traitorous acts like, "RUN!"

But I remained paralyzed as Mike beat them all. He roared as he shot from the sea of tuxes and preppy assholes. None stood a chance with him. He jumped up, leaving them on the ground and pointed at me. His voice cracked. "Let's go."

My feet wouldn't move. I was frozen.

He looked defeated. "Why? Why are you so scared? Come on."

I opened my mouth to say something, but my voice was gone. He turned, shaking his head and staggering out of the church.

The rest of us stood there, motionless and silent.

Phil got up, humiliated and bleeding from the lip. He gave me a look and walked from the church after Mike.

My chest rising and falling was the only hint that told me I was alive. Everything else felt like it was gone. No sense or voice or spine.

Finally, it hit all at once. I grabbed my sister's hand and ran down the aisle.

"STOP!"

I halted, looking back at my father. His face was seven different shades of red. He snarled. "You will get nothing."

"I already have nothing, Father. What can you take from me? I have nothing—no pride, no respect, no love, no feelings. Keep your money. I see what it's done to you. I don't want that."

Muriel stepped from the seats, grabbing my hands. "Go find your love. If you need anything, let me know." My mother watched us with burning hatred in her eyes.

She kissed my cheek. I nodded and turned and ran, holding the hand of my sister. Phil was gone. Mike was gone. There was nothing but a ton of cars and silence. As we jumped into a limo, I shouted, "Grand Central Station. FAST!"

I pulled my cell phone from the waist of my panties and dialed.

I ended the call when I reached voice mail.

The driver couldn't go fast enough.

Brandi sobbed. "I'm so sorry. I should have helped more."

I kissed her. "Stop. Just stop. I know."

She looked at me, and for the first time, I actually saw her. "We don't need them, JD—Mom and Dad are fucking insane. Let them have each other."

I kissed her again. "We have each other."

The limo stopped and I dashed from the car. I sprinted inside the train station, but he wasn't there. Everyone looked at me like I was crazy as I spun in a circle, desperate to see him.

I sat on a bench in case we had beaten him there.

People looked at me like I was insane. My sister came and sat next to me. "I checked the restrooms. I don't think he's here."

I dialed again, but he didn't answer.

I looked like a jilted bride. It made me laugh. Not a normal laugh but a crazed one.

We walked back to the limo. I wrote down the addresses of the next five places. We drove for hours and I grew more desperate with each place he wasn't at.

"The Empire State Building."

The driver gave me a shitty look and turned back toward the city. When we arrived there, we ran inside. Brandi paid the sixty dollars for us both as I pressed the elevator. Brandi gave me a weird look. "Why here?"

"I made him watch Love Affair with Irene Dunne and Charles Boyer and the remake, An Affair to Remember, with Cary Grant and Deborah Kerr. He hated both but suffered through them for me."

The elevator stopped at the observatory deck. We stepped out onto it, getting a breeze and looking around. There were other people and a saxophone player. Brandi went right and I went left. I ran, imagining I would see him any second.

I met her back at the sax player. She was staring at the case. I looked down, seeing the pink sash with bachelorette written on it.

"He came here." I picked it out of the case.

The guy stopped playing. "Dude, Mike France gave that to me. He signed it."

I bit my lip. "I'll give you a thousand dollars for it."

He cocked an eyebrow. "Two."

I looked at Brandi. She fished cash from her purse and slapped it into his hand. I looked at his signature and tried not to cry.

Brandi and I walked back to the elevators. I felt sick. "He hates heights. He came here to show me he would do anything for me—even the 86th floor of the Empire State Building."

She pressed the button on the wall. "It's not like you won't find him. You will. He's got to be at one of his houses. He only has two here. There must be somewhere he would have gone."

"South Carolina." I dialed the number again, but he didn't answer.

"It's fucking 2013. How is it this hard to find someone?"

She snorted. "We can pay someone and track him like a rabbit."

I dialed the other number I didn't want to.

He answered, "I'm sorry, Jacqueline."

I nodded and followed my sister back to the limo. "Me too. Can I meet you at the house? No parents, just me and you?"

"No. I have all your things being boxed now, and they will be shipped to your mother and father's. Your father is here doing it."

I pressed my lips together. "Okay."

"I put five hundred thousand into the account you and I share. He doesn't know. Take the ring back to Harry Winston. Brandi has the receipt for it. I gave it to her in case. Between those two things you should be okay until he calms down. I'll close the account in a couple of days so be sure to get it."

"Thanks."

"Of course. You have to know how sorry I am."

The lump in my throat was huge. "I know. Me too. I'm sorry about Mike and my parents."

"Take care." He hung up the phone.

I looked down at the ring on my hand.

We walked back but the limo was gone.

My father was pulling everything away from me.

Friday

Six months later

I put the glass on the table. "This is the Carano I had while I was in Italy for the Alto Adige tasting. It's perfect and peaking this year. It's Baron di Pauli."

The man smiled at me. "You actually went to the tasting there?"

"My friend is a sommelier. She invited me to join her."

He stuck his nose in the glass and nodded. "It's fruity."

"It finishes off with dark chocolate. The fruit and chocolate are delectable."

The lady gave me a blank look. "Can we get a cheese board with the wine?"

I bit my lip, but couldn't hold it back. "The reds don't go with cheese. That's a white wine food. Did you want to try something else?"

Her cheeks flushed. "No. I'd like the cheese, please."

"Excellent. How is the wine?"

The man gave me a thumbs up. "Fill us up. It's beautiful."

I poured them both a glass and placed the bottle back on the table. I walked back to the kitchen and nodded at Jon. "I need a cheese board."

He grimaced. "Didn't they get a red?" His French accent was noticeable when he said "they."

I folded my arms. "Americans. What can you do?"

He swore in French and muttered things I didn't catch. He had given me a job, something I had never had before, when I was alone in the world last May. My family and friends had all abandoned me when the wedding was over. Rebecca, Helena, Angela, and Brandi still saw me, but it was in secret. I was a pariah of the blue bloods. Phil was already engaged again. Ashley would make a beautiful bride. It grossed me out, but the fact he was marrying her, seemed to make it okay that she wasn't even legal drinking age yet.

France had not taken a single call from me or returned any of mine. He hadn't returned a single email or made a single appearance in my life. The small wine bar was the only solace in my life.

Jon handed me the cheese board. "I hope they choke."

"No, you don't. Then I have to do the Heimlich, and no one wants to do that to a two-hundred-pound man."

He scoffed. "They think they know everything."

I laughed and walked the cheese out to them. The wife plucked a grape and some Brie as I laid it down. The husband glanced at my ass, making me uncomfortable and annoyed. I smiled. "Enjoy."

I walked to my other tables, clearing and refilling. Jon had taught me how to serve. I had no idea how to do anything, beyond fill a glass.

I looked at the time and hurried back to the kitchen. "I have to go."

He looked at the time. "Oui. It's time for your appointment, non?" I loved his blended French and English.

I nodded and pulled my apron off. He nodded. "I will get Beth to finish the tables and make sure you get your tips."

I winked at him. "Thanks." I needed those. I needed every dime I got. My rent was paid, but the ring had only fetched me forty thousand, even with the receipt. I hadn't taken the five hundred thousand from the account. I daydreamed about it sometimes, like when I really was hungry or cold, and wished I had just a few of my things from before.

The whole world had opened up and closed simultaneously for me. I had never seen or experienced the things I was now, both good and bad.

I ran down the street to see the people I had been dreading all along.

When I got inside, the two men were already there. Will smiled and opened his arms. I felt sick; I was so embarrassed. I hadn't seen him in the six months, but we had run into each other at a bakery the week before.

I almost slumped into his chest. He squeezed so hard that my back cracked and then he pulled me back. "You look so different."

"Poverty changes you." I blushed and ran a hand through my hair.

"No." He shook his head. "You look beautiful, but different in a good way." He nodded at the guy next to him. "This is Vince. He just plays for Boston. He was actually the reason I hunted you down yesterday and asked if you would meet up with me."

Vince took my hand. He looked like a hockey player, burly and thick. His sweater was exactly what I could imagine France wearing.

I sat as Will pulled the coffee shop chair out for me.

Vince smiled. I could see where he was missing a tooth in the back. It seemed all hockey players were missing teeth or constantly bruised.

Finally, I said what I was thinking about, "Have you guys heard from France?"

Will shook his head. "No. His contract was up, and he said he was taking a leave for a year. Went to play in the Italian league."

I knew that. The whole world did. It had been on the news. "Yeah, I've felt the brunt of numerous Rangers fans being pissed at me."

Will snorted. "The whole team is pissed at you."

I winced. "Sorry."

"Vince just got back from Italy."

My eyes widened. "Did you see him? Is he okay? He doesn't answer my messages."

Vince sipped from his cappuccino. It was a contradiction watching him drink from such a delicate cup. "I saw him in Rome. He came and met up with me and the other guys who went."

"How did he seem?" My heart was beating through my sweater.

His eyes couldn't hide the truth of it. "He seemed okay. He wasn't upset or anything. He's coming back. Signed his contract. Said he'll be back in America after Christmas."

My heart skipped beats. "Really?"

Will gave me a smile. "He's a stubborn guy, JD. I think he believes the reason you never got married was because Phil broke it off after the whole spectacle. I think he suspects you're still together."

I almost started to cry. I felt my eyes trying to tear up. I shook my head. "I tried to catch him. I was just so stunned, I think." I looked down at my hands as Will slid a piece of paper across the table.

"Go get him."

I looked up. "What?"

"Go to Mike." He nodded.

"I can't."

He smiled. "His address is in there with a plane ticket. He isn't coming back here for Christmas. Go get him. Tell him everything."

"I can't accept that."

"You will accept it."

I scowled but put my hand on the ticket. I couldn't be foolish and let it ride again. I didn't have the money anymore to go on my own. Tears filled my eyes. "I have to pay you back?"

His face was so stoic, but I heard his voice crack, "It's not me you need to pay back. It's your sister. She came and found me a few weeks ago. Came to a game and stood outside the locker room. The guys thought she was a good-time girl, but she wanted to find me. Told me how she couldn't see you often without losing everything herself and how her husband works for your father. She had already risked so many things helping you, but she told me the story—the whole story."

I winced, ashamed that he saw how I had chosen Phil to stop my father from taking everything.

But he smiled after a minute. "She told me about the threats your father made against Mike and you. She told me that you were living in a shitty little apartment and working as a wine server because your father made sure no one would hire you or help you. I waited outside the wine place and followed you to the bakery." He reached into his pocket and slid an envelope to me. "She said to give you this as well."

I took the envelope, not opening it in front of them. I was ashamed of the fact that she had snuck money to me, and a ticket. I was broke, almost completely.

"I don't know how to thank you."

He looked at Vince who shook his head. "We didn't know people were so fucking evil. Your dad is a piece of work. Coach revealed to me he was told that Mike France was not to be given a contract this year or next. He said something like it came down from the high-ups, trying to teach him a lesson."

Will nodded. "Same in Boston, but the owner is a bit of an asshole himself. He isn't one to be told how to do anything. He knows Boston needs Mike. He doesn't give a shit about anything else, and he doesn't need the finances from wealthy investors. He needs wins. That's what he cares about."

Vince laughed. "Our owners and managers felt like it was a trick from the Rangers' owners to make sure that Mike didn't get snatched up. They offered him double to go there."

"What?"

He nodded. "And some crazy lady named Muriel Lawson sent in a huge donation to the team, incentive to offer Mike a contract. He's coming to Boston, not New York."

I opened my mouth, stunned and speechless.

Will shrugged. "New York is going to miss him, but they were too slow to offer him a great contract. Boston is lucky. Best right winger there is in hockey and a dirty scrapper."

I put my hand over Will's. "Thank you. I don't even know how to thank either of you—but thank you, anyway." I leapt from the chair, launching myself at Will. He wrapped around me. I had never done a kind act for someone for no reason. I had done it as charity work and for the ability to say I had done it. I had never been good to someone just because it made me happy. Here were the two of them, almost complete strangers, helping me because it was the right thing to do. They didn't have to hunt me down and help my sister help me, but they had.

I jumped up and hugged Vince. They both laughed.

Will nodded his head. "Your flight leaves in a few hours. You better get a move on. A car will be waiting outside your apartment in an hour to get you to the airport."

I wiped my teary eyes. "Thank you." I shook my head. "Thank you."

I turned and left for the wine bar to tell Jon I was quitting.

Of course when I got there, he already had a glass poured for both of us and a huge grin that told me he too had been visited by the fairy named Brandi.

He hugged me and sent me on my way.

When I got home, she was sitting outside my building on the stairs.

I started to cry. I hadn't seen her in weeks. I had been alone almost all the time.

She got up, sobbing and wrapping herself around me. I felt something hitting me. I looked down at her belly. It wasn't perfectly tight and flat like before. It had a tiny little bump. "Oh my God, is that a baby belly?"

"I wanted you to know before you left."

I snuffled. "Thank you."

She shook her head. "I should have told them to go fuck themselves years ago. Shawn got a job in Boston working for Muriel. He and I, along with Muriel, are moving out there to have the baby."

"Why is she helping us so much?"

She shook her head. "I don't know. She just decided she was moving to Boston and came and asked Shawn if he was happy at his job. He said no, of course. She offered him the same position at her new company in Boston. She has a bunch of family there. Her kids moved there. She hates the old house, reminds her of Mr. Lawson. So we bought a house and sold the one here. Dad told everyone he fired Shawn and tried to smear his name everywhere, but I think people are starting to see the little weasel he honestly is."

I gripped her hands. "I am so happy for you."

"Yeah, well. Just wait. You are being named godmother."

I hugged her again. "What's the date?"

"End of June."

"Congratulations to you both."

She pulled back. "Hurry up and grab a small bag of stuff for Italy. You have to go."

I started to tear up again. "Thank you."

She grabbed my face. "It's the least I could do after abandoning you."

"I never wanted to take you down with me."

She kissed my forehead. "You have ten minutes—run."

Saturday morning

My eyes burned, but I lugged my bag through the airport. I had never taken a red-eye flight before. It was unbearable. At least she had booked me in first class. I couldn't imagine coach on top of a red eye.

I didn't know where I was going, beyond the address in my pocket.

It was colder than I recalled Rome being, not that I had traveled there in December before.

I walked up to an elderly taxi driver and tried my best Italian on him. He smiled. "You an American?"

I narrowed my gaze. "Maybe."

He opened the door for me. I passed him the address. "You know this place?"

He nodded. "I know it." His English was far superior to my Italian. He looked back. "You a cowgirl?"

"No. New Yorker."

He pointed. "Rudest people in the world. I saw the show the other night on Discovery Channel."

I laughed and nodded. "That sounds about right."

"I don't care. I still want to go, one day. Is my dream." He drove like a madman through the streets to a hotel, not just any hotel. He was staying at the Boscolo Aleph.

"This is it?"

He nodded.

I got out and looked up at the huge stone building with the large red flag and beautiful red front door. I had never stayed there, but I knew of it. The architecture of it was something I had studied.

"Isn't this the 'five sins' hotel?"

"Yes! You are a smart New Yorker."

I paid him and walked up to the door. The handsome doorman got the door for me. I walked inside and went directly to the elevator. The piece of paper had the floor number for me. I pressed the button, surprised there was no elevator operator.

When the elevator got to the floor, I walked out, praying he was home, and yet somehow also not home. I didn't want to face the music and explain everything. I just wanted us to be like we were before.

I put my hand up to knock, but I heard a sound I hadn't been prepared for, like an idiot. A woman laughed. Of course. It was France. Of course some hot Italian woman was there. I almost turned away, but something inside me forced my hand to knock.

A lady answered. She was stunning—a model for certain. She cocked an eyebrow. "Can I help you?" She had a thick accent.

"Is Mike here?"

She looked me up and down and laughed. "Mike, the door is for you." Her mocking tone almost made me jump her, but she didn't know me. She underestimated me. I looked like slightly warmed shit, I was sure, but Mike didn't care. The minute he saw me, his face grew into a huge grin. "No fucking way!" He pointed at me. "Are you real?"

I nodded.

He nearly shoved her out of the way and scooped me up into his arms. He nuzzled into my neck and took a deep breath, like he was breathing me in. He dragged me into the room.

"Michael, what is going on?"

He put me down and looked me over. "You okay?"

I nodded again, unable to speak without crying and telling him everything all at once. He lifted my wedding finger. "No ring?"

I shook my head.

"Getting a divorce already?"

"I never got married. You knew that."

The model stomped between us. "Michael, who is this? Your little sister?"

I felt my eyes narrow, but he ignored her. "You never ended up marrying him afterward? I knew the day was ruined but the relationship is over?"

"Where have you been? It was in the paper."

"Jack, I never read a single thing. I just shut down and came here. I knew Phil had followed me out that day. He was pissed, but I figured your dad would have everything patched up by now."

I glanced at the model, putting my hand out. "Jacqueline Croix."

She smiled sarcastically. "Daniela."

He didn't notice us talking. He just stared at me. I looked at him and then her. "If I'm interrupting, I can just wait for you downstairs."

She nodded. "I'll call down and have a room readied for you."

I was being dismissed. I slapped France on the shoulder. "I'll meet you downstairs then."

He nodded. "Meet me in the red library in five minutes."

I left the room, not looking back. It wasn't the reunion I had expected, but all I could do was hope he would listen. And maybe not bring the model.

I took the elevator to the lobby and asked about the red library. The front desk person pointed me in the right direction. I was a little weirded out that it was a library without books, but the whole hotel looked like an Ikea showroom, instead of the huge stone Roman building it was on the outside.

I sat and waited. My stomach was in my throat. The modern decor made it worse.

I was lost in space and a terrible place mentally, when the door opened and he slipped inside. He closed it behind him. The initial joy of seeing me was gone. He looked nauseated. It made me feel worse.

He sat across from me on the odd and uncomfortable chair. He looked like he might break it. He was bigger, beefier than before. He must have been working out hard.

"How's it going?"

"I don't know."

He gave me a hard look. "Look, I owe you an apology. I acted like an asshole and ruined your wedding. I know you never chose me, and I had no right to do it."

I shook my head again. "France, I chose you. I still choose you."

He flinched. "Jack, me and Daniela, we're uhhhh—"

I put a hand out. "I know. I gathered that. I just needed to see you. I missed you."

He looked sickened. "I miss you too."

I stood, clearing my throat. "So, I'll see you around then." I quickly ran out the door. Daniela was at the front desk, beaming at me. She pointed and a man came over. "Ms. Croix, of course you must stay the night with us. Ms. Rabissi was just telling us who you are."

I smiled. The breeding and good manners were there for life; there was no fighting that. I couldn't just walk away. I had to be polite. "Thank you, sir. You are too kind."

He passed me a room key. "We have you in an executive suite. Is this your only bag?" He eyed up my small carry-on bag. I nodded and passed it to the bellhop, awkwardly standing in the circle.

He turned for the elevators. I smiled again. "Thank you so much. Good evening."

I turned and followed the young man with my single bag. I had no nice clothes or shoes or anything. I had only the jeans, tee shirts, and sweaters I had packed. My room was nice, but again modern. It didn't have the romantic feel of Rome, which might have been good, considering where my heart was. I tried to feel something but there was nothing. I was blank inside. I started unpacking when there was a knock at the door.

It was Daniela and France.

"Hi."

She walked into my room. "We were wondering if you wanted to have dinner with us?"

I opened my mouth to say no, when France shook his head. "She is probably beat. That's a long flight."

Daniela took my hand. "You must."

I smiled. "I didn't come prepared for dinner out. I came on a whim, hoping to see Mike play with the Italians."

She beamed. "He plays tomorrow. It is the last game before we go to Boston, and I say goodbye to my beloved Roma."

I smiled through the pain of the reality that she was going to Boston, not me. "Why don't we just agree to meet tomorrow then, and I will watch the game with you."

She tilted her head. "Yes, all right. That works well too." She looked over at France. "Doesn't it, Michael?"

His face was still stunned. "What? Yeah, sure." I could only assume he was shocked I was there. Or that he was with someone else and I was available. We just never seemed to get it right.

My tears were barely holding themselves at bay. He gave me a desperate look. "So dinner then?"

"No, the game tomorrow."

"I'll have some clothes sent up. Take a nap, and we'll see you this evening downstairs. Seven?"

I wanted to argue, but I was about to burst so I just nodded. "Sure."

Daniela smiled like she was my mother. She latched onto France's arm. "See you in a few hours." They left the room, but as I closed the door, I caught something on France's face: a look of confusion. I shook my head, closing the door and leaning against the back of it with a sigh.

I crawled into the bed and closed my eyes before the tears started.

Saturday night

The knock at the door woke me. I had drooled all over myself in what I would forever call the greatest nap ever. Groggily, I stretched and climbed off the bed. When I answered it, I was stunned. France was standing at the door with bags from what looked like boutiques. I frowned, fighting the heartache. "What are you doing?"

He held his arms out. "I phoned the hotel we stayed in and got them to tell me the stuff you had ordered."

"What? What hotel?"

"The one where you hired the private shopper."

The one where he made me orgasm over and over—right. How had I forgotten that hotel? How had he remembered so well?

I blushed, thinking about it. He smiled. "Yeah, that hotel." He looked funny, off a little. Like he was unsure of how to be around me.

I laughed and opened the door for him. He walked in and placed the bags on the bed. His eyes darted to my bag. "So, uhhh, seven?"

I rubbed my eyes and climbed back onto the bed, pushing the bags over. "Yeah, sure."

I pulled the blankets up. He got up and walked to the far side of the room. "You have a good flight?" It was weird the way he said it.

"Whatever you're avoiding asking me, just do it. I'm beat, and we don't do small talk."

He looked like he might say something, but he stopped himself short and shook his head. He looked a bit lost as he walked back over to the door. "I need to go do something. I'll see you at dinner."

"Whatever." I waved and pulled the covers up over my face. "Night."

I closed my eyes and let the sleep claim me again. I woke to the alarm that I should have woken to an hour earlier. It was six. I had an hour to be hot. I dumped the bags out on the bed and grabbed the shampoo, conditioner, and frizz control he had bought for me. I stumbled into the bathroom and started the process of not looking like I was no longer caring about my looks.

The hot water was wonderful and the idea of being in a hotel with France made me think about the last shower we had taken. I blushed, smiling and scrubbing.

I got out, dialed Brandi and started changing into the sexy underwear and bra he'd purchased for me. They were stunning and not the same as I had ordered last time.

"Hello?"

I spoke softly, "He has a girlfriend. An Italian-model girlfriend."

Brandi sighed. "I know. Will told me when I met up with him the other day. They're engaged, JD. You need to home wreck on his ass and get this to end. Will thinks she's looking for a green-card, rich-husband combo, and Mike is so desperate to get over you that he's making this mistake."

My mouth was dry. I grabbed a bottle of the Swiss mineral water and guzzled it. I coughed. "You sent me here, knowing he was engaged? Do you hate me, Bran?"

"Baby, I know you and him are meant to be. You need to tell him how you feel and don't do your prim and proper bullshit. Belt it out."

I nodded, feeling faint. "Okay. I hate you though. You and Will. You're dead to me."

She chuckled. "That's fine. Call me later."

I shuddered. He was engaged—already? It had been six months since he asked me to run away with him. Asshole. I felt a bitterness creeping up inside me. Not a jealous bitterness but an "I want him jealous" bitterness. Fucker.

I pulled on the dress that he had bought me, hiking it up a bit and adding the padding back into the push-up bra. I slid my feet into the Versace patent-leather black pumps. My hair was in its natural state of curls, falling loosely around my shoulders. The black dress was sexy with the harsh push-up of the bra. I looked classically beautiful. Not Italian-model beautiful, but I wasn't going to beat myself up over that. She had to have flaws too.

God was fair.

I lined my eye makeup on a little heavily and smoky and then ran anti-frizz product through my hair. I sprayed a touch of perfume and gave myself a final look.

It was good. He had done well.

My lips were red. Nothing beat a strawberry-blonde with red lipstick. Not even an Italian model.

I left the room and made my way downstairs to the dining room. The maître d' brought me to my table. They weren't there yet.

I sat and waited, perusing the wine list.

I smiled when I saw one of my favorites.

"Can I get you a drink to start?"

I made a face. "It's going to seem presumptuous of me to order wine for the table, but I must have a bottle of the pinot noir. It was made at a vineyard in the Alto Adige region." I had tried it when I was there for the sommelier tasting. The region was well known for its pinot noir grapes. It had a history of thousands of years of winemaking and grape growing. I found it fascinating.

The server grinned. "The lady knows her wine."

I smiled. "I do. I love wine. I actually spent a little time in Alto Adige, in Tyrol and a few other places."

He looked taken aback. "Wow. That is impressive. The area is so rich with wine."

"It flows everywhere."

He smiled. "I will be back with your selection."

I sat there alone until he came back with the bottle. He poured my taster. I smelled and drank, swishing it about in my mouth, and letting it get air before I swallowed. I nodded. "Perfect."

He poured me a full glass and looked around the room. "Are you dining alone?"

"I'm not supposed to be."

He frowned. "Who are you waiting for?"

"Mike France."

He scowled. "Of course. Some of the others he plays with, the other foreigners, are at that table." His eyes flickered to a table across the room.

"You don't like Mike?"

He looked around discreetly. "I am a huge fan of his. That woman, Ms. Rabissi, is another story."

"Excellent. I think you and I will be great friends. Can I tell you a secret?"

His dark eyes lit up. "Of course."

"I'm here to ruin their engagement."

His face glowed. "Oh, how wonderful. You are here to save him from that money-grabbing man-eater?"

I took a drink of my wine. "No. I want him for myself."

"This bottle is on the house. You dine for free. Wait until I tell the others there is hope for him. We assumed it was the hits to the head that have made him stupid."

I laughed and drank another big gulp. I wasn't savoring my wine. I was chugging it. I needed liquid courage.

"My name is Romeo, and if you need anything at all while you are here, you tell me."

I looked around. "I don't think they're coming. Can you introduce me to the other hockey players?"

He clapped his hands. "Wonderful idea." He grabbed my bottle and glass and carried them over to their table in the corner. Six beefy guys sat there. They didn't all look like hockey players—well, maybe one didn't.

"May I introduce Miss Jacqueline Croix. She is a friend of Mr. France. He has been delayed, and she is dining alone tonight."

Their faces lit up. One guy smiled. "Come sit with us, sweetheart." He sounded like he was from Texas maybe.

Another guy with a German accent shoved his chair over. "Sit next to me."

I smiled. "Thank you. I didn't want to sit alone." Actually, I wanted France to come in and see me with everyone else. Let him be the awkward one—him and the model.

I sat, nestled into the small group.

"This is Bill from Vermont, Sal from Germany, Luce from Israel, Daniel from Sweden, Arthur from Ireland, and I am Tex from Texas."

I waved. "Jack or JD."

Tex gave me a squeeze, not realizing I hated being touched by other people. "JD, now that's my kind of girl."

I laughed and let him keep his arm wrapped around me. I hoped that France would walk in, accidentally seeing another man touching me.

Of course he didn't.

We started drinking.

"So, Jack, where are you from?"

I looked at the eager faces of the men. "New York."

"D d he just call you Jack?"

I turned around to see France standing behind us, alone. "Yeah."

"Her name is JD or Jacqueline. No one calls her Jack, okay?"

They all stopped for a second and then immediately started laughing. His face got red.

I looked around at the laughing men. Arthur from Ireland nodded. "You're that Jack? Shit, I thought you were bisexual, France."

Mike's face got even worse. He put a hand out for me. "Can I talk to you?"

"Where's Daniela?"

"Upstairs."

"Is she coming down?"

"No. Can you guys excuse us?" He tossed down a hundred-dollar bill. I grimaced. "That's not enough for the bottle."

He pulled me from my chair. "Tex, you got the rest of that bill?"

"Yup."

France dragged me out of the dining room. I pulled my arm from his grip. "What are you doing?"

He paced for a minute and then pulled me down the hall to the elevator. He pressed the button. "Why did you come here?"

Tara Brown

The elevator arrived, but before I could answer he pushed me inside and against the wall. His face was savage as he reached inside his pocket, ripping the pink bachelorette sash from his pants. I frowned for a second. "Did you go through my bag?"

He held it in my face. "How did you get this?"

I shoved him back. "I went to the Empire State Building that night, you meathead. I went to the train station, your apartment, your house in Jersey, my house, the coffee house we once accidentally made out in, and then it dawned on me—the Empire State Building. Of course. The place that would show me you loved me, more than anything in the whole world. I paid the sax player two thousand dollars for it."

He clenched his jaw. "Why?"

I shoved him again. "Because I wanted your fucking signature. Why do you think?"

He pounded the wall of the elevator. "Why are you doing this to me?"

I jumped, feeling my lip quiver. He was angry in a way I had never seen before. He closed his eyes. "Why did you come here? Because I finally met someone? Because I was finally happy?"

I felt my nostrils flare. "Firstly, you've known her like a week. Finally happy—my ass. You are rebounding with that poor girl. Secondly, you truly believe that I would come here just to sabotage your engagement? How was I supposed to know you were engaged, dick?"

He flung the pink sash at me. "That is a low blow and you know it. Just tell me how you got it. Who did you pay off? Did Will tell you where I left it? Did he go back and get it and give it to you?"

I pushed the main floor button. The door opened. I realized then, we had not actually moved. I stormed from the elevator and looked back at him. "I went to the Empire State Building, looking for you. Same as today. I came looking for you. I flew across the fucking ocean. I wanted to tell you that you were right. You were right all along. You and I love each other, and no one is ever going to love us the same way. So

124

fuck you." I flung the sash back at him as the door closed. I turned and stormed into the dining room and sat back in my chair.

The guys gave me a look. "You want some more wine, JD?"

"Call me Jack. I like Jack better anyway."

Sunday morning

The knock at the door woke me. My jet lag and wine hangover were savaging my brain and body. I stumbled to the door. Daniela was bright-eyed and bushy-tailed and at my door with a supermodel smile.

"Brunch?"

I squinted at her. "What time is it?"

"Eleven, silly. We are all meeting downstairs for brunch. Mike didn't want to wake you, but I figured you'd balance out faster if you got up now."

"Be down in ten." I closed the door and prayed I had at least one cute brunch outfit.

I didn't, but Mike had bought me a couple of cute dresses and skirts. I slipped on a skirt and a blouse, and attempted to get myself close to not puffy.

I ended up with so much eye brightener, I looked semi-high. I ran from the room, hoping a little exertion would get me looking better.

When I got downstairs, I was flushed and glowing when I passed the mirror. I hurried into the breakfast room. The server sat me with a wink. I didn't know what that meant, but I smiled at the guys. "Morning."

They all nodded at me. Tex slapped me on the back. "How ya feelin,' Jack?"

I caught an evil glare from Mike but smiled anyway. "Great. Little jet lagged but that'll wear off." I leaned into Tex. "You let me drink too much last night."

He beamed. "With a name like Jack, I figured you would drink us under the table."

"Wine, I bet I can. You guys drink wine with me tonight." I waved at Romeo. He came rushing over. I smiled brightly. "Can we do a post-game wine tasting for these guys, you and I?"

His eyes lit up. "Of course. What a fabulous idea. Yes. We will make it wonderful for you all. Red and white?"

I nodded and clapped my hands. "Yes, please." I grinned wide, opening my brunch menu.

Romeo winked at me. "Leave it to me."

"Thank you."

Tex gave me a scowl. "Now, I don't drink wine."

Mike scoffed. "Me either."

Arthur shook his head. "More of a draft sort of lad, myself." His accent was adorable.

I cracked a wide smile. "You will all be converted by the end of the night."

I batted my lashes at them all. They all blushed and joked, apart from Mike. He scowled and grumbled. Daniela seemed to be compensating for his horrid mood. She didn't know he just needed a nap and some video games. That always got him into a worse funk, and then even he couldn't stand his own self. Then he would go for a huge workout and come back a new man.

I avoided his face. I didn't know what to say to him. He didn't believe I went to the Empire State Building. He thought I had used my money and influence to get the sash back.

Screw him.

Daniela fed him a bite. His eyes darted at me before he bit. I rolled my eyes and smiled at Luce who was telling a story.

We finished breakfast and walked out of the dining room. I was stuffed and ready for a nap, but Luce asked if I wanted to go for a walk and sightsee a little.

"Let me just get my sweater. I'll meet you in the lobby in ten minutes."

He smiled and I sighed. If I wasn't so angry with Mike, I would have paid more attention to the fact Luce was hot. He was dark haired, green eyed, beefy, and five-o'clock-shadow gorgeous. He had that foreigner hotness that Americans just couldn't do. He wore Armani and smiled with brilliance and confidence. I had a naughty thought as I stepped into the elevator.

Mike climbed in after me.

He pressed his back against the wall and pushed the door close button several times.

"So what's the plan for today?"

I shoved him. "No way. You can't be a dick to me yesterday and today be all 'Hey, Jack, what's shaking?'"

He smiled and I sighed again. I shook my head though and muttered, "I hate you."

He grabbed my face and pressed his lips to my forehead. It was seductive and more than a forehead kiss. "I am so sorry I suspected you were here to ruin my chances after I ruined yours."

I pushed him back. "You're getting married. Just stop this. No more kissing." When the elevator stopped on my floor, he got out, walking me to my door. I sighed as I opened it and looked back at him. "You can't come in." I barred the way with my arms. He grabbed each hand that was clinging to the frame and pushed me into the room. He closed the door with his foot and looked down on me. I felt tiny.

"Just tell me that you love me, again."

"No."

He nodded. "Do it."

"I hate you. You did ruin my life, Mike. You ruined everything, and then you disappeared and left me there alone. I had no one. My sister, my friends, no one. My family doesn't speak to me. My father took my things from Phil's and burned them. I picked you, but you were gone so I was stuck alone. Do you know what that felt like?"

His face was stoic, but I could see the pain in his eyes. "I just assumed you had picked him when you didn't move."

I shoved him back. "You stormed into my wedding and started a huge fight. I was terrified and shocked."

He nodded. "I know. I see that now."

"But now is too late. You didn't answer one phone call or one email or one message. You didn't hear the message of me calling from the Empire State Building? You had to have heard the sax in the background on the message I left you."

He winced. "Jack—"

I shook my head again. "No. Don't Jack me like that. Screw you, Mike." I grabbed my sweater from the bed and walked out, brushing past him.

He grabbed my arm. "Where are you going?"

I jerked my arm free. "To hang with Luce. He wants to be with me, Mike." I didn't mean it the way it sounded. I saw a fire lit in his eyes.

I turned and ran for the stairs.

"Jack!"

I hurried down the stairs, but his legs were strong, longer, and in considerably better shape.

He grabbed my arm, spinning me. "Stop calling me Mike. I hate it when you call me that."

I shoved his huge hand from my arm. "I hate when you act like I'm being unreasonable. You came and ruined my wedding day and my life, and somehow it's my fault that I never hopped down from the altar quick enough. You fucking started a brawl at my wedding. A brawl. How did you think I was going to react?"

His dark eyes burned down on me. "I thought you'd see the romantic gesture."

I moaned in disbelief. "You came drunk. Romance was not what I saw. I saw a drunk hockey player making a huge scene."

"What do you care? You don't even like any of those people."

I shoved him again. "THOSE WERE THE ONLY PEOPLE I HAD! YOU LEFT ME THERE AFTER YOU MADE A FOOL OF ME! YOU DIDN'T EVEN GIVE ME A CHANCE TO REACT!"

He grabbed my face and lowered his, but I shoved him off me and turned and ran down the stairs.

He didn't follow.

Luce was waiting for me in the lobby. He looked like a model. He looked like he and Daniela should be going sightseeing. But it was me he smiled at. "You ready?"

I nodded and followed him out of the hotel. The streets and buildings were ancient looking. I loved it. That part of the city had such a romantic feeling to it. The crisp winter air was surprising. It wasn't New York cold, but it was not as warm as I expected. The entrance to the hotel wasn't at all what a five-star hotel in New York would have for a grand entrance. It was old and stone, and the cobblestone streets made it feel like I was suddenly part of the history. We walked down the one-way street until we reached a huge five-way stop. The traffic was nuts. It reminded me of Manhattan, but the buildings were incredibly old and beautiful. The smell of the old city was interesting and surprising.

Luce pointed at the building next to us. "Gallery of Ancient Art. Let's go in."

I had been to Rome shopping many times, but never had I seen the side the tourists saw.

We walked through the huge iron and stone gates into the plaza. It was stunning. When we got inside, it smelled old and dusty, but the paintings, ceilings, and woodwork captivated me. He paid and pointed. "My favorite is down this way."

He took my arm in his and led me along. "You know, the painting we are about to see is my all-time favorite."

If I hadn't been so angry, I might have liked the fact he had a favorite piece of art in a gallery in Rome. He wasn't just a hockey player. He was a worldly man from a humble and war-torn country.

Each painting was more impressive than the one before until suddenly we stopped. My eyes scanned the painting, overcome by it all. *St. John the Baptist in the Wilderness.* The shadows and subtleties were perfect. I was drawn into the dark places I couldn't see and captivated by the young man whose face was cast to the side. He looked like he was crawling from his bed. The date was the detail that struck me with overwhelming awe: 1603–1604. It was over four hundred years old.

"Makes you want to see what else is there, what is in the shadows, and what he is looking at."

"It's stunning. It makes me sad, and I don't know why."

"He was beheaded for speaking against King Herod's marriage to his niece. He called it incestuous. He was the man who baptized Jesus but refused to be more than him.

He was a humble man, always trying to be smaller and make Jesus bigger."

A tear grew in my eye and slowly trickled down my cheek. I was certain it had little to do with John the Baptist and more to do with Mike the asshole, but I let the painting be the reason I was overwhelmed.

Luce looked down on me with a soft smile. He wiped my tear. I smiled back. "Thank you for showing me this."

He nodded. "No, thank you." He pointed. "Do you want to see another one that's breathtaking? The ability of the painter is remarkable."

I nodded. He pulled me gently to a dark painting of a man lost in his own reflection.

"Narcissus," I read. It was older than the one before. It looked as if it were mocking vanity maybe, like the man was stuck staring at himself.

We walked, not speaking, just taking everything in. There was a stone archway that looked like a reproduction, sculptures, paintings, and carvings. They started to blend into each other until we reached the tapestries. They were like rugs held on looms high in the air. The art made of thread was impressive in both size and detail. I felt like a different person with Luce. Someone who could be quiet and just appreciate the things around her.

We linked our fingers into each other's at some point, walking like lovers in Rome, people we weren't. He pulled me out another doorway to a long corridor of arches. It was so big, and yet ornate. I felt like I could be that backpacking student who was seeing everything before her life started.

He walked us to a column and pressed my back against it, looking down on me. My heart was in my throat. He ran a hand down my cheek. "You are so beautiful."

I swallowed hard. "I can't do this. I'm so sorry, Luce. I am still recovering from something."

"France?"

I winced and nodded.

"He's engaged."

I looked down at his waist. "I know. I made a mistake coming here. My sister and his best friend back home, they bought me the ticket to come see him and set it up. I didn't know he was engaged."

He lifted my chin. "You deserve someone so much better than a man who would even look at a gold digger like Daniela."

"I think I drove him to Daniela, unfortunately. France is the greatest guy in the world, but he makes terrible choices when he's upset."

Luce smiled. "We will get a gelato, and you will tell me this terrible story of the breaking of Mike France."

I laughed. "Deal."

I linked my arm into his and pointed at the pillars. "If we're both still single in six months, can I get a rain check for that pillar kiss?"

"Yes. But I don't think I can wait six months."

I laughed harder, feeling the blush taking over my face.

Sunday night

Daniela passed me a hot chocolate, which to Italians is a thick and delightful drink you dip your biscotti into. You didn't drink it, so much as savor it with baked goods. She dumped some Frangelico into both our small cups and winked at me. "It's good."

As it turned out, it was pretty hard to dislike her.

She was sweet. I saw the money grubbing she did, but she was no different than the girls I had always hung out with. She was like a soul sister to me, really.

My life had been spent in pursuit of a man to marry me, buy me expensive things, and get me into the right circles—oh, and love me.

Daniela looked excited as we waited for the teams to hit the ice.

"So you watch a lot of hockey?"

"No. Not so much."

She frowned. "But you're American."

"I'm more of an after-party sort of girl."

She nodded. "The after-parties are fun. That is where I met Mike."

I grimaced. "Yikes. They are usually pretty nasty. One time when Mike and I were about nineteen, he came home for Christmas from wherever the hell he was. We went to a party, and one of the guys he was teammates with, came up and asked me to take his wife out for a smoke. I smoked at the time. So I asked her to come with me. She was excited someone was even talking to her. I had my smoke, and she got into a conversation with another girl. I left her there on the deck and went back inside to go to the bathroom. I opened the door to find her husband screwing some random chick in the bathroom. I closed the door and went back out onto the deck. He came out about twenty minutes later and wrapped his arm around her, like nothing had happened. I learned then, the difference between puck fucks and wives. I also lost a lot of respect for the players."

I dipped my biscotti and took a bite. She looked disturbed. "That doesn't happen now though?"

"It happens every day. Why do you think there are so many divorces with sports players? They are surrounded by adoring fans who want to give them everything and anything they could possibly wish for." I wrinkled my nose. "That's why Mike is still single. His best friend Will is the same. He won't marry until he knows he is almost done with the game."

She swallowed hard. I felt the tiniest bit of remorse, but it was washed down with the delicious biscotti and the vision of the players as they skated out onto the ice. They looked sexy in their gear.

The anthems were sung and the announcer got the game going. The puck dropped and it was on. I didn't realize how much I did enjoy watching hockey until it was the second period. I was out of my seat, screaming as Mike was on a breakaway. He scored. Daniela and I hugged each other and jumped up and down in our heeled boots.

The game ended with a win: Italy over Germany, 6–3. We waited in the seats for a few minutes. The game was over and the box was quiet.

She finally touched my hand. "I want you to know I love him. I know he is like a brother to you, and you watch out for him and worry. But you don't have to. I adore him."

I smiled. It was the fake plastic one my mom had taught me. "I'm glad." I wasn't. I was dying inside, but he had chosen to be with her, even when I had professed my love for him. Even after I had flown to Rome. Even after he had seen the sash and knew the truth.

He had chosen her, and if I wanted him to still be my France, I had to accept his wife.

She stood. "We can wait downstairs in the heat."

The box we were in was warm enough, but I could sense the awkwardness coming from us both and agreed. We walked with only the sound of our heels clicking on the floor. I had bought myself boots when I was out with Luce. He had shown me where the Italians bought their footwear, all designer but discounted. I had found a pair of gray A. Testoni knee-high platform boots for three hundred euros. It was a steal. The pair I had bought the last time I was in Rome cost me eight hundred. These were a mixture of leather and suede.

Daniela nodded at them when we got downstairs. "Those are beautiful."

"Thanks. I went shopping with Luce."

She smiled wide. "He is a beautiful man."

"Yes. He is trouble, I can tell. Smooth and sweet and dresses well. He scored three of the goals."

"He's going to Boston to play also. When the owners came to speak with Michael, they saw him play. Offered him a huge contract too."

"How old is he?"

"Twenty something."

I bit my lip. "Oh. I wonder why he never got scouted when he was young?"

Her eyes widened. "He was in a terrible accident. He has a huge scar on his leg. He was in rehab for it for two years. He was drafted as a young man, but he never made it to America. Now he's a little older and still playing just as well, if not better. They want him now."

"That facial hair and confidence definitely make him look older."

She nudged me. "He is not too young for you. Besides, that is an Italian way. Older woman, younger man. Very common."

I was clearly older than him. What was I thinking? She had me distracted from France. She was good. Too good.

I wanted to hate her and destroy her, but I couldn't.

The group of foreigners came from the dressing room together. They had to stop and sign autographs. Girls were crying and kissing cheeks and making a spectacle. Daniela tried to look stoic, but I could see the annoyance on her face. I had created the doubt that now sat in her eyes.

France came over to us, looking confused. Daniela wrapped her arms around him. He hugged her to him, but I could see the way he wasn't all in. He was half-assing the hug.

Tex grinned at me. "Ready to drink some wine, Jack?"

France made a face, but I ignored him and nodded. "I am if you are."

Luce walked up, inspecting my boots. "They look lovely." I almost melted into his green eyes. I nodded. "Thanks for helping me pick them out."

He cut Tex off and looped my arm into his. "Tell me about this obsession you have with wine."

I let him lead me out to the cab. Some of the Italians on the team joined our group suddenly. Tex nudged me. "We invited the team."

"Okay."

France sighed. "Red wine tasting as our after-party?"

Daniela poked him. "I think it's a marvelous idea."

He glanced down at her, maybe catching the glare of doubt in her eyes, and shrugged. "Whatever."

When we got to the hotel, Romeo had prepared a magnificent spread. He had red, white, and blush wines set up at three separate tables. He was grinning from ear to ear as we walked in.

"Ms. Croix, welcome to our wine tasting. I have selected what we here at the Boscolo Aleph consider our best wines. Some are top shelf and others are surprisingly good for their cost level and popularity."

There was a member of the hotel staff at each table to pour the wine and discuss it.

Daniela's face was glowing. "This is a smart after-party."

France glared at me. "Leave it to you to wreck my last night with the guys."

I stuck my tongue out at him. "We aren't even close to even."

Luce was hovering over me. "Which should I taste first?"

I turned my back on France and took Luce's arm. "White." We strolled over to the table to taste the best whites I had ever had.

Luce nodded on the last glass. "I can taste peaches, but it isn't sweet. It's like the essence of peach is in the wine."

I smiled at his accent and palate. "Exactly. Aging wine in oak is a great way to add flavor to the wine. The oak barrels will make the wine take on whatever flavor is present while it ages. So if ripe peaches were in the room as the wine aged, the oak would soak up the flavor in the air and infuse the wine with it."

He sipped from the glass that looked like a toy in his huge hands.

I cocked my head. "I don't know a lot of people from Israel, but you seem huge."

"I am above average for an Israeli man, but I'm not Israeli. My mother is actually a Brit from Saudi Arabia, and my father is half Bahraini and the other half British. My mother was raised in Saudi because her father was an ambassador, and my father was raised in Bahrain until he was thirteen. Then he was sent to school in England. He and my mother met there, at Oxford. My father works in Bahrain in banking. His family has always been in oil, banking, and trade. I was raised the same way he was. When I was thirteen, I was sent to London for school, but I wanted to play hockey. My uncle lived in California so I was sent to stay with him when I was fourteen, and played at nearby prep schools. I was drafted from there."

"How are you from Israel?"

"I'm not. I lived there before I came here because I was in rehabilitation there. The best doctor for my injury was in Jerusalem. I was in a car accident. Technically, I was drafted into the Italian league from Israel. I am not from there though. It is a beautiful place but not my homeland. I think of California as my home."

I grinned and walked to the red wine table. "So what are you?"

He chuckled. "I am exactly what most Americans are. Heinz 57. I am mostly British with a quarter Bahraini, and being born there, that is my nationality. I have duel citizenship."

"Luce is an odd name. It sounds Italian."

"It is. My mother's favorite teacher when she was a girl was an Italian named Lucian Merino. He was her philosophy teacher. I am Lucian Nooruddin."

I whistled. "That must have been a blast when you were a child."

He scoffed. "Luce has always been my nickname." He nudged me. "What are you?"

"Same as you. My father is French. Croix is pretty obvious. My mother is English. Her family came over on the Mayflower, very old money. Unfortunately, they lost it all. My parents both grew up on the East Coast. My mother was in the Hamptons and New York mostly, and my father was in New York."

France poked his head into our conversation. "Your parents would love Luce's." His tone was harsh.

I scowled at him but Luce just laughed. "She explained them to me earlier. I doubt even I would get their approval." He was giving France a compliment, but he didn't get it. France shrugged indifferently. "They'll love the improvement in her. Caring about art, music, and theatre. You'll be a great influence on her. I mean, Philip brought her so far; you should be able to get her the rest of the way, make a lady out of her, and get her the right connections. His family is friends with the Bush family and the Kennedys, you know that?"

My jaw dropped but Mike continued with his mockery. He pointed. "You never know, Luce. I thought she came here to ruin my engagement like I did hers. But maybe her parents sent her to snatch you up instead. We both know you're the better catch. Any guy here, technically, could have had her with the way she was throwing it out there, but I'm glad it's you."

Luce shoved him slightly. "France, watch it, huh? You're drunk. Stop. We're friends. You're being a dick."

Mike shoved him back, but Luce was sober. He pulled Mike's shirt over his head and held him down. "Calm down, Mike. Stop. We're on the same team, man."

Mike tackled him into the table with the blush wines, crashing everything to the floor. The bottles smashed.

I jumped at Luce. "Are you all right?"

Mike got up and shoved me back and grabbed Luce, lifting him off the ground and punching him in the jaw. Luce took the hit well and tackled Mike into the wall. The plaster cracked.

"STOP!" I screamed.

Tex grabbed Mike and Arthur grabbed Luce. They held them back with the help of the rest of the team. I could see blood on Luce's back from the bottle. I lifted his shirt and winced. "You're going to need stitches."

He was breathing heavily when he shook his head. "Fuck with me again, Mike, or her—" He pointed. France looked at him from under the most evil face I'd ever seen grace his brow.

Daniela grabbed my arm. "JD, you okay? I'm so sorry. I'll take him upstairs now. He'll be so sorry he said that tomorrow. You know how he feels about you. You're like a sister to him." She turned and gabbed France. "You are an asshole, and you owe her a huge apology." She scolded him as she dragged him from the room. I stood there, frozen in the silence of them all. I looked up at Luce. "I'm so sorry. Excuse me." My words were barely audible.

I turned and ran from the hotel. I ran down the street in the direction I hoped was the right one. I passed the piazza we had been at earlier and ran down the cobblestone street. My boots clicked against the stone. I ran past a road but stopped when I realized it was the turn to the *Piazza di Trevi.*

I slowly entered the square, awestruck by the pain in my heart and the lit up piazza. The whole fountain had a warm glow to it and the lights under the water made it magical. I sat on the stone ledge and tried to breathe. A terrible lump formed in my throat. I heard footsteps, dreading seeing Luce. The sound of the running water was overtaken by the footsteps of the man I really didn't want to see right now.

"Jack." His panicked face was twisted as if he were in pain.

Tears started instantly. The lump took over. I couldn't talk or breathe. All I could do was sob.

"No." I hugged myself as he drew closer. I put a hand out, shaking my sobbing face. "Just stay back."

He stopped. "I don't know what's gotten into me. I just don't know which way is right."

I looked down, crying silently in the dark and nearly empty piazza.

He walked to me slowly. "You and me, we're crazy and explosive and fun. I wanted you my whole life, and you refused to come down to my level. You let me touch you and be with you, but you never gave me a real chance. I thought if I did a grand gesture, you would see how much I loved you. I didn't have the courage to do it so I got drunk and the courage came." He was right in front of me. He dropped to his knees, taking my hands in his. "I fucked up so bad, and I don't know how to fix it."

I closed my eyes and let the silent tears drip down my cheeks. Small raindrops started to hit me sporadically.

"You just make me feel so unworthy."

"I never meant to."

He nodded. I could see the tears in his eyes. "I know."

I sniffled. "I just never was as strong as you. I needed you to be brave. You made me strong. I could stand up to them and walk away because you were there for me."

He ran a hand down my cheek. "But I wasn't, was I? I made you be brave, and then I left you to deal with it all." He leaned in close to me. "I'm sorry, Jack."

"We can't do this. You're engaged."

He looked down. "It's like you said. I was just rebounding."

"You never even gave me a chance, Mike. You assumed how my life went and never gave me a chance."

His words became a whisper, "You broke my heart."

"Then I guess we're even." I pushed him back and got up. I hugged myself and walked to the road I had come in on. The skies opened and rained down on Rome.

"No, we're not."

I looked back at him, barely able to hear him through the bouncing rain. "What?"

"We're not even, Jack. Not by a long shot."

"What more can you ruin for me, Mike?"

He got up and stormed across the piazza, lifting me up into his arms. "I can ruin you for every other man in the world." He brushed his soaked lips against mine. The rain poured down on our kiss, mixing with my tears, washing them away.

"You already did."

He whispered into the side of my face, "Then be mine, Jack. Be my girl."

I nodded and let him kiss me harder.

Monday morning

I stared at the ceiling of the room and wondered how it had gone. He was breaking things off with her. It didn't feel right or wrong. It was too big to try to classify.

A knock at the door interrupted my pondering the essence of life and why God was against me. I got up, surprised to see Luce there. His lip was puffy.

"How's your back?" I asked quickly.

He grimaced. "Six stitches." He turned around and lifted his shirt. There was a huge bandage covering it all. I could see bruises over his back muscles.

I ran my hands over the skin. "Oh my God. Have you seen Mike?"

He turned back around. "No. Have you?"

"He followed me last night." I pointed to the room. "Please, come in."

He walked in and sat on the couch in the corner.

I sat across from him on the chair, pulled my legs up, and wrapped my arms around them. "He followed me to the *Trevi Fountain.* He told me he wants to break up with Daniela and be with me."

He flinched. "What? Is that something you want, after everything that's happened?"

I almost said yes, but I froze. My mouth hung open. I didn't have an answer. I had my mother's smile and nod. I had the fake answer of least resistance. But with Luce I didn't feel like I had to say it. I could be conflicted. He expected nothing, either way. I shook my head. "I don't know what I want."

"I think you need to think about that, Jacqueline. You are young, crazy, vivacious, and fun. You need to embrace that and be the person you want to be. I got the impression from Mike that you sort of mold yourself to be the person you need to be to match the man you're with. That is a mistake. My mother has done that, and I have watched her die inside every day, just a little more. My father is a respected investment banker. She is expected to be a dutiful wife. He shouldn't have married a white woman, but he did. My father isn't even Islamic and my mother wears the garb. She is a strong woman, always has been. You would never know it if you met her." His green eyes were dark and beautiful under his thick black lashes. "I like that about you. You seem like you are full of passion. To listen to you talk about wine is like listening to you pour your soul out. I think if you were smart, you would take this as an opportunity to find yourself. You're already in Europe. Go see the art and architecture and the vineyards. Go and live this and see where you end up."

"How are you so smart for so young?"

He smiled back, but it was filled with something else, and I didn't know him well enough to read what it was. "I almost lost the thing I loved the most in my life: hockey. I didn't care if I walked or made love or ran or drove again. But I cared that I might not skate again. My father was so excited to be free of the hockey, the burden of it, and the influence of the West in my life. I had no support. I know what you have been through. I found the best doctors, I made the arrangements, and I got better because I wanted it." He stood up. "I am going to California for Christmas and then Boston to work. I hope I see you again. The real you." He left me there, dumbfounded and alone.

The next knock on the door was also surprising. I wanted it to be him, but it was Mike. He looked exhausted and sad.

I grabbed his hands. "Tell me fast, what did you love about her?"

He frowned. "What?"

"No, answer the question as quick as you can."

He looked stunned. "Silky brown hair, smoking hot, funny, kinda subservient, but spicy when I needed it. I don't know. Why? Why are we doing this?"

"I have a challenge for you."

"Jack, I'm beat. This has been the most tiring six months of my life."

"I know, me too. We are both single right now. We are both completely available. I want that to last for six months. Go to Boston alone and love the game again. No one-night stands and no random puck fucks. Just you and your team and your love of the game."

He pinched the bridge of his nose. "Baby, I just broke off an engagement with an Italian model for you. Whatever this stupid challenge is—I passed—trust me."

He stepped toward me, but I stepped back, holding my hands in between us. "Mike, me and you need a chance to be me and you before we are a we. I need this. Can you grant me that? The freedom to find myself? You were right last night in one respect: I always find a way to fit the man I'm with. I think I'm me with you, but I need to be sure."

He grabbed me, scooping me up, and then laid me down on the bed and spooned me. "Fine, but I want to sleep, nap like before."

I closed my eyes and let him hold me until he was asleep. When I was sure he was snoring, I climbed from the bed and packed my things. I had to pack it tighter with the new clothes and makeup. My sister had sent me twenty thousand dollars. It would have to be enough to get me through Europe. I called from the bathroom and changed the return date of my flight to May 7.

I wrote him a letter and left it there next to him. I glanced at it once more, tearing up as I reread it.

> France,
> I am not letting you go. I am not giving up on you and me. I am putting me first in the least selfish way I can. You need to go to Boston and establish yourself without anyone else there to define you. I need to find out what, besides wine and little blue pills, defines me.
> You have always been the person in my life that I could count on. I am counting on you now to trust me

and let me trust you. I don't want to regret following you on your dream and never experiencing mine.
I love you,

Jack, your Jack

I grabbed my bag and slipped from the room, not waking or kissing him.

Romeo was in the lobby as I was leaving. He beamed. "You leaving early?"

I nodded and placed my bag next to the counter. I wrapped my arms around him, even if I hardly knew him.

"Thank you."

"I saw Ms. Rabissi leaving today. She seemed upset, but that husky Texan went after her."

"Maybe you won't be rid of her."

He pulled me back. "But you will be."

"She seemed nice."

He scoffed. "Not to anyone she thought was lower status. Women like her are like a vase. They are pretty to look at but that is all. They serve no real purpose."

"I hope you have a merry Christmas."

"You too, Ms. Croix."

"JD." I stepped on my tiptoes in my boots and kissed his cheek. I grabbed my bags and left the hotel. The air was fresh and crisp and exhilarating. I had no rules and no expectations. I was free, truly free.

Saturday morning

Four months later
The wedding day

I fumbled with my dress and hat. Italians always wore hats to weddings. I still smelled like the bar from the night before. We were soaked in wine by the end of the night. Greeks were crazy like that. I could see there was still a bit of tannin on my knuckles.

I looked once more at myself and nodded. It was as good as I was going to get.

Brandi gave me a cockeyed look. "That's the best you could do? It's a March wedding. You need something springish."

I rolled my eyes. "Bran, I'm here as the ex-girlfriend of the guy she almost married. I was stunned when France brought you the invite for me."

She shrugged. "He said Tex wanted you here. Now let's roll." Her New York accent was more noticeable. Probably because I'd been speaking Italian and Greek for months.

We walked out of the flat I had rented for the week.

"How are you for money?"

I shrugged. "Still about ten thousand and two months left. I'll probably be okay."

She nodded back at the apartment. "I stuck another forty in the dresser for you. It's in a sock."

I snorted. "Wow. So I take it things are going well?"

She nodded. "Beyond being five-months pregnant, yeah. You have to come and see the new house. It's amazing. Shawn loves working for Muriel. She is kicking ass in Boston."

I glanced at her. "How are Mom and Dad?"

She sighed. "Mom has snuck over to see me a few times. Dad isn't speaking to me. He blames me for you and

146

blah, blah, blah. Whatever. Let him think what he wants. He gets no part of my babies and my future."

I hugged her. "I'm sorry."

She shook her head. "Screw him. He's a mean old goat."

I laughed.

"So how's the traveling going? Any hotties on the roster?"

I nudged her. "No. You know I made that pact with Mike."

She smiled. "You know he's gonna be here tonight."

"Yeah. Temptation to the extreme."

"No one is going to judge you if you give up two months early on this fucking pilgrimage of working at wineries around Europe. What kind of pilgrim are you anyway?"

"I know but I want it. I've learned a ton. I know what I want."

She gave me a sideways glance. "What?"

"My own label at my own house. I want the vineyard more than ever."

"In Boston?"

I shrugged. "I don't know."

"Muriel will do whatever you want. She thinks the sun rises and sets on your ass."

"Crazy old woman. I am not taking a dime from her unless she wants to be an investor and make money." We walked to the car she had hired for the week.

The drive to the villa was incredible. Grassy hills, beautiful old houses and structures, and the sea. It was intoxicating. I couldn't believe it was my life. There were no pressing matters or charities or creepy men groping me. There was nothing but wine, vineyards, and friends who were like family even after only a few days. The villa was an old castle with vines growing up it and faded stone fences. There were fragrant trees and flowers blooming, even on the Ides of March.

The castle was a giant building with arched windows and a huge circular driveway. France was waiting outside with Will when we pulled up. He looked sexy, fucking sexy. His white dress shirt and black dress pants were tailored to perfection. Will looked the same but in a gray suit. France's sleeves were rolled up, and I could see new ink on his forearms. When the car parked in the courtyard, I jumped out.

His face lit up when he saw me. "Jack!" He pointed at me. "You really here?"

I laughed and attacked him. He held me, taking in a deep inhale of me. "My Jack!" he mumbled into my nape.

"Yeah." I sighed, melting into him. "I missed you."

He nodded. "Me too, baby."

I pulled back and ran my fingers over his scruffy face. "Already?"

He grinned something sly and nasty. "You know you like it."

I slapped his shoulder. "Shut up."

I turned and smiled at Will. "There he is." He held his arms open. I hugged him hard.

"How's it hanging, JD?"

A laugh slipped from my lips. "You bastard. You set me up so bad. You and Brandi are dead meat."

He nodded. "I figured as much. Poor Tex has no clue what he's getting himself into."

Brandi shrugged. "Whatever. Not our problem."

France snorted. "Least I dodged that bullet." He slapped Will on the arm. "You knew what to send to make me change my mind."

Will squeezed me again. "She is your kryptonite, my friend. If anyone could make you see, it was JD."

"Good to know you are comfortable with the fact you used me."

France snatched me from Will's arm. "It worked. 'Course then she snuck out of the hotel, and the next thing I know, I get a postcard from some vineyard in Greece."

"It was so nice, I had to send a postcard. I stayed for three weeks and helped with the winter cleanup. I got paid in wine. Best week I ever spent, anywhere. The Mediterranean and wine and the food. Oh God. The lamb was so tender, I almost married the cook, but she wasn't my type."

"No playoffs beard?"

I nudged Mike. "No, she had that. She was missing the shitty attitude and penchant for Doritos."

He laughed and carried my bag inside.

I looked at the arch and the artwork. "Oh my God, France. Look at this place. It's stunning. The artwork is incredible. Imagine if this were your house."

"Yeah, Jack, it's a castle. Come on."

I let him pull me past the stunning marble foyer and arched hallways to the lady who was planning the wedding. I was running my hand along the marble and woodwork when she passed me a champagne flute and a room key. Will and Brandi stayed outside talking. It looked heated. I looked back. "Are they screwing?"

"I suspect they might be."

"She's pregnant. That's disgusting."

"How long did she and Shawn try to get pregnant?"

I ran my fingers along the hallway. "Look at the art. This is like a museum." It took a second to hit me. I grimaced. "Oh God. It's not Will's kid?"

He shrugged. "She comes to every game, they talk all the time, and a few times I saw her walking away crying."

"How did they even meet? I thought she was pregnant when they met."

He shrugged. "I don't know or care." He opened the door to my room for me. He leaned against it. "So, did it work?"

"Did what work?"

He grinned. "Did I ruin you for every other man?"

I smiled. "Not telling."

He leaned in, brushing his lips softly against mine. Almost four months had past since we had last seen each other and my feelings had not changed.

I was unsure of everything about myself, and therefore unable to thoroughly commit to feelings for him. The intensity with which I had always loved him scared me into wanting to feel nothing. I stopped him. "I don't want this to change the rules."

"You suck."

"Not on this trip."

The room had a melon-green bed with matching chairs and drapes. It looked dated, and yet pristine, if that were possible. "God, I love it here. If I ever get married, I want it to be somewhere like this. A castle with arches and history."

His eyes were burning. "Marry me."

"We agreed to wait to start our relationship. I need this time, France. I'm having fun, probably for the first time in a decade. Apart from the times you and I had fun."

"I'm scared I'll lose you in all this freedom and fancy-free traveling."

I laughed. "Then you never had me from the start."

He rolled his eyes. "Baby, I had you. That's what I'm talking about. I want you again."

I pressed my hands against his chest as he got close. I realized what was happening. "Oh my God, are you horny from lack of sex?" I cupped my hand on his massive erection and smiled wide. "Dirty bastard."

He moaned. "Just let me put the tip in. Please. I'm going insane without sex."

I laughed harder and shoved him back. "No. The tip counts."

He adjusted himself. "I'm going to die from this, Jack. Die. Will you be comfortable with that?"

I folded my arms. "If I'm your beneficiary then—maybe."

He tossed me over his shoulder and threw me onto the bed. He dove on top of me, squishing me the way I liked. He rubbed himself against me. "Just one quick little check to see if we still like seeing each other naked." I wrapped my legs around him, aware of the fact my underwear was pressed on his zipper. He moaned. "You're enjoying this."

I bit my lip and nodded.

He brushed his beard against my neck, lightly kissing and sucking. He slowly lowered himself to my chest. He dragged his lips over where my nipple was. I moaned. "France, no. Not here. The wedding is in two hours. Your ex-fiancée's wedding."

"Goddamn."

"Yup."

We were weak so I got up and left the room, before I made a huge mistake.

Saturday evening

The wedding

The wedding wasn't huge, maybe a hundred people. The foreigners from the Italian team were all there except Luce. I had wanted to see him badly.

France didn't say anything to me after I had left him there hard and annoyed. He was one of the groomsmen, which was weird. At least, I thought it was. He and the other groomsmen were all up at the front of the chapel talking with the priest. Tex had crazy, obviously Texan, relatives who were loud and funny.

I saved my sister a seat when I entered the long arched corridor where the service was going to be held. I hadn't seen Daniela or Tex. I felt awkward being there.

I was staring at the paintings on the ceiling when I heard a voice. "It was commissioned by a cardinal. He was a patron of the arts. Most of the house was built in the 1600s."

I looked back, smiling wide. "You came."

Luce nodded. He looked the same, but maybe better. His accent had lessened maybe or he looked more American. Something about him was different. Maybe it was the way he looked at me. He held his hand out to me. "You have to see something."

I placed my hand in his and let him lead me through the massive hallways and small clusters of wedding guests. We entered a room with high arched ceilings. Instantly, both our faces went to the artwork above us.

"My God."

"It's called the ancient library."

The ceiling was covered in stunning paintings that all came together with a Pegasus in the middle.

"Imagine if this were just one room in your home."

He smiled when he spoke. I could hear it. "Have you seen the spiral staircase yet?"

"No."

"What about the Pannini gallery?"

I looked at him. "The wedding starts in ten minutes."

He made a face. "We better hurry." He walked from the room. "How is the traveling?"

"Great. I don't even know who I was four months ago. I feel so liberated."

"You look different."

I gave him a look. "How so?"

"Your eyes are clearer and your sadness is gone."

I liked that answer. I smiled and followed him into the chapel. We sat next to each other. I still didn't see Brandi.

Luce leaned into me. "How are things with Mike?"

"Complicated as per the usual." I looked at him. "We are still not seeing anyone, including each other."

His eyes flinched. He nodded. "Really."

"What do you know?"

"No way. He can tell you himself. I'm not having any part of this."

I felt sick, and yet at the same time I completely expected it. His being a slutty hockey player was not something that was new. I sighed and leaned into Luce. "How's Boston?"

He chuckled. "Cold."

"Yes, it is."

My sister and Will came in and sat together. She glanced back around at me and waved. I cocked an eyebrow, but she turned away. The music started as the seats were filled and the wedding began. The bridesmaids came down the red carpet first, looking gorgeous. Of course, they were probably all models as well.

Luce whispered, "Were you surprised Tex and Daniela decided to tie the knot?"

"I was." I glanced into his dark-green eyes. "Were you?"

"They were having an affair for months. Will, Mike's friend there, came to visit the team in August. He caught them in a compromising position. He told me when we were drinking in Boston one night."

"Did he tell Mike?"

"No. The dynamics of the team were already a bit tight. Mike came and some of the other guys felt threatened by him. Who leaves the NHL to come and play for Italy?"

I smiled. "He was running away from me."

He nodded. "I know, but a lot of guys said he was being a diva. They said he couldn't get a contract so he said screw it and came to Italy to prove a point. His New York teammates were pretty angry."

"That was entirely my fault." I looked down the aisle to where Mike stood next to Arthur and the rest of the groomsmen. His dark eyes were burning, watching me and Luce talk.

The music changed and we all stood.

Daniela looked stunning. Her dress was by far the most beautiful wedding dress I had ever seen. Against her olive skin and dark hair, the cream was the perfect contrast. She looked warm and glowing.

I smiled at her as she walked past. She winked at me. I felt the blush creeping up my cheeks. I hadn't seen her since the wine tasting. She looked happy, oddly enough, considering I had broken up her last relationship. Not to mention, Tex was a big lug and she was a delicate flower.

Tex looked like he had won the lottery. His smile and the emotion in his eyes were unmistakable. He was smitten with her.

The ceremony was beautiful. The padre made me weep with the Italian sonnet he added to the sermon. It was a dream wedding.

I wiped my eyes, but Luce handed me his handkerchief. I loved that he had one.

I handed it back to him, but he put a hand up. "You keep it."

I smiled, but he gave me a cocky grin. "What?"

"Nothing. It was a beautiful ceremony."

"It was."

The happy couple walked down the aisle and the Texans started to hoot and holler. The groomsmen each took their model on their arm and followed behind. Mike winked at me as he made his way out of the chapel.

Brandi came over. "Is she pregnant?"

I scowled as we walked out of the chapel together. "I don't know, but you should probably be the last person on earth to judge her."

Her eyes narrowed. "Who told you?"

I wrinkled my nose. "How could you?"

She shrugged. "I couldn't bear the thought of Shawn's wimpy DNA, okay? If I have a son—and I am having a son—I want a warrior."

"Oh my God, Bran. What the fuck?"

"Don't say fuck in church."

I looked down at her belly and tried hard to hide my rage. "You are despicable."

She sneered. "Shawn has his female friends, and I have my male friends, and we don't question each other. As long as the house is clean and the dinner is ordered and the babies are made, I'm free to be me."

"What about Will?"

She laughed softly. "JD, be serious. No one like him would ever be with someone like me."

"You sent me here to be with Mike."

She gave me a patronizing but also loving look. "You had already screwed yourself. That ship had sailed. Dad may not talk to me, but honestly, I'm a victim of your circumstances to the rest of society."

My mouth hung open.

She lifted a perfectly manicured finger up and closed my jaw. "I love you and I want you to be happy. You have never been one of us. Good society has never suited you, JD. Your name alone says it all. Jacqueline Croix is a beautiful name, and you go by JD and Jack. You hate your name, first and last. You hate the fact we have arranged marriages and planned lives. I don't. I have always enjoyed my life. I loved my place in the world. I don't need to see the art and buildings and the vineyards of the world. I don't give a shit about some priest who built this dumpy old castle. It doesn't even have turrets so he didn't do a great job." She squeezed my arms. "I love you the way you are. Quirky and complex. I'm a simple person, lots of money, lots of fineries, lots of galas and events. That's all it takes to make me happy. You have never been that girl."

I felt sickened, and yet thrilled by her weird and insulting speech. I nodded. "Thank you."

She hugged me. "I love you as JD and Jack. The girl who can't just drink the wine—she has to know how it's made, how old the fucking vineyard is, and which monk made it first. No one actually cares about that."

My brain made a funny remark in my head. That wasn't entirely true. There was someone who cared about that. He was standing under a lemon tree, watching me.

I smiled at him.

"That is trouble, by the way. Is he a model?"

"No. He's a hockey player. He plays in Boston too."

"Oh shit. Is that the Lucian guy that every girl on the East Coast is in love with?"

"Probably."

"Yeah, his family is crazy rich. Old money too. Ambassadors, bankers, and oil money. He is loaded. Too bad he wasn't the one you picked. Dad never would have had a problem with him."

I glared at her. "I need to get a drink." My head was spinning.

"Get me one."

I looked back at her. "Seriously?"

She shrugged. "A little bit doesn't hurt."

"Yeah, it does." I sighed and walked to the bar inside.

I sat at the old bar, running my fingers over the ornately carved wood. The bartender interrupted my appreciation, "Can I get you something?"

I smiled, without looking at him. "Red wines. What do you have?"

The list was slid in front of my face. I glanced at it and pointed right away at the Valpolicella.

"You look like you could use a goblet of wine."

I lifted my face to see Luce behind the bar. "What are you doing?"

He shrugged. "I'm getting the lady wine." He reached for the bottle I had selected and opened it. Watching his hands working the corkscrew was sexy. He didn't notice me staring. He was too busy telling me the history of the bottle he was opening.

"The region is known for its method of using dried or partially dried grape skins in the process. This bottle in particular is a Superiore because it is made of the dried skins left over from the fermentation of dessert wines. The fermentation of the skin is part of the flavor in the wine. It gives it that sour-cherry flavor the wine is known for. Because the region is more north and cooler, the grapes typically are lighter in flavor. The fermented skins make the robust flavors come to life." He passed it through an aerator and slid a massive crystal goblet in front of my face.

I leaned forward, smelling the cherry of the wine and sighed. He poured himself a glass and picked mine up. He walked out behind the bar and through the doors to the veranda out back. He sat us down at one of the lit tents overlooking Rome.

"Imagine this was your view every day."

I sat across from him. "Would you ever leave the house?"

"The house yes; the yard maybe no. I love this villa."

The sun was setting and the tents were lit and spread across the backyard in amongst the hanging garden. The view of Rome was incredible. The warm air and the smell of my wine and Luce's subtle cologne were as if my wish list had been granted. Every item was ticked off.

Of course the aching guilt in my stomach was something I hadn't asked for. I felt sick, knowing I had nearly slept with Mike. That was bothering me more than anything. I had missed him. I hated that truth as I faced it.

Luce never spoke. He sipped his wine and looked at the valley below us.

My heart was racing. Not from the mistakes I was making, but from the experience I was having. I felt more alive in that moment than I ever had.

I took a deep breath and closed my eyes. "Can you imagine this in the 1700s? The villa, the view, the vino, and the food?"

I could hear the peaceful smile upon his lips when he spoke, "I can. I can see all of it. It's like a Henry James novel or Jane Austen."

I opened an eye. "You read?"

"I was forced to in the beginning, for school. But as I got older I learned to love reading. I read science fiction and fantasy, like The Lord of the Rings and Stephen King's The Dark Tower series. I never appreciated Austen until the remake of Pride and Prejudice. I saw it with a girlfriend. She forced me to go, and honestly, I only agreed because the blonde from James Bond, Die Another Day, was in it. She is gorgeous, and of course, Keira Knightley. That changed it for me. The music was a perfect match: Dario Marianelli was the composer who did V for Vendetta. That's probably one of my favorite movies."

"I've never seen it. I loved the music in Pride and Prejudice though. I loved the scene where she was walking in the morning, in the mist, and he was there."

He nodded. "Yes, exceptional score for certain."

I was no longer at a wedding in Italy. I was on a hillside with a guy who felt like he challenged me and made me think about things.

I panicked, standing up abruptly. "I should go find Brandi. Thank you for the glass of wine."

He looked confused but nodded. "See you at dinner."

But he didn't. No one did. I ran to my room, packed my bag, and called for a car.

A knock at the door startled me as I finished grabbing everything. I opened it to find Mike, looking feisty.

"What is going on in there?"

"What do you mean?"

He pushed past me. "Shit, I thought I'd find Luce in here, and instead, I find something much worse. You're leaving?"

"I am leaving before I make a fool of myself. I'm not ready for this, for us. I don't even understand why I was invited."

He sighed, closing the door and pulling me into him. "Jack, don't piss me off tonight, please. We need to finish what almost happened earlier."

I shoved him back. "No, we don't. We have done that half a dozen times. We have never needed to talk about it. I actually don't want to talk about it at all."

He pulled me into him harder. "We never actually did it though." I closed my eyes and smelled him. He was home and safety and strength, but I needed to find those things on my own. I hugged tightly to him. "I love you."

"No, you love torturing me."

"I do."

He pulled me back, and I could see it. I was hurting him. I hated that. He faked a smile. "Don't go."

I stood on my tiptoes and kissed him softly. "I love you, forever and always. You're my best friend, Mike."

He winced. "Best friend? Is there something going on with you and Luce?"

"He's a friend. He was a friend when I needed one and that is all." His eyes narrowed, but I put my finger to his lips and smiled. "Whatever mean, hateful thing you're about to say—don't. Just stop. You always say the shittiest stuff when you don't get your own way. I'm going back to Greece to finish my two months of work at the vineyard. I will see you in May in Boston or New York."

I held my pinkie out. He rolled his eyes and wrapped his massive pinkie around mine and shook them.

I winked. "Thanks for the almost booty call."

He chuckled. "I hate you sometimes."

"I know. Make sure my sister doesn't break your dear friend's heart. He has no idea what he's in for, and he is awfully sweet."

"Not my problem."

I slapped his chest. "See you later." I turned and walked out into the hallway—the most beautiful hallway I had ever seen.

The cab ride back to the room I'd rented was refreshingly free. I hadn't a single worry in the world. I had run away from them both. Luce was a safe temptation and Mike was easily distracted. Neither was a real threat to my discovering myself, not yet.

The next morning, I had just finished packing up my

room in Rome, when there was a knock at the door. I pulled the towel off my head and opened it, instantly disappointed. It wasn't just Mike. It was an unmistakably drunk Mike.

"Thank God you're here. I fucked up, Jack." He staggered in, still in his tux and smelling like hell. He collapsed on my rented sofa and groaned. "Baby, I did something bad last night. I didn't even know I did it until it was over."

I frowned and closed the door. "What?" My stomach was aching.

He shook his head and gave me a heartbroken look. "I almost slept with Daniela last night."

I winced. "Oh God, why?" I lifted my hand to my mouth, covering it. I didn't want him to see the disgust on my face, but I couldn't help feeling it. He was loaded and stupid. I felt tears slipping into my eyes. "Fuck, Mike. Why would you do that? Tex is going to be heartbroken. It was his wedding night. You're an asshole."

He nodded, covering his eyes. "I know. I just got so drunk and then the next thing I knew, we were in one of those rooms. She was undoing my pants, and then I blinked and we were almost—but I called her your name and she got mad and left."

I covered my eyes, holding back my pain. Technically, we were not together. I had tried to be his friend, and it suddenly became clear that a friend was all I was. "Did anyone see you?"

"I don't know. I don't care. I shouldn't have done it." He got up quickly and dropped to his knees in front of me. "I don't want it to fuck things up for me and you. That's why I had to come and tell you right away. I can't hurt you, Jack, but I can't lie either. I don't want secrets."

I laughed and cried a little at the same time. "That has kind of happened though, hasn't it? I am hurt and Tex will be too." I didn't know how to feel.

I closed my eyes, wishing I had blue pills for the first time in a long time. I wanted the exploding feeling in my chest to go away. I let the sunset amongst the tents, the charming smile of Luce, and talking about movies and wine take over my mind and become my new blue pill. I dropped to my knees too. "Mike, there is no me and you. You're drunk right now, so it feels like maybe that almost sex we had yesterday was something. But let's think about this for a minute. Me and you have never had anything beyond having fun and having sex and taking naps. We have always been that couple who was never distinctly a couple. You're funny, cute, and sexy as hell, but we won't ever be anything but what we are."

He looked impassioned. "I think I knew that. I watched you slipping away. I can feel it, I'm losing you." A tear slipped down his cheek. I wasn't sure drunk tears counted, but it was an effort. He sniffled. "I don't want to lose you. I need you. Can we go back? Can we be friends again? I miss you."

I kissed his cheek softly. "I miss you too, but I mostly just miss being your friend. I miss being your family. I miss listening to your stories and laughing. Like the one about you and your brothers when you went fishing and one caught some underwear and chased you with them. I like us as friends.' I wasn't sure if it was true or just words I spoke to avoid my broken heart.

He looked devastated. "I can change, Jack. I can be what you need."

"I don't want that. I like you just the way you are, but I can't love you the way you want me to. It took me all this time of not having you around to see that we are always going to be best friends. Always. I will always be your Jack."

"Baby, I love you. I know I do."

"I know you do. I know you love me in your special way, and I'm the only girl who says no to you and makes you crazy, but that isn't the marrying kind of love."

"You love someone else? Someone like Luce, who your parents will love? Fuck you! Don't tell me you love me but don't want to be with me." He got up and walked to the door. I grabbed the back of his shirt and dragged him to my bed. I shoved him down on it and lay beside him. "We are not arguing right now. You are drunk and stupid."

"Don't sneak away this time."

"I won't." I closed my eyes. "I don't want to lose you,

Mike. If you want to be with me, then you need to prove it. You couldn't even do three months of celibacy. I know you were with other girls."

"They don't ever mean anything, Jack. And I did cut back, a lot. I only slipped twice when I was at a couple of parties. I woke up and realized what I'd done. I tried to tell you, but I didn't know how. I knew you'd be disappointed in me. I am trying."

I kissed his forehead. "I'm not kidding around. I'm disgusted you would almost sleep with Daniela and hurt Tex and me like that."

"Tex did it to me first."

"That's mature." And that was exactly the point my heart was making. "Mike, this careless, sexy, slutty, hockey player thing you have going for yourself was hot five years ago. It's not hot anymore. You're getting older, time to grow up."

He nuzzled into me. "I'm like Peter Pan."

I shook my head, trying to stifle my laugh. "No, you aren't. It's time to see what big boy Mike is like."

"I can show you big boy Mike right now."

I nearly gagged. "You stink, and you just had almost sex with another woman. A married woman."

He chuckled. "You walked into that one, Jack."

I watched him fall asleep, forcing myself to see slutty, gross Mike.

Later that night as he shoved my bags into the back of the cab, he gave me a sour-looking expression.

I nudged him and smiled sweetly. "I'll see you at the end of May."

Mike scowled. "Just come home. I swear you can watch me grow. Muriel will be excited to see you."

I shook my head, folding my arms over my shirt. "Sorry. I need this."

"Why are you doing this?"

I narrowed my gaze. "My sister is having sex with Will, who probably loves her, and she probably loves him. But you know what's sad? She will never be with him. She won't sacrifice her social status and choose love. Tex was screwing Daniela the entire time you were with her—she's a whore. Let's face it. You wait for him to marry her and then try to pay him back—that's sick. I nearly sleep with you and then nearly bed hop from you to Luce." His face darkened, but I shoved his chest. "Stop. You have no right to judge me. To top all that shit off, I nearly married a sadistic bastard because my dad told me to. I have NEVER just been away from the toxicity of it all. All these near misses would have happened, had I still been taking several types of prescription medicine. You see how fucked up that is? My life sounds like a soap opera. I'm waiting for someone to come back from the dead, and I'm just going to find a scriptwriter and produce this shit."

He snorted. "You're making it sound worse than it is."

I shook my head, exasperated. "NO. That's the worst part, Mike. I'm not."

"STOP CALLING ME MIKE!"

I leaned into his savage look. "THEN EARN MY LOVE, FRANCE! STOP EXPECTING THAT YOU DESERVE IT BECAUSE WE HAVE HISTORY!"

He grabbed my shoulders but stopped himself. We hovered in that awkward silence for a minute. The one where we stared at each other's quivering lips and prayed desperately that the other person would move that last ten percent. Both stubborn and scared, neither of us did.

He gave me a hurt look. "I went to the Empire State Building for you."

I smiled. I couldn't fight it. "I loved that."

His ragged breath sounded like it might catch in his throat. "I can't lose you."

"Then act like it. Act like missing me isn't just a concern for you when you're sober. Act like I am the person you want to be with and think about the person I want to be with."

I moved the last ten percent, but I pressed my lips against his flushed cheeks. He pressed into the kiss. I whispered, "See you in May."

I turned away from him and climbed into the cab. Before I closed the door, I turned back to him. He looked tragic and on the verge of doing something crazy. I hoped he would, just a little bit.

"Tell Brandi I said she is a hateful slut, and I will see her in May too."

He started to laugh, but it sounded close to crying. "I love you, Jack."

"I love you too, France."

When I got onto the flight for Greece, I pulled the handkerchief from my pocket. I smelled it and sighed. It was the smell of the hillside, the setting sun, and the Valpolicella. I opened it up to see a note written inside.

It made me smile.

> *Jacqueline,*
> *As per our previous agreement, I will be waiting for you May 9th at the Gallery of Ancient Art in Rome at 7 p.m.*
> *Yours,*
> *Luce*

My breath hitched as I reread it. He had planned all along to give me the handkerchief. He had planned it like a romantic movie, long before we had even spoke of movies.

My stomach tightened as the plane took off. He would be the right choice. I could love a man like Luce so easily.

Tuesday

The end of April

I shelved the last of the bottles. "I think this is it. Now we just have to go and see if the guys are ready with the pruning and burning."

Rita smiled at me. "You work hard for an American. I have never seen anyone work so hard."

I smiled, proud of that. "I like it here. I like this kind of work. Every bottle feels like a member of my family."

She rolled her eyes. "You sound like my pappou. He always said the wine was the blood of our family."

I dusted my knees off and nodded. "See, that's so romantic and inspired. I like that."

She winked. "He drank almost as much as you."

"Nice. What did you want anyway?" Rita, being an owner, rarely came down into the cellar. She did the "fancy work in nice clothes" part of the job. Things like tours around the vineyard and dinner parties.

She pointed at the ceiling. "A very persistent American is here to see you."

I scowled and walked after her through the old tunnels. "No one knows where I am, except my sister." I couldn't imagine her wanting to fly at seven months pregnant. We emerged from the dirty basement, but it wasn't Brandi.

It was Muriel.

She looked stunned. "Jacqueline, you look positively filthy. Come with me this instant."

I smiled and walked over. She was the ball of fire she had once been. No longer broken by a bad marriage and too many pills.

She opened her arms for me. I wrapped mine around her. She squeezed my biceps. "You are getting muscles.

This is most unbecoming. No doubt too much hard work and fighting off Greek men."

Rita snorted. "She doesn't fight them off. She just gives them that look, and they know not to go near her."

"What?" I asked, scowling.

Rita shook her head. "No, not that one—the really mean one with the wrinkles in the eyebrows."

I gave her a look. She laughed. "Yes, much closer."

Muriel put a delicate hand out to Rita. "Muriel Getty." She was going by her maiden name.

Rita smiled. "I am Rita Barontis."

Muriel's eyes widened. "Why then, your grandfather must have been John."

Rita nodded. "Yes, he was."

Muriel gave me a sly smile. "Very attractive man."

I shook my head. Rita gave her a surprised look. "You knew my pappou?"

Muriel winked. "A girl never kisses and tells."

Rita laughed. "That sounds like him. Well, you must have lunch on the patio."

Muriel glanced at my tee shirt, shorts, and boots. I shoved her toward the patio. "We will, thank you."

Muriel linked my arm. "I suppose if I didn't want men to notice me, I too would dress like a young man."

"How are things in Boston?"

Nick, the maître d,' brought us to a nice seat in the midday sun. He smiled and passed us the single piece of papyrus with the menu on it.

Muriel placed hers on the table. "What are you doing, Jacqueline?"

I glanced at the menu I knew off by heart and shook my head. "Running away, I suppose."

"Are you done?"

I looked up at her. "I don't know. I don't know what to choose for myself so I figured, why go back? What is there for me in New York or Boston?"

Her eyes narrowed. "You're about to become an aunt. Your father is in the hospital. The man you love is winning every game under the sun, and Boston is probably going to win the cup this year."

She could see the hold I had on my emotions, even if my father was in the hospital.

"I found a vineyard I was thinking about investing some money in, if I had the right person to buy it and run it."

"Oh, that was a low blow, Muriel."

She sipped her lemon water. "I know. The joy of getting old is that you may speak your mind. Let me speak mine."

I took a sip of water. "Let me order us some wine first."

Her eyes darkened. "No, that's all right. I prefer the water."

"Okay." That was odd.

She ran her fingers over the silverware. "The day you came to my house and found me in the corner, I had dished out enough pills and booze to end my life. I wanted to die. You came there and you saved me. You made me remember that a man wasn't worth giving up on myself for."

I hadn't seen that coming.

She continued, "I don't drink or take anything anymore." She looked at me with emotions filling her eyes. "Let me save your life, Jacqueline. Let me be the beacon of light you were for me."

My heart stopped.

"Let me invest in your dreams and help you make them come true." She pulled a folder from her oversized purse and laid it in front of me.

"They aren't listing it until we have had first refusal on the property. A friend owns it and is getting too old to run it any longer. His children have never been interested in it. He doesn't want it to pass to anyone who isn't completely in love with wine and wine making."

I stared at the stunning photos of the old vineyard as she spoke, "The grapes originated from the mother vine—the oldest cultivated wine grapes in North America. The blended wines from the vineyard all have some of the mother grape in them, her fermented skins. The vineyard is beautiful, and he is willing to give his label, as long as when you create your own, his legacy doesn't die with the transfer of ownership."

"Sounds fair, but I don't see how I can do this. I don't have enough money. How much is he selling it for?"

"Let me worry about the finances. Come home and start your own dreams."

"You have no idea the significance of what you are offering and how much it means to me, but I can't accept that kind of generosity."

She took a drink. "You saved my life. I want to help you."

I closed the folder. "Muriel, I didn't save your life so you would help me. I have asked too much of you already. You protected Mike from my father and Phil, and gave my sister's husband a job. You got Mike on with Boston. You have done enough." I smiled. "I have never had to work for anything in my entire life until now. I want to earn what I have. I never want anyone to give me anything and have something they can hold over me. I'm not saying you would do that, I just don't want to put us in that situation."

Her eyes glistened from the tears sitting in them. "You never realized you saved my life. The tiny bit of care you showed me was all I needed. I never truly wanted to die. The moment you arrived, I had just finished praying that one person cared I was dying. You walked through the door like an angel. I was about to give up and take it all when you got there, answering my prayers. Let me answer yours."

I reached across the table, taking her hands in mine. "You have already."

She let a single tear drip down her cheek. She sniffed. "The air here seems to be bothering my allergies. Please excuse me." She got up slowly, squeezing my hands and leaving me there. I looked out over the valley and imagined what it would be like if I had something like that.

I flipped open the folder again. The North Carolina mother grape was fascinating. The history was as rich as the fields.

It was a tempting offer, there was no doubt. I flipped through the pages, noticing the old homestead on the property. I could refurbish that, making it a tasting spot, and tear down the crummy barns. I could build my own castle, my own villa. The sea air and the storms would be incredible. The beaches there were incomparable to any. I could buy it for myself, but how? I was deep in thought when she sat back down. "What is good here?"

I smiled at her. "The lamb is second to none."

She nodded. "Lamb it is then."

It was a sacrifice to eat at a vineyard and not have wine, but for her, I would do anything. I owed her everything. That one afternoon was nothing, compared to what she had already done for my family. Not to mention, I knew the struggle of the little pills that made everything feel better. I had craved them for months when I was a waitress in New York.

We finished and I walked her back to her driver.

"Thank you for coming and seeing me."

She scowled. "You don't even want to know why he's in the hospital?"

"He is as dead to me as I am to him."

She took my hands. "I know that isn't true. I know you are not hard like him, not when it comes to matters of the heart. Maybe the head. He is your father."

"Fine. What is it?"

"Cancer. He has cancer in his stomach, liver, and bowels. He has months to live. I don't want to tell you how to run your life—well, that's not true. I do, but I won't. I will say, the regret of not saying goodbye can become your own cancer. I am leaving tomorrow if you want to come with me. I will have a seat ready for you on the private jet. I think we are having chicken."

"I'll think about it."

She tapped the folder. "Maybe I can help you write a business proposal for the vineyard while we are flying."

I rolled my eyes. "You are so bad."

I couldn't sleep that night, even though I was exhausted from working all day. The vineyard and the possibilities and my dying father plagued me. I woke, stressed, puffy, and fully convinced Muriel was right. I would never have proper closure if I didn't say goodbye to him, even if he had already said goodbye to me. I scrambled to get dressed and pack my bags. I knew I most likely wouldn't be coming back. That bothered me.

I ran across the grounds from the staff housing to the main house. Rita's maid answered the door. I breathlessly explained my situation and left a note with her for Rita who was still sleeping.

Francis, the driver, was awake when I got to the car barn.

I slung my bags over my shoulder and walked into the barn. "Can you call me a cab? I need to go to the airport."

He scoffed. "It is too far. I will drive you."

He was a grumpy man with terrible social skills, but he had warmed, slightly. I stuffed my bags in the back and climbed in the front seat. He started the car. "How fast we need to go?"

His thick accent made me smile, that and his dark mustache. I looked over at him. "Pretty fast."

He nodded once and raced the car from the barn. He didn't speak until we were at least half an hour into the drive. Then he gave me a serious look. "You go to America?"

"My father is dying."

"They will miss you, at the house."

I smiled, knowing he meant he would miss me too. "I'll miss you too."

He scoffed. "Not me—the house. Rita, she likes you a lot. She never likes anyone."

"I know. I'll miss this place a lot. It's been an amazing spring."

"The summer will be hot and the grapes will be sweet. It will be a good year."

"How do you know that?"

"Lots of rain in the spring means lots of sun in the summer. Hot spring means rainy summer and the grapes are not as sweet. We will have a good year."

He drove into the small airport and stopped at the private jet. "Thank you for the ride. Tell everyone I said goodbye." I got out. He got out too and passed me my bags. When I took them, he wrapped his arms around me once, hugged tightly, and then turned and left without saying another word.

Muriel walked off the jet. "Well, look what the cat

dragged in."
I sighed and climbed aboard.

Wednesday

The hospital smelled funny. I hadn't been there since my bachelorette party. That party had been the beginning of the end in many ways.

I had come directly to the hospital from the airport, fighting Muriel on it the entire drive over. She felt I should have showered and changed and looked the part, but I liked the new me. I was strong by myself.

I stopped at the nurses' station. "Hi. I'm looking for my dad, Peter Croix."

Her eyes were panicked for a second. She shook her head. "I am so sorry. He passed about two hours ago. He's still in his room if you want to go and say goodbye. To the right. Room 708."

My heart stopped beating.

I turned and ran.

My mother and Brandi were standing outside the doorway.

I dropped my bags, ignoring them and walked into the room.

He was still on the bed.

I had nothing.

A vast emptiness.

Seeing him made me want the little blue pills and a dark room to hide my shame. I hadn't made it. He died thinking I hated him, but I didn't, not anymore.

Silent tears fell, blurring my vision. I walked to his bedside, placing my hand over his cool one. He was gone.

I lowered my face, scanning his. He looked the same, like Victor from The Young and the Restless. He hadn't aged a minute since I'd gone. There was, at long last, peace on his face. I lowered my face to the blankets on his chest and searched my brain for a happy memory.

The best I had was when I was nine, and he took me Christmas shopping for my mother. His assistant had become sick and was unable to buy the gift, so he brought me. We walked the shops. I tried to hold his hand, but he shook mine off, complaining it was sticky. I was scared of all the people on the streets, but still he would not hold my hand, so I clung to his jacket. He wasn't aware I had gripped to him for dear life. He had never been aware of the times I had reached out for him, and he hadn't been there.

Only one person had.

I sat up and whispered, "Goodbye, Dad. I'm sorry I was such a disappointment, and I'm sorry I never made it back."

My mother came into the room. I could hear her sniffles. They bothered me. I hated that she was sad. Neither of them had ever loved each other or us. There was no love in the hollowed halls of our mansions and vacation homes.

"He hoped you would come home."

I looked back at her. "He did?"

She nodded. "He knew he had been wrong to cut you out. He knew in the end."

"I should have called, at least once."

She wiped her face. "You came. That's what matters."

Why was she being so sweet to me?

Brandi came rushing in, wrapping herself around me. Her baby bump was huge. She sobbed into my shoulder and I hers. Our mother, completely unaware how to cope with emotions, straightened the blankets on our dead father and muttered, "The funeral will be in three days. Where are you staying? Will you stay at home?"

I almost said no, but I knew she would need the help. Brandi was useless, and she was worse.

"Sure. If that's all right with you?"

She nodded. "It would be nice to see you again."

Venomous things floated about in my brain. Things like the only reason it was nice to see me was because my dad was dead, and she was allowed to see me. I held them back.

The nurse came in. "I'm sorry to interrupt, but we have to move him."

My mother looked at me. "Will you go ahead to the

house and get Brandi settled in?"

I didn't know what she meant, but I nodded as I grabbed my bags and led my sister from the room to the desk.

"Brandi, do you have a car here?"

She shook her head.

I leaned in the nurses' station window. "Can you call us a cab, please? Meet out front in ten minutes?"

She gave me a look like she might tell me to go screw myself, but then she looked at Brandi and nodded.

We walked to the elevators.

"How was he in the end?"

Brandi shook her head. "Bad. He was mean and cruel to her. He wouldn't let me come and see him. Forbid you and I both entry to the hospital room. Two days ago he fell into a coma. I phoned Muriel and told her she needed to find you. I've been in the room with Mom ever since."

I sighed and walked into the elevator.

The cab ride was silent. I assumed it was our loss and grief, but when we got closer she finally spilled, "Shawn left me."

I glanced at her. "He found out about Will?"

She nodded.

"Are you going to be with Will?"

She started to cry harder. "No. He won't be with me."

I almost laughed at her and told her it was because he was a nice guy. Instead, I wrapped my arm around her and kissed her head.

The old house looked bigger than I recalled it being. It was stately and ridiculous, but it had suited them perfectly. The vacation houses had always been more my speed.

Seeing the luxury filled my mind with memories. My shoes, clothes, and handbags had all gone there to die. All those things I had placed so much value and love in, that now seemed silly. My father was dead and my mother would want to rekindle our relationship. I could and she would pay for the vineyard I wanted, out of guilt, but that didn't feel like me working for it. It just felt like I was moving back into my old house to be my old self.

I hated that girl.

I looked down at my boots and shorts and smiled. I could still be the girl in the vineyard in New York. I loved that girl, even if I was freezing here.

We got inside and switched on all the lights.

I looked around. "Where is the staff?"

Brandi scoffed. "He got so paranoid in the last three months, he fired everyone except old Les. Poor man was waiting on them both, hand and foot, and doing all the driving."

I winced. "Good God."

The house was huge and dark. It reminded me of a haunted house.

I climbed the grand stairs to my room. When I opened it, I was stunned. It was exactly the same as it had been the last time I had seen it.

Brandi leaned in the doorway with me and sighed. "She wouldn't let him touch it. She threatened to burn the fucking house down—is how she put it. Your clothes and shoes are all put away, stored lovingly. She doesn't know how to love us, but I think in her way, that was an attempt."

Tears filled my eyes. It was like a hug from her cold, stiff arms. Arms that would never wrap around me, were cradling me in her special way.

I turned and hugged my sister, letting it all hit. My shoes hadn't burned. My clothes were still there. My mother had taken care of my things. And my father had died and never loved me once. I didn't know how to meld the feelings of grief over his death with the love my mother secretly snuck me. Or the joy I felt over finding myself in Greece and Italy, and yet finding another version of myself there in that room with my things. I didn't know how to be all those things at once.

Brandi patted my back and nodded. "Night."

I wiped my tears. "Night."

She looked at me with a grin. "It's good to have you back."

"It's good to be back." I closed the door and dragged myself to my shower. My shampoo and conditioner were in the cupboards. My makeup was there. Even a new toothbrush had been placed in the holder in the cupboard.

I cleaned, shaved, and scrubbed until I felt human again and heaved my naked body to my closet. Inside, with the light on, it sparkled with possibility. I touched everything: boots, sandals, wedges, Gucci, Chanel, Louboutin, and Choo. They were all there. I dragged my fingers over my dresses and stopped when I saw something impossible.

I closed my eyes and opened them to see it still there.

My Chanel dress had somehow made it back into my closet. The last time I'd seen it was in the back of Mike's car. I pulled it down and slipped it over my head. I ran my fingers along the petals and smiled. *Lucky dress maybe?*

I turned and left the huge closet and climbed into my bed. It all smelled the same. It felt the same.

My eyes grew heavy, but I heard something. I looked up as Mike climbed through my window like we were nineteen again.

"Are you really here?"

He kicked off his shoes and climbed into my bed. "Jack, I'm so sorry about your old man." He wrapped himself around me.

I closed my eyes and let myself dissolve into the puddle I needed to be.

Only he could make it okay for me to feel all those things at once and not need a blue pill.

He kissed my head. "Just get it out. I'm here now. It's okay, baby."

I clung to him, feeling the whole world land on me, squishing me in a bad way. I pulled my dress off, careful not to ruin any petals and tossed it to the chair next to the bedside table. I turned back to him, pulling him into me. "I want you."

His eyes were glistening in the dark. "Not tonight, Jack. Tonight I'll just hold you, keep you safe."

He had no idea the depth those words had for me. I nodded and just let the tears fall until I finally fell asleep.

Thursday

Friday

Saturday morning

Pre-funeral

I could smell food, but my eyes refused to open. They protested the light coming in the blinds.

"Miss Jacqueline, Mr. France says you must eat today and get dressed."

I squinted at the elderly lady in my room. She put a platter and a tray on the dresser and left the room.

I rolled over, but I heard him coming. I groaned before he was even in the room.

"Jack, don't make me drag your naked butt to the showers. Let's go."

"I need to sleep. I'm so tired, France."

His weight shifted the bed. "You've slept for days. This is enough of this nonsense. Laying in here, feeling sorry for yourself isn't going to get you past this." He spanked my butt. I groaned, but he laughed. "I think someone likes her butt being spanked. I smiled, turning over. "You're nasty."

He winked at me and lifted the lid off the platter. "Eggs Benny, your favorite."

The food made my stomach ache. I didn't know when I'd eaten last. I didn't think I had in days.

I sat up, pulling the sheets around my breasts. I noticed the laundry basket next to him. "What's that?"

"Rosa wants the sheets. She says you're becoming one with the bed. There isn't enough staff to do the entire funeral and clean up around here, so I've been helping them out."

"My mom is okay with you being here?"

"She's been in a drugged-out state for two days. Your sister has been crying, but I think it's 'cause Shane came back."

"Shawn. His name is Shawn."

He shrugged. "Whatever. He's a douche. He's been down there watching TV and barking orders at the staff like he's taken over as man of the house."

"What?" I snarled, making him laugh. "There's the spitfire I wanted to see. Now get down there and tear him a new one."

I held my hands out. "Eggs first."

He passed me the tray. I ate slowly, trying to let my body get used to food again.

I wrinkled my nose. "Sorry, I sort of flaked out."

He gave me a look. "Your dad died before you made it home, Jack. I don't think anyone would be okay with that."

"I'm not." I shook my head, wanting to say more, but my mom walked into the room. "Jacqueline, you need to be downstairs in fifteen minutes. We have to go over the plan and preparations." Her eyes darted to Mike and then back to me. My bare shoulders were probably making her uncomfortable.

I looked at Mike. "I'll see you downstairs in a few minutes."

He got up and left, nodding his head at my mother. She smiled at him, but I could see it. I hated seeing it. I hated the way she judged him. It made me want to rage on her and maybe kill someone. I placed the tray farther down the bed. "Mom, I just wanted to say thanks—my room and clothes and stuff."

She sat on the bed with the tray between us. I could see the effect of the drugs in her eyes as she spoke, "Jacqueline, I love you. I have never truly known how to show it. I had a wet nurse and a nanny until I was old enough to leave the house. I was raised the old way, and I don't know how to share my feelings. I don't even know how to feel them. But I will say this, I am sorry your father died, but I am not sorry my husband died. I hope that you will not judge me too harshly for that."

I jumped from the sheets, wrapping my naked body around her. I held her tightly and whispered, "You're free now, Mom. Just be like Muriel and have some fun. You deserve it."

She made several noises and patted my arms. "Muriel, yes. Of course. Okay, well. Uhm, that's good then. I'll see you downstairs." She got up and left the room.

I sat back on the bed and wondered how it had taken me so long to find, not only myself, but also my way back home. How had we all been so petty and disgusting that we couldn't even find it in our hearts to just love each other? Even I was guilty of it. If I even looked at Brandi, I wanted to slap the hell out of her.

I got changed, slipping on my CHANEL dress again, but with underwear this time. I styled my curly hair into an updo and put on light makeup. The months spent in Greece and Italy had me golden colored. I looked at myself and felt a hateful satisfaction that he would have loathed my outfit. He would have been disgusted at the dress, the hair being up, and the whole nine yards. The tan from manual labor and the way my hands had calluses from work wouldn't have gone unnoticed.

I looked like I was going to a garden party, but I didn't care. They all knew about the things he had done to me— the ways he had humiliated me and treated me like I was a second-class citizen. Everyone knew that. Let them look on at my pale dress and judge, but I would not wear black for that man. I was sad my father was dead, but it was an incomplete type of sadness. I was glad the man was dead, but I wished he had made an effort to change the way he was before he died.

I walked down the stairs to the kitchen slowly. The bravery in my bedroom had been overwhelmingly strong. On the main floor of the house, where even the staff was giving me a sideways glance, I was scared.

"Looking good, Jacqueline. The Mediterranean suits you." Shawn gave me an appraising nod and an off smile.

"Thank you." I noticed he was watching TV and eating a huge breakfast. The staff was rushing about frantically. Mother was in the kitchen leaned over the counter and Brandi was helping set the utensils and folding the cloth napkins.

"You don't think maybe you should change into something black, show some respect for the man?" He didn't even look up from the golf game he was watching.

"No, I don't."

He looked over at me, most likely hoping I was still the weak person I had been when I'd fled. "Change. Stop being so stubborn. You're going to shame your family. I think you've done enough of that already, don't you?"

I stormed to his plate, flipping it into his lap. "GET THE FUCK UP AND HELP OUT! IF YOU CAN'T BE OF HELP, THEN GET OUT!"

He stood up, leaning into my face. "YOU CRAZY BITCH! YOUR FATHER HATED YOU! HE WAS ASHAMED OF YOU! GO AND PUT SOMETHING DECENT ON!"

He dragged a hand across CHANEL, wiping his spilled breakfast over my dress, and ripping a flower from it.

I slapped hard, harder than I thought possible. He raised his hand to me. I felt my face flinch involuntarily, waiting for the impact. It never came. A blur whizzed past my face, taking him to the ground. Mike had him on the ground, punching him. Shawn tried to fight back, but his efforts were futile. Mike was in peak shape with the Stanley Cup playoffs starting in a few days.

Mike hauled him up from the ground and dragged him to the front door. He opened it and tossed him from the house, shouting, "You don't come back or me and you are gonna finish this." He sounded distinctly country when he was angry. The South Carolina accent was brutal.

I stood there, vibrating with anger and agony. My dress was ruined.

My life was ruined.

Everything was ruined.

Mike turned back to me. "You have two choices—you can lose it now and realize later it looks like you're freaking out over a dress. Or you can lose it later and be grateful you still looked like a lady."

My lip quivered. I turned on my heel and walked back to my room gracefully. I changed into a black CHANEL that made me look like Audrey Hepburn, but with a slightly frizzy updo, instead of sleeked back. I laid my CHANEL down on the bed and turned away from her broken and damaged body. She was gone forever. I felt broken inside, like there should be two funerals that day. Her importance to me was huge.

"At least you got to wear it on the beach at my place."

I looked at Mike in the doorway. "I know, but still. To die so young and prematurely."

"Try not mourning the dress harder than your dad."

I blushed. "I will, but she was there for me in the beginning, when things were at their worst."

He opened his arms for me. "I'm here too."

I collapsed my face into his huge chest. "Thank you. I know I'll never be able to repay you for being here for me."

He pulled back and looked down on me. "That's what people do for you, when they love you. You don't repay me or thank me. You let me love you."

I realized then and there what being loved by Mike meant. It meant warmth and family and loyalty. It was the best kind of love.

Saturday afternoon
Post-funeral

Muriel took my arm, leading me about the room and into the den. She gave me a grave look. "Sorry you never made it home."

"Thank you for saving my life, Muriel."

"You're a brat. Anyway, the figure we have come up with is four million. He will sell everything—the equipment and everything—for four million. He will also stay on for a season and help out. You have two weeks to make the decision. The 15th of May, this property goes on the market for eleven million dollars."

"But he'd sell it to me for four?"

She nodded. "He phoned the place you've been these last five months, and they all raved about the time you spent with them. True wine lover is what they called you."

I blushed. "They are too kind."

"Your father will leave you four million, at least. You should buy this. We both know you should."

"It's not working for it if I am given the money."

"You have worked for that money, my dear girl. No one has worked as hard as you. You have always done that man proud, even when you showed true character and refused to marry someone who didn't love you."

Her words made sense but it felt wrong. I shook my head. "I can't."

She grabbed my shoulders. "Two weeks, think about it. Don't decide this today. Never make a decision on a bad day. My grandmother always said that. Never make a decision on a day where it's rainy and shitty. Always wait for the best and brightest day to see if it's truly the heart's desire."

I smiled. "Smart lady."

She nodded. "She was." Muriel kissed me on the cheek and walked from the den. I turned and stopped, frozen in a thousand different things.

The person staring at me from the doorway made my heart stop in a flustered way. I beamed. I couldn't even stop myself. "Luce."

He nodded. "The whole gang is here: Arthur, Tex, Daniela, Sal, me, and Will. We all came."

"Thank you."

My mother bustled in, no doubt smelling the money and position all over his Armani suit. "Jacqueline, who is your friend?"

I nearly laughed. "Lucian Nooruddin, this is my mother, Mrs. Jillian Croix."

My mother held her hand out like he might kiss it. Of course he did. She blushed. "Not of the Nooruddin family in Bahrain?"

I would have to murder my big-mouthed sister.

He blushed. "Yes, but I'm more like Nooruddin who plays for Boston."

My mother's face got tight. "With Michael?"

He nodded. "Yes, ma'am."

She gave him the fake smile and me a slightly worried look. "It was lovely to have met you. Thank you for coming, but I must get back to my guests."

He gave a subtle nod. "I am so sorry for your loss."

She didn't even try to accept the condolences.

He gave me a look. "If you ever have the misfortune of meeting my parents, you will see that look perfected."

I rolled my eyes. "I am so sorry."

"Jacqueline, never apologize for other people. I have long been the wrong kind of Nooruddin. Your mother has nothing on my parents."

"I know that story all too well." I stepped closer to him, wanting so badly to mention the handkerchief, but I loved the mystery and romance of it.

He looked down on me. "How are you holding up?"

I bit my lip. "I would love to be sad for his death, but I am sadder for his life."

His dark-green eyes sparkled. "I pity our parents. They have no idea what a simple glass of wine and a sunset can feel like."

"Or a painting of a man when he was a young man. Long before he was beheaded for his beliefs and humble ways." He lit me up inside with a joie de vivre. I could have gotten drunk off the inspiration he put into the air.

He wrapped an arm around my shoulder and led me back into the rest of the house. "The funeral was lovely."

"It was far too lovely, but his friends are as fake as he is."

Will walked up to us, opening his arms for me. I hugged him. "Thanks for coming."

"Of course. How are you?"

I smiled. "She is upstairs, crying still, but I sincerely doubt it has much to do with our father's death."

He narrowed his gaze. "Does everyone know?"

I nodded.

"I came to be supportive. That's all."

I gripped his hand. "Thank you."

Sal, Arthur, Tex, and Daniela made their way over to me. I hugged each and stepped back into our circle. "Thank you for coming."

Arthur shook his head. "Sorry about your father."

I smiled. "Thank you. Are you making a trip out of it?"

Daniela gave Tex a pout. "No. We have to go back. They have games."

Tex wrapped a beefy arm around her. "Now come on. We talked about this. We'll be stateside all summer long." He winked at me. "I heard someone might be opening a winery, and we could all stop by for a tasting, since Mike ruined the last one."

"Who told you such lies?"

He nodded his head at Will. Will put his hands in the air. "I heard it through the vine of doom."

I cocked an eyebrow. "I'm not sure. I doubt I'll be able to pull it off."

Will crossed his arms. "Well, the way I heard it, you

wouldn't have much choice."

I shrugged. "I have two weeks to think about it."

Luce looked down on me. "A villa of your own to drink your own label and make the whole experience as phenomenal as that castle in Rome?"

I couldn't stop the smile crossing my lips. Noticing the hateful looks I was getting from the people at the funeral, I toned it down a little. "Yes. It would be mine."

Luce shrugged. "I think you should do it."

Arthur and Sal nodded. Tex slapped me on the arm. "Make a villa like the one in Rome, and we'll be there all the time."

I laughed. Even with that threat lingering in the air, I couldn't stop thinking about it.

Mike came over to our little chat with a tray of drinks. I smiled. "What are you doing?"

He looked back at the kitchen. "There aren't enough people to serve what's made. Your dad firing all the staff really put your mom in a bind."

I took a drink and shook my head. "You are too nice to my mom. She hates you."

He whined at me. "Jack, that's all an act. She hit on me an hour ago." He nodded at Will. "Get a tray, slackers."

I stood back and watched as three NHL stars and three Italian league stars served the drinks and food at my father's funeral.

Daniela slid over next to me with her drink. "What's up with you and Mike?"

"Nothing. Friends." I looked up at her. "I am sorry for what happened."

She shook her head. "Not me. Tex is the right one. He keeps me on my toes. Mike was too easy."

"He is still too easy."

She winked. "I know."

I almost sneered, but I managed to keep my hateful expressions to myself. If he was having sex with her, that was his choice. Of course, the fact that I'd offered myself to him, and he'd turned me down made me feel a little sick.

Eleanor came slinking over in a cute gray dress and

huge crimson heels. She smiled. "I am so sorry to hear about your father."

I smiled politely. "Thanks."

She glanced at Daniela, noticing she was no longer the prettiest girl in the room. "How is your mother holding up?"

"Devastated."

On cue, my mother laughed from the kitchen with Muriel. They just needed one more widow to complete the Bitches of Eastwick, the Hamptons version.

"So you are still friends with Mike France?"

I smiled again, desperate to keep the plastic look on my face. "Yes. He's a dear friend."

She winked. "You can give him my number if you want."

Daniela laughed. "Let me guess, you tried to give it to him, and he turned you down?"

Eleanor's face grew tight.

Daniela waved a hand. "It was lovely of you to come." And with that, Eleanor was dismissed.

I snickered and pointed at the group of women I used to call best friends. "Can you come with me to see the mean girls of the party?"

She winked at me. "*I* am the mean girl of the party. Let's go."

She linked her arm into mine and walked with me to Angela, Helena, and Diane. They all gave me a sympathetic smile and tilted their heads perfectly. "Oh, how are you?" Diane asked, giving me a pathetic hug. I smiled at the three of them. "Wonderful. I mean Dad died, but whatever. I've been traveling Europe for months, living at vineyards, and drinking wine. I was just at Daniela's wedding just outside of Rome. It was held at a four-hundred-year-old castle. Amazing. How are you all?"

Diane smiled. "Great. The kids are busy with activities and our eldest is in school now, so we have a lot on our plate."

Helena gave me the same sweet look the others were giving me. "Spending the summer with my mother in the South of France again. Richard is working hard this year with land deals. You know how I love the South of France."

I smiled and looked at Angela. She shook her head. "Miserable. I have missed you. My mother forced me to go to Phil's joke of a wedding to that child. She is a spoiled bitch who I heard has him nearly broke. His dad is footing the bill for things because she is so high maintenance. Speaking of high maintenance, my kids are driving me insane and it's not even summer yet. I wish I were traveling with you."

I gave her a genuine smile. "Well, I wish I were married and having babies with someone I loved." I paused. "Maybe not babies, maybe wine. But same idea. I wish I had something that was mine. The traveling is a lot."

Angela rolled her eyes. "Sounds horrid."

Helena finally stopped faking it and started acting normal. "I love that the NHL is serving at this funeral. You know you're rich when."

"It was a fundraiser."

She cocked an eyebrow.

"I'm kidding." I shook my head. "Father fired all the staff a few months ago. Mother has been roughing it."

All three made a face. "Dear God."

I glanced at Daniela, but she had the same look. I nodded. "Yes. It was horrible." I felt like that first world problems commercial.

Diane took my hand. "Your father was so crazy the last year. Your family has been through a lot."

I was sick and tired of fucking smiling. I gave her a sad face. "Yes, it was an ordeal." Little did they know, how much of one. If they knew how my year had been spent, they never would have believed it.

Daniela excused herself and immediately they started the gossiping, "Who is she?"

"She is sweet. Stay on her good side, but she is sweet."

Luce circled over, kissing my cheek and passing me a drink. "There you are, my love." He walked off with the full tray.

I was stunned, but I didn't speak.

Daniela, no doubt to blame for that little act, was back with a drink herself. She nudged me. "You scored. Who else would be so lucky to snag one of the richest men in the whole world, and have him so well trained that he serves at your father's wake?"

I opened my mouth to correct her, but she leaned into my friends. "Lucian Nooruddin's family are some of the wealthiest bankers in the world, and he is the only son of the family. He is smitten with Miss Thing here."

I blushed and looked down. "He is not."

She nudged me harder. "He absolutely is."

The girls were green-eyed with jealously. I let it slide. It wasn't entirely true, but it would make my mother happy to have it circulate."

Angela's face fell into a horrified look.

I followed her gaze to where my mother was letting Phil hug her. Our young neighbor, his bride, was standing next to him, gushing all over my mother.

I gagged a little bit just from seeing him. Daniela also followed her gaze. "Let me guess—that is your ex that Mike told me about?"

I nodded, helplessly.

She took my hand in hers, leading me away. We reached the kitchen where the men were reloading trays.

Daniela clapped her hands to get their attention. "We have a situation."

They all stopped. She looked at Mike. "Philip is here—with the young girl he married."

Luce, Mike, and Will all made a face. She pointed. "Luce, we need you to pretend you are dating and madly in love with Jacqueline."

Mike opened his mouth, but Daniela shook her head. "He is a catch, worldwide." She grinned and I could see her enjoying his pain.

"I can't ask that of you."

Luce put down his tray and swept my arm through his, dazzling me with his green eyes and thick lashes. "I am honored to be asked." He looked at Mike. "We cool?"

Mike looked broken momentarily and then snapped back. "Do it. Make Philip look like a chump. It's better than me beating the piss out of him again."

I didn't understand why Mike agreed, but Luce was

dragging me out into the great room before I could argue.

We walked back over to Angela, Helena, and Diane. I pointed. "Diane, Angela, and Helena, this is Lucian."

They all blushed and instantly became silly girls. I loved that about them. A rich man made them crazy.

My mother noticed the way we were standing and motioned for me to come over. I smiled. "I have to go see my mother."

The girls all giggled. "Of course. It was lovely to meet you."

Luce laughed. "Yes, you ladies as well." We walked to my mother. "Are you sure?"

He stopped me from walking and looked at me like I was the only girl in the room. He tilted my chin and pressed his soft lips against mine. My head spun as he pulled me into the kiss. He let me fall back to earth slowly and smiled. "I want nothing more than to make you happy." I felt giddy. I was blushing and grinning like a fool when we got to my mother.

Luce made Phil look like he was mini-sized, and he was not a small man. Luce was Mike's height and just as thick. My mother beamed when she introduced us, "Phil, this is Lucian Nooruddin. His family are the Nooruddins of Bahrain. Friends with the Bush family, if I'm not mistaken."

Luce laughed. "Guilty as charged—and the Kennedys. He held out a hand for Phil. "Pleased to meet you." Phil's wife couldn't take her eyes from his face. I looked up at him and smiled. "Phil is my ex-fiancé, and his wife Ashley was the neighbor girl at the home we bought together."

Luce pointed at the young girl. "Red Jimmy Choos and a cape?"

I slapped his chest. "Yes. That is the story." Ashley's face was bright red and my mother was confused. Phil looked furious but before he could speak, I cut him off, "Ashley, I owe you big time. I might have married this giant asshole if you had not let him fuck you like a dog on my bed, in my shoes. For that, I will be eternally grateful."

She gasped and my mother started to laugh. Phil leaned into me, but Luce stepped in front of me. "I think it's time for you to leave. Your being here is disturbing my fiancée."

I was nervous, giggling into Luce's back when my mother grabbed my hand. "We are going to be the laughing stock from the Upper East Side all the way to the Hamptons."

"Who gives a damn? You have all of Daddy's money, Mom. Have fun with it."

I kissed her on the cheek and sauntered back into the kitchen with Luce. Daniela raised her eyebrows. "Well, how did it go?"

"You certainly are a crack team of evil people. I thought the girls I grew up with were bad, but damn. I think, besides the girl who once tossed a full milkshake in my face, you have redeemed me to everyone I know."

Daniela winked at me. "I owed you one."

Tex wrapped his arm around her shoulder. "She surely was a mean girl in modeling. This is her stage and these people are her props."

Daniela kissed his cheek, and I had no idea how they made their relationship work, but they did. The cheating and the weird drama were like foreplay.

Tex gave me a grin. "Well, Jack, we better be heading to the hotel. This has been fun and all, but we have an early flight."

I hugged the four of them hard. "Thank you so much for coming." I hugged Daniela. "Thank you for not making me a prop any longer."

She whispered, "You have always been one. That'll never change. You are fun to play with, Jacqueline."

"You are awful."

She shrugged. "I detest being bored." She waved and let Tex lead her from the room. I shook my head and looked around to find the kitchen was nearly empty. Will had vanished, no doubt upstairs to see my sister. So when the four of them departed, Luce and I were left in the kitchen with the staff. I didn't know where Mike had gone. I turned to go find him, but Luce walked toward me. He wrapped his arm around me. "There is something I want to talk to you about."

"No. Don't ruin it. Just wait and see if it happens. You never know, and I like the surprise of it."

Mike came walking into the kitchen, looking exhausted. He put the dishes he had picked up into the sink. He cleaned like he knew how, because he did. He was the only one who had grown up cleaning and cooking. He glanced at Luce and me. The look was the most painful thing I had ever seen or felt. I could see the defeat on his face, and it broke me inside. I looked up at Luce. "I better start cleaning up as well. Thank you for everything."

He bent and kissed my cheek. I heard Mike growl something. Luce grinned from ear to ear. "See you tomorrow, buddy. I'll get your mother to see me out." He waved and left the room.

When he was gone, I walked up and shoved Mike. "You have something you need to tell me?"

He leaned on the huge sink. "I have a lot of somethings I would like to tell you."

I poked him in the ribs. "About Tex's wife, by any chance?"

He turned around and pinched the bridge of his nose. "Jack, what in the ever-loving hell? Are you bugging me?"

I folded my arms. "She told me you two hooked up. Spill."

"It's not what you think. She came to my place in Jersey. I wasn't there. A friend was staying at my place. He called to let me know she was there. I drove out to end this, once and for all, and never have it come up again." I could see the guilt all over his face.

I winced. "So while I was sleeping and depressed, you were doing Daniela?"

He shook his head, grabbing my hands. "NO! I swear. She attacked me, started undoing my pants and kneeling and—"

I put a hand up. "Ewwwww. Stop. Okay, look—this is who you are—I get it. I don't want you to feel bad about yourself. I just don't want to hear any more details. I want to go upstairs and pretend my house isn't full of a bunch of people I don't like and sleep. Will you come with me?"

"I never touched her. She tried and I ran away like a little girl. I think I even screamed."

"Okay. Sleepy time?"

"You don't believe me, do you?"

I shrugged. "It doesn't matter. It doesn't change the way I feel about you. You're my best friend, Mike. You have slept with far worse than her."

His eyes grew heavy. "I know. But I didn't this time. I swear it. All I thought about this whole time was you. I've been here all along." He wrapped around me and steered us to the back stairs where no one would see us slipping to my room to hide.

We stripped to our underwear, locked the door, and climbed into the bed.

I curled into the crook of his arm. He kissed the top of my head, taking in a deep smell of my hair. "What did Phil's face look like when Luce and you went to talk to him?"

I smiled against his chest. "He looked humiliated. Luce made him look like a giant tool, and I made Ashley look like the whore she is. I am going to try to feel bad for it tomorrow, but I don't think I can. It was so evil, and yet so fun."

He kissed my head again. "Those people deserve everything they get. If you mess with them and make them think you and Luce are getting married, then good."

"I know. They do deserve it. Especially Phil."

"I told you he was a douche."

I nodded again. "Shawn too."

"You gotta start listening to me, Jack. I know assholes when I see them. I spent a lot of years trying to blend in at that fucking school. It was a nightmare."

"I know. You always spot the guys, and yet somehow end up with the wrong women."

"I can't always be right." He held me closer to him. "If this is all we ever are, it's okay with me. I'm sorry I let you down so much, Jack."

But he hadn't, not really. He was the only person who had made my father's funeral possible. He was the reason my house had functioned. He didn't even see what he had done. He didn't have to be asked. He just came and did it because he loved me. I could have cried, but I didn't. I just let him hold me.

May 9

7 p.m.
The Gallery of Ancient Art in Rome

I had changed my mind a thousand times on whether I should go or not. It seemed like an adult decision, and he was the choice I would make, if I freed myself to make one. If I got my fifteen-year-old heart back from Mike, it would tell me Luce was the right choice.

I stepped out of the cab and walked along the ancient street to the front of the building. I didn't go inside. It was exactly 7:00. The sun was getting ready to set and the romance of Rome was starting to hit. The city was stunning in the evening.

I walked to the place we had agreed to meet—the pillars. He wasn't there yet. I leaned against them and wondered for a second if I had made a mistake. My love for Mike was never going to go away. No matter how much I fell for another person. I pushed the thought away and leaned my back against the pillar. The marble and stone arches were stunning with the cobbled road.

The smell of flowers starting to bloom wafted by me on a warm breeze. May in Rome was warm. Far warmer than December.

I closed my eyes and imagined how it would happen. He would come around the corner, and I would see him there, waiting for me. We would run into each other's arms and finally kiss. The kiss I had wondered about many times.

The warm wind was gone as quickly as it had come, but I still felt something. Suddenly lips brushed against mine. My instinct was to open my eyes, but I didn't. I let the kiss be frightening and exciting.

Hands grabbed at my arms, pressing me into the pillar.

Lips caressed and sucked, massaging mine slowly. The stranger's tongue brushed lightly against my lips, as if asking permission to go farther. I could feel the intensity of his body against mine. He vibrated as if he wanted much more but forced himself to remain controlled.

I caught a scent I would know anywhere and smiled against his face, still not opening my eyes. "France?"

"Hi, Jacqueline."

My arms shot up, wrapping around his neck. He lifted me up into his arms but pressed me against the ancient pillar. His body against mine was familiar, and yet exciting and somehow new.

His tongue still never made its way into my mouth. He still teased with the kiss, regardless of the fact our bodies were begging for everything all at once. He stopped kissing and pressed his forehead against mine, breathing ragged breaths against my chin. "You aren't disappointed?"

I shook my head.

It was odd but true. I was excited it was him. It was the sweetest display he had ever done, and it made him the person I wanted him to be.

He put me down and took one of my hands in his. We were shaking with need and excitement, but he did the unexpected. He led me to the door of the art gallery.

He paid and pulled me through the familiar surroundings. He dragged me to the painting of the man staring into the reflection of himself.

He stopped and stared at it. "This is my favorite. I don't see it the way everyone else does. I think he's looking at himself and seeing all the mistakes he's made and all the regrets in his life, and he's stuck there, trying to find the point where it all went wrong. He doesn't see perfection. He sees regret and mistakes."

My eyes filled with tears.

He looked back at me. "The day I left your parents' house like a chickenshit after Phil proposed. That was the day it all went wrong. I should have walked out of that room, punched Phil the douche in the face, thrown his ring at your father, and dragged you out of that house. I should have married you and made you happy every day. I think I've been like this guy here, just stuck staring at the reflection and trying to find a way to fix it all."

My lip quivered.

He wiped my tears. "I am so sorry it took me so long, Jack." He got down on his knee, stunning me. He pulled something I never imagined from his pocket. "I'm not going to rush into a wedding and a relationship; I expect to win you over the right way. You deserve that. But I wanted to give you this as a symbol of my love." He handed me the deed to the vineyard in North Carolina. The paper shook in my hands. "Sometimes you just need something good to happen to you. You're the good thing for me, and I want to be yours." He reached up, drying my tears. I was frozen.

He smiled. "Stop doing that freezing up thing and say you love me."

I dropped to my knees too, in front of him. "I don't deserve you. I should have said no to my father and Phil faster."

He leaned over, kissing my face. "Jack, I always knew we'd find our way here, eventually."

I sniffled and leaned into the kiss. "You've always been home, France. Always." I realized then that home wasn't so much a place as it was a feeling. I had never felt at home in my house. I had never felt at home in my life. But with him, I had always felt at home. The only time I ever truly slept was when I was with him. The safety wasn't strength, it was the comfort of being loved and accepted, regardless of the flaws.

"I will pay you back every dime."

He chuckled. "Stop being a pain in the ass and come home with me."

"Home." It was wherever he was.

"Somehow we always take the long way home, Jack."

I wrapped my arms around his neck and let him lead me from the Gallery of Ancient Art and out to the car he had waiting.

"What's the rush? We could stay overnight."

"I have a playoff game in fourteen hours. It's eight and a half just to fly back."

"You came here between games?"

"Yeah, when me and Luce worked this out, we didn't take into account playoff games. Not smart."

"He told you about the meeting?"

"It's a long story."

"It's a long flight."

He winked. "I don't want to talk, Jack. I wanna join the mile-high club."

I wrinkled my nose. "Ewwww."

When we reached the airport, I understood. He had Muriel's jet.

"I can't do that to her plane."

He winked. "I was kidding. I need to sleep, and besides, me and you are on that celibacy kick."

"Yeah, right."

"I'm not kidding. We aren't having sex until we are sure of where we are."

I hugged him. "I am sure."

He kissed the top of my head. "Don't tempt me."

I sat next to him and snuggled into his arm and had the best sleep I'd had in a week.

Saturday

The end of May

The sounds of Muriel and my mother cackling and telling stories, which I wouldn't ever be able to drink away from my memories, had filled the air for hours. I was excited to see my mother so free. Muriel had been a terribly good influence on her.

Brandi looked haunted but gave me a fake smile. Suddenly she understood what heartbreak was. It was refreshing, seeing her suffer. It was her first time really feeling something.

Luce nudged me and pointed at the old barn. "What's the plan for that?"

I beamed. "Tasting bar."

He nodded. "I like it."

We stepped into the cool shade of the decrepit old barn. Vines and webs made up the air around us.

"Were you disappointed it wasn't me?"

I looked back at him and bit my lip. He smiled. "I knew you wouldn't be. I saw how you looked at him. Did he tell you how it happened?"

I shook my head, looking around the old barn. It would make an interesting structure, once refurbished.

"He came and gave me his blessing. He told me that I was the right choice for you, and he would accept it."

I spun around. "He said that?"

"He never meant it. He was sacrificing his happiness for yours. It was a big step for him. I told him that I was certain if he applied himself, he would make you far happier than I ever would or could."

"Thank you."

He nodded. "I will regret it the rest of my life, but I have never seen him this focused on something unselfish before.

It's good for him to need to try."

I winked. "You set the bar pretty high for him."

He chuckled. "If you find he isn't meeting that bar, you come find me."

I put a hand out. "Deal."

France came into the barn. "Dude. What the hell?"

Luce grinned at him. "Just making arrangements for stealing your girlfriend's heart after you go back to being a lazy slob."

"Screw you guys." He wrapped an arm around my shoulders and kissed the top of my head. "This barn is fucking creepy, Jack. I'm going back into the sunshine. It looks like that movie The Ring in here." He shuddered and walked back out.

Luce frowned but I laughed.

We finished the tour of the grounds with a glass of wine in the small building currently used as a tasting room and restaurant. The old man, Mr. MacKenzie, poured me a glass of the cabernet. He smiled as I took the first sip.

I closed my eyes. "Plums and tobacco?"

He nodded. "Yes. Some people get a hint of black cherry but only the good palates can pick up on the plum. It's fruitier than the French cab sauv, but that is a New World taste. The grapes have reacted to the New World with a slightly more fruit-driven flavor. Still nice and dry though."

I smiled. "It's delicious. The mother grape skins went into this as well?"

He smiled. "She goes in every bottle, even if it's just a little. The tradition was taken from the old Valpolicella wines."

I looked at Luce. He sipped and nodded. "That's smart. It gives it an Old World flavor."

Mr. MacKenzie pointed at him. "Exactly."

Mom and Muriel took him by the arm. "Show us the rest of the vineyard, Stanley."

I grimaced. France laughed. "Your mom and Muriel are like cougars."

Brandi wrinkled her nose. "Oh gross. I don't even want to think about it."

France came and took my hand, leading me to the far side of the small room. "Are you happy?" His eyes were worried. I stood on my tiptoes. "That isn't a strong enough word for it." I brushed my lips against his softly.

He smiled. "I love you, Jack."

"I know."

Luce interrupted our kiss. "I'm taking Brandi back to the hotel. She is feeling the heat."

"Thank you."

He nodded at me and waved at Mike. "See ya later."

Mike waved. He looked down at me. "I wish he was less awesome."

I laughed and slapped his arm. "You go through what he's been through and try to not come out either bitter and horrid or totally awesome. He was prepared to never play again, and that's when his father started to love him. That's awful."

"You rich people are weird."

"I agree."

He led me from the small building to the long grassy trail. It led to the beach. We sat down in the sand and watched the waves. The warmth on the coast was amazing.

He lay back and pulled me with him to lie in the crook of his arm. We looked up at the clouds.

I pointed at the cloud above us. "A sailboat."

"It's the van from Scooby-Doo."

I started laughing. "What?"

He pointed. "See the side has those designs."

I laughed harder. "When was the last time you watched Scooby?"

He looked over at me. "Well, a couple of weeks ago I woke up and it was on, and I didn't feel like getting up to find the remote so I watched it. It was pretty good."

I kissed his cheek and shook my head. "You are crazy."

He rolled on top of me, spreading my legs with his huge body. "I'm crazy about you. Always have been."

I ran my hands through his playoffs beard. "When do you shave that off?"

He cocked an eyebrow. "I'm saving it for when we decide

to have sex again."

I pulled him down to my lips. "Let's start now."

He kissed but muttered into my lips, "You do realize that you are saying we are officially a couple. You are mine if we are doing this?"

I gripped his cheeks. "Ditto."

He gave me his sexy grin and kissed me again. It was slow and sexy. The kind of warm kiss you want from the person you love. He ran his hands up my sides, pulling my shirt off. He sat back and pulled his off. He spread the two of them, making a blanket. I crab crawled onto them. He smiled. "I wanted to go to the bottom."

"No, I want to feel you squish me."

He gave me a look. I laughed. "Trust me, I like it when you do."

He undid his pants and crawled between my legs again. He made a small stop to lift my bra up and suck one of my nipples into his mouth. I moaned, undoing my pants and dragging his down. He was in a push-up position so I slithered down to his cock. He dropped to his knees. "Jack?"

I took him in my mouth, grabbing his ass and forcing thrusts into my mouth. I sucked like I had in the hotel, moving my tongue and hand in sync with my mouth. He was thrusting on his own after a couple of strokes. His body started to get into a rhythm. He stopped abruptly. "It's been a while, Jack. You gotta stop."

He pushed me back and pulled his pants back up to stop the sand from getting in. He dragged my panties to the side and rubbed his beard against my thighs. I bit my lip, waiting for it. He lightly rubbed it against my lips as he spread them. He buried his fuzzy face into my slit, licking and sucking.

I dug my hands into the sand. He licked my clit with circular strokes. I moaned, but he stopped just as it was getting good. I could see the shitty grin on his face as he crawled up between my legs. He opened his pants again, rubbing his cock head in the wetness he had made. He slowly pushed in, taking long strokes. When he was fully inside, he bent down and sucked my bottom lip. He squished me and filled me up exactly the way I liked. I wrapped my legs and arms around him, pinning him there. His thrusts were shortened by it, but I didn't care. I just wanted him there.

He kissed my neck and shoulders while moving rhythmically over me. It was nice, but it wasn't going to get the job done. I pushed him back a bit.

He chuckled. "You want me to make you come?"

I nodded.

He cocked an eyebrow. "What do you say?"

"Please."

He laughed. "No. Say what you want."

I smiled. "Make me come, France."

He nodded. "Yes, ma'am."

He sat back on his knees. I put my feet on his shoulders to get the angle. His hands dug into my hips and lifted me slightly. He slammed his cock into me. I moaned something awkward and bleat-like.

He did it again. "This what you want, baby? You want me to fuck you?"

I nodded, not even a little ashamed that I had never liked sex like a lady.

He pumped hard, pounding me until my toes clenched, my hands grabbed fistfuls of sand, and my pussy gripped him hard. He came at the same time, muttering things that didn't sound like words.

He collapsed onto me. "The sand is getting everywhere."

I laughed. "I know. It's in my bum. I can feel it."

He nodded. "Yeah, mine too for some reason."

I laughed harder, pulling him onto me more. He squished me into the sand, making me sigh. I closed my eyes. "Let's go back to the hotel and shower off. This is brutal."

He nodded. "Yeah. I have to get back to the city anyway. We have a game in Boston tomorrow night."

I opened my eyes. "What? Already?"

"We just got back from Chicago, so yeah. It's our home game tomorrow. You should come and watch."

I smiled. "Okay. I hate the way I become a savage though, screaming and yelling."

"I kind of like that about you. The guys think it's funny.

New York socialite screaming and shaking her fist at the ref." He shook his head as he laughed.

I covered my eyes. "Oh God."

He got up and helped me up. "It's funny. Your mom has quite the mouth on her."

"I told her she can't come anymore. She has held shit in for so long that she's crazy now. She and Muriel are probably molesting Stanley right now."

France grinned. "He's a widower. He's probably thanking God right now."

I shuddered. "So nasty."

We pulled our clothes on and made our way back up the grassy trail. I took one last look at the vineyard and smiled. "This is ours, Mike."

He kissed me and whispered, "This is yours, baby. When you get it all shiny and new and appealing, I'll take credit then."

I laughed and shoved him. "You are a pest."

He nudged me. "Stop for a gas station burger on the way home?"

"Fine." I wanted to protest, but I had a dirty love for them.

He opened the car door for me. "We never did finish that road trip, taking the long way."

"Trust me, we took the long way."

The end of June

My mother had never looked so in love. She stared down at the perfect little bundle we had all agreed was a definite Abigail, Abby for short. She was pink and cute and sweet. It was as if all the good things in Brandi rolled themselves into one little bundle of joy. She yawned and everyone in the room gushed. Even Mike was lost, staring at her. The nurse held a piece of paper out. Mike signed it. She was lit up.

Luce laughed when it was his turn to sign. "We should have brought the cup. It would have made the baby pictures that much better."

Mike laughed, but my mother and Brandi both got a terrible look on their faces.

That made me laugh.

I pulled my phone out and sent another text. Mike wrapped his arms around my waist. "What are you doing?"

"He deserves to know. His name is on the birth certificate. Even if he and Bran can't make it work, that's his baby."

"He's pissed. He isn't coming."

I looked at him, examining his eyes. "If it was your baby?"

"Why? You got something you wanna tell me?"

"Uh, hell no. I just took possession of the vineyard. Don't even kid around. In fact, just looking at that bundle of joy, I think maybe we should probably abstain for a while."

He chuckled. "I won the cup for you."

I rolled my eyes. He kissed me softly. "If you ever had my baby, I would make you marry me and never let you get away."

"So you would go all caveman on me and drag me off to your cave?"

He kissed me again. "Don't tempt me to show you what I would do. I told you, this is it. I gave you your chance to get away. It's me and you forever now."

I loved the sound of that. I kissed him back. I pressed send on my text. The noise of a cell phone behind me made me turn around. Will gave me an emotional look. "Hey."

I smiled. "I knew you'd come. She's inside." I stepped out into the hall. Mike hugged Will and slapped him on the back. Luce followed us into the hallway. I watched as my mother placed the baby into Will's arms. He started to cry, hugging the small bundle. He shook his head. "She's perfect."

He looked awkward and smitten in the same breath. Brandi's hands lifted to her mouth. Her eyes were filled with tears, and her hands shook as they rested on her lips.

He carried his new daughter to Brandi and the three of them embraced. Mom left the room, closing the door. She gave me a look and then gave Mike a scowl. "Just marry Jacqueline before you impregnate her, please. It's bad enough the celebrity gossip pages are saying she had a nervous breakdown and Lucian left her."

She patted him on the chest and walked down the hall with Muriel.

Mike gave Luce a look, but he just shook his head. "So weird your mom is gay now."

I looked at my mom and Muriel, suddenly seeing something I had been missing all along. The two of them linked arms and my mom leaned her head on Muriel's shoulder.

I felt shivers all over my body. "That explains so many things."

Mike folded his arms across his chest. "I like Muriel way better than your dad."

"Me too." I looked at him. "What a year."

He smiled. "Things are never dull with you rich people."

Luce snorted. "To say the least."

I swatted at them both. Slowly we crept back into the room to see smiles and tears.

Will looked at me. "Thank you."
I winked at him. "I owed you one, I think."

Saturday morning

June, one year later
The day of the wedding

The bottles on display were lined up perfectly. I dusted the table once more and looked around the room. The barn renovation had been done without a hitch. The old beams and glass were all that was left of the ancient structure. We hadn't built like the Romans; it didn't last.

The fresh paint smell had finally started to fade. I looked at the boys I'd hired from the university to pour and serve. "You are good if I go and check on the rest?"

They nodded, giving me an odd look. I was being a control freak.

I walked out onto the path of trees we had just planted in amongst the old black walnuts and willows. I touched one of the lemon trees and smiled. It would one day be my legacy. Albero di Limone was the name of my label, or Lemon Tree Winery for Americans.

The path led to the villas I had built for the guests. There were two. Each functioned as a sixty-room inn. It was perfect. They were mock-ups, but not exact, of the villa where Daniela and Tex had been married. The view was of the vineyard and the sea. The hills with the vineyard was my favorite viewpoint, but I was alone in that. Everyone else loved that Carolina coastline.

We even had storm reservations for storm watchers who could come on short notice. If a storm was hitting, the room was immediately reserved for them. Some people were crazy and liked watching storms. They made me nervous.

The butlers were in proper attire and ready to serve. I scanned each one as I walked past. "You ready?"

They nodded.

I walked to the far side of the property, where the best view was. Our house was there, tucked away in the trees. It matched the villa in Rome but with considerably better updates. I walked in the front door. Mike and my mom were arguing.

Or rather, she was yelling at him, "You can't, Mike, stop being such a—"

"Mom!"

She looked at me and blushed. "Sorry dear, we were just discussing the fact that he was going to sign autographs at the winery. He, Lucian, and Will are all in protest."

I lifted my hand to my heart. "I think I'm having a heart attack, and you two are fighting about autographs? Where the hell is Brandi? Jesus. I need someone to make sure those boys don't drink anything. They looked shifty. Has anyone made sure the rooms are all clean? Vince, Tex, Daniela, Sal, and Arthur will be here any moment. Sal and Arthur have women with them. I had the driver bringing them from the airport, but I didn't know about the women. I mean, I should have assumed there would be dates, and I didn't. I am not good at this planning stuff."

Mike ignored everything I had said and walked toward me. He scooped me up and carried me up the huge stairs. I wiggled. "France, stop messing with me. Mom! Mom, go and get Muriel and tell her that she can't feed those boys liquor. MOM!"

Mike opened our double doors and walked across the room to our bed. He tossed me onto it and walked back to close the doors.

"Mike, I can't do this right now. I have a thousand things to do. I don't have time for this."

He jumped onto the bed, making it rock like a boat. "Deep breaths, Jack."

I gave him my dead-inside look. He snorted. "You are so dramatic. When we got out in the second round of playoff games, you never saw me getting all dramatic. I shook gloves and skated off the ice. Now you gotta just let tonight be what it will. You have a whole team helping you here, but it doesn't work if you don't trust them."

I almost growled, "France, I need to make sure everything is going to run smoothly."

"Stanley has helped every step of the way. The sommelier has tasted everything we are about to serve. You have all the right people in all the right places. The chef already let me taste everything he made and it was good. Real good. The decorations look top-notch and the bride and groom are in their room with Abby, getting ready. Why don't you just lie back here for a minute with me and think about how nice it is that you can do all this stuff."

"I can't even relax here. I thought this would be more relaxing, but I owe you so much. I was looking at the villas and our house and it hit me; I will probably never make enough money to pay you back. Ever. What if it's never mine?"

When he didn't answer, I glanced over at him. He looked dead inside when he spoke softly, "Your mom gave me all that money. She didn't want me to tell you. That's what we were fighting about. It was all yours anyway, all your inheritance."

My stomach dropped. "My dad paid for it all?"

He pinched the bridge of his nose. "Jack, you paid for it all. Your mom had your trust fund reinstated. You own this whole place. She and Muriel wanted me to make it look like I paid, even though I didn't."

I felt sick. "I can't talk about this now." I got up, but he followed quickly and pulled me back to the bed.

"Too bad 'cause you're going to."

My tone dropped down to calm anger, "I can't believe you would lie to me like that."

He dropped to his knees, between my legs. "You have made me live in sin with you for a year, as your mother calls it. You don't want to talk about marriage or babies or us ever being anything beyond what we are now. You want your own identity, and you want to earn this place so bad that you're pushing me away. I don't want this money to be between us anymore. What's mine is yours, and if you had just let me do it, I would have given you the damned vineyard. But I know you. I knew you would insist on paying for it. So your mom took money from your inheritance and gave it to me to cover the vineyard and all the renovations. Now you know."

I had a thousand excuses for what he'd revealed, but I didn't know how to say them. I sat there staring at him.

His eyes filled with something not good. "I guess now that you don't owe me and you own this place, you will have to choose if you want to be with me or not. But I'm done with this living arrangement, and I'm done with you holding that fucking money over my head." He got up and left the room.

I sat there and watched the door close. It felt bad.

I got up and followed him out of the room, but he was gone when I got downstairs.

Muriel gave me a look. I nodded. "I know."

Mom came into the room with a sheepish look. "We just wanted you to have it. We never thought about the fact that it would make a wedge between you and Mike. He wanted to tell you from the start, but we made him promise not to."

Muriel got up from the chair and stood next to my mom. I sighed. "Thank you." I forced a smile on my face.

Muriel laughed and my mother gave me a scowl. "Oh, if you're upset, just say it."

I slumped into a chair in the nook. "Mom, how could you?"

She sat across from me and picked at a bowl of grapes. "How could I what? Use the trust fund money that I had protected for you to purchase your dream that your father stifled? Yes, how dare I try to make up for the fact I was never much of a mother." She got up and walked away from the table. None of us knew how to fight in a healthy way.

Muriel gave me a nasty look, but my mother turned back around with a vengeance. She nearly spat at me, she spoke so harshly, "Your grandfather left you that money because he loved you. He always loved you and Brandi. He always wanted you to be safe and happy. If he had known you wanted a vineyard with a bunch of villas he would have bought it and made it so. You will not be ungrateful. I never raised you to be rude. Not to someone's face." She turned and left for real this time.

Muriel gave me a smile. "I like to think of it as payment

for all those years of wearing the right thing and saying the right thing and being the right thing. A minute is precious and shouldn't be wasted being unhappy. Every minute had a dollar value. Your father got a bargain, if you ask me." She winked and walked out after my mother.

I looked out at the trees and gardens. I got up and ran from the house until I reached the grass path. I raced down to the beach. He was sitting there in the spot where we had gotten sand in all our bits.

I sat next to him, but he didn't move. The sea looked gray and ready to storm, regardless of the beautiful day.

I nudged him. "I am grateful I have someone like you who gives me what I need, even when my stubborn ass can't see that I need it."

He sat stoic so I continued, "I'm grateful that no matter what, you didn't give up on me. You let me finish the renos and make this place what I wanted it to be before you told me I was actually borrowing my own money. I never would have finished if I thought it was my father's."

I looked out at the choppy water. "But most of all, I am grateful that two years ago, when my pride and my heart and my mind were all broken, they managed to think of you in their moment of despair. The first thing I did when I caught Phil cheating, was drive to you. You were my autopilot and my safe haven. You were home, safety, and happiness, and I knew that then."

He wrapped an arm around me, pulling me into him. He kissed the top of my head. "Will you marry me?"

I smiled. "I will."

"When?"

He smiled. "I'd say in an hour, but Will and Brandi are getting married. How about in a week?"

I looked into his eyes and saw myself. I hoped it would stay like that forever—me in his eyes like I was the only thing he saw.

"I'm sure Mom and Muriel can whip something up, and we'll just keep the decorations up."

"Promise, 'cause if I call my momma there is no turning back."

I leaned in, brushing my lips against his. "Let's go call her now."

He kissed me hard, pressing himself against me and pushing me back in the sand. "Let's call her in an hour."

I laughed and pushed back. "No way. I had a hell of a time getting all that sand out of my butt."

He looked into my eyes and brushed his hand along my face. He brushed the hair out of my face and nodded. "You know you have to change your name to mine, right?"

I scowled. "No Croix?"

"No. Croix-France sounds completely insane."

I laughed and nodded. "Okay."

"Do you have any demands?"

"Just you." We were about to seal the deal with a kiss, when I opened my eyes. "And no signing autographs in my winery. Mom's right, it's tacky."

"I was the one saying no. She was saying yes."

"What has become of that woman?"

"When she decided to stop taking pills and drinking away the pain, all those feelings came out with force. Now she's damned near crazy."

I would have laughed, but I knew that feeling. The time I'd spent in New York as a waitress had been the same for me. I had felt things for the first time and it was bad, horrid even.

I closed my eyes and let him try to convince me to take my clothes off. It was my beach, after all.

Saturday night

The wedding

It felt like Italy. I took my glass of wine and walked onto the back deck, overlooking the other villa and the sea. I sat under a lit tent and watched the waves.

"This is it, Jacqueline. You did it."

I smiled at Luce as he sat in the chair next to me. He held his wine glass up to me. I clinked it.

"To new beginnings."

I glanced back at the girl he had brought. "She is beautiful."

He nodded. "Inside and out."

"Best kind."

We sat in silence. It wasn't awkward with him like it could have been. We understood each other too well. He knew every minute of the journey I had been on and vice versa.

"Do you think you will head back to Rome after the harvest?"

I smiled. "I do. We are planning a little excursion. Stanley wants to stay on and help out. He's not loving retirement. I am in the process of building him a caretaker's house. So he will be able to hold down the fort. After the harvest and the processing, we will be done by October."

"Have you considered ice wine?"

I wrinkled my nose. "No. I think it's disgusting. I can't get into it. My sommelier, Sandy, wants me to—but blech."

He laughed.

Brandi came out onto the deck. She sat next to me, sipping her wine slowly. "Some view, Sis."

"It is. I got lucky with this place."

"No, you never. You got exactly what you deserved."

She looked stunning in her wedding gown. Luce held his glass out for her. "We all have."

I clinked my glass with theirs and sat back to enjoy the view.

"I'm pregnant again."

I coughed on my wine a little as Luce snatched the glass from her hand. She laughed. "It's cranberry juice."

I choked for a second. "Wh-wh-what?"

She smiled like I had never seen before. "Yup. Just over a month we figure."

"Wow, so soon? Abby is only a year."

She nodded. "I want them close so they'll play like you and I did."

It made me smile. We had played. She had been my friend more than she had ever been my sister. I had assumed that was what sisters were, friends who slept over.

Luce handed her back the glass after checking. He knew her well enough. He held his glass up again. "Congratulations."

I clinked my glass again. "Yes, congratulations to you all. The wedding was stunning, and the baby will be an amazing addition."

She gushed. "I know. Thanks again for the wedding. It was perfect, with none of our old friends. Just what I wanted. Will is up for contract this year so wherever he ends up, I will get a fresh start."

I smiled. "I know. This place has been like a retreat. If he ends up somewhere sucky, you know you can always live here."

She gave me a smile. "I can't live without him, JD."

I looked back at Mike talking with Sal and Arthur. "I know that feeling."

He gave me a shitty grin when he saw me looking at him. My mom walked past him. I jumped up. "Excuse me." I ran over to her. I grabbed her hand. She gave me a look of shock and annoyance. I wrapped my arms around her. "Thank you."

She hugged me back. "We can fix all the things we left broken for so long, Jacqueline. I do love you very much."

I nodded into her shoulder. "I know you do. I love you too, Mom."

I hoped my dad was watching.

The whole wedding was a hit, and the photographer got hundreds of shots for our portfolio in the bridal magazines. Experiencing the Italian villa wedding in the US was economical and easier. No passports and foreign planners. Just me, Mom, and Muriel.

God help them.

I put the last of the dishes into the staff kitchen and thanked everyone. I turned and walked back to my house, excited to crawl into bed and sleep for a week.

When I got to the house, it was dark. Everyone had gone to bed, eager to sleep for a week too.

I opened the door to our room, stopping when I saw the lanterns lighting the way out to the porch.

I walked out to the deck, then stopped, stunned by what I saw. The entire yard was filled with lanterns that were lit and glowing bright. Mike was on the deck holding a lantern. I looked at the lights everywhere. "Mike?"

He dropped to his knees. "I never got to ask the right way. Jacqueline, will you do me the honor of being my home and my heart forever and ever?"

I nodded, feeling the emotion and exhaustion starting to blend. He let go of his lantern and in his hand was a ring box. He lifted the ring and placed it on my finger. The diamond sparkled in the lights. He stood and kissed me softly before turning to the lights in the yard. "She said yes!"

The lanterns all sailed from the hands of the people I hadn't seen. They sailed up around the yard and out to the ocean. It was stunning to see.

I pointed. "Is that going to burn my vineyard?"

"They burn out fast. And Stan said the wind was going out to sea so we were good to go." He kissed my head. "I have a bunch of guys with hoses on standby."

The crowd below erupted as the lights filled the sky for a second and then sailed away and went out.

Mike wrapped his arm around me and waved to the people below. I saw my mother waving like a madwoman.

I looked at the diamond on my finger. "Is it colored?"

He nodded. "You already had a white one. I figured mine could be a different color."

"I love it."

He reached behind me to a box and passed it to me. "I have one more surprise."

I frowned as I opened the box. Inside was the dress. CHANEL. She was alive and well. I pulled her from the box. "How?"

He smiled. "I stole it from your mom's and took it to the store. I explained that I needed another one, but I wanted it a little different."

I let her fall open and noticed the weight difference right away. She was a gown. In the light I could see the flowers and the gathered fabric. She was stunning. The flower petals moved in the wind. I shook my head. "I have no words."

He kissed my forehead. "Good. I have something else in mind." I put her back in the box carefully as he waved goodnight to our family and friends below.

I placed CHANEL on a chair and turned to see Mike closing the drapes.

"Thank you."

"No, thank you."

"How did I get so lucky to find someone like you?"

He turned and grabbed my hands, pulling me to the bed, "You didn't find me, Jack. You made me this way. You make me better."

"Mike, that's all you."

He kissed me on the shoulder as he pulled my shirt off and tossed it on the floor. "No, Jack. You make me want to try."

I closed my eyes and savored those words.

The End.

HERE IS A SNEAK PEEK OF PUCK BUDDIES, AVAILABLE NOW.

Prologue

Matt

February 28, 2015

I stumble down the stairs, leaning on my friend Brady and laughing.

We stagger along the path from my boathouse to the main house, both of us cooling off quickly in the frigid wind.

"Good game tonight, Brimstone." Fairfield nods at me as he passes us, leading some brunette back to the boathouse at the bottom of the property. She giggles and trips but he catches her, lifting her into the air and making noises like he's a car. He's such a douche.

I hate that Carson brought him to my house. We both dislike the asshole. But it's how society works. Had we slighted him on the invite there would have been parental issues. As in mine would have a shit fit. It doesn't matter how old I get or removed from it, escaping this world is like getting out of Alcatraz.

But it doesn't mean I have to like it.

"Did you see that dipshit?" I point behind us when I know Fairfield can't hear me.

"The brunette with the big boobs?" Brady spins, confusedly.

"No, the dick with the brunette." I chuckle. "Of course you only saw the girl."

"What?" Brady scowls. "What does that mean?"

"Nothing."

"What about the dick?"

"He's dating this girl—not the brunette—some other girl. Anyway, he breaks up with her randomly so he can get with other girls. And then when he's done with them, he gets back with the girl afterward, so technically he didn't cheat."

"Bro." Brady lifts a swaying finger. "That's a legit play, bro.

Don't hate the player, hate the game. That's a real way to get off scot-free. No drama."

"You're a moron."

"Whatever." He grabs his groin. "Men have needs." He laughs, leaving his hand there too long.

"You mean to tell me if you met the one—the girl who just did it for you—you'd cheat on her if you could get away with it?" He can't understand the way I do, he's never been in love. Brady doesn't believe in it.

"Naw, man. But that's a unicorn you're talking about. That girl doesn't exist. I'm never going to be dumb enough to fall in love. It's a pain in the ass. My brother used to be cool. Now he's whipped as hell." He loses the cocky grin. "But for real, if I ever did fall in love like how he is, and I didn't kill myself, I wouldn't cheat. Cheating is something scum does."

"Right. I enjoyed the kill yourself part though. You're an idiot." I steer us toward the house, fighting the breeze the whole way.

"Girls aren't part of the schedule. Finish my degree and get to the pros, that's it."

"Good luck with that schedule." I chuckle, remembering how I'd had one too. I used to have all kinds of rules.

"My dad never cheated. He was married for a pretty long time, and he never cheated before he died." He nods his head at the house casually, like he hasn't just dropped the dead-dad bomb. "I think I need to take a piss. This isn't the kind of house where you piss on the grass, is it?"

"No. My mom will kill you." I point to the large door at the far side of the courtyard. "Go through there and go to the first door on the right. I'll meet you upstairs."

"Roger that." He lifts a thumb in the air and staggers for the wrong door. We've been friends for years but he rarely comes here. There's a good chance of my mom hitting on him here.

"He's going to piss in your mom's planters."

Spinning around I come face to face with the girl I was just talking about. "He probably is." I don't even turn back to check on him. I don't care and I can't look away from her. I have a terrible feeling she won't be here if I do and this will be a drunk-induced hallucination.

Only she doesn't appear the way I would imagine her in this moment. She's different from everyone else at the party. She's in jeans, a parka, and a wooly hat—something Laramie would call a toque. "It's a cabin fever party." I point at her jeans. "Bathing suits and flowery shirts." I glance down at my own bare legs and flip-flops.

"Yeah, I gathered."

"How are you?" I ask too quickly, desperate for her. It's the weirdest feeling, but I don't bother fighting it. I gave up on that the moment I lost her.

"Good. I just came to bring a bunch of your stuff. I wouldn't have stopped in if I'd known there was a party."

"It's in the boathouse. Everyone's down there." I shiver slightly from the cold air on my bare arms and legs but fight looking cold. "Wanna come in?" She came to this house to be rid of me and my things, knowing I never come here. She wanted to avoid me.

"No." She says it breathy, in almost a whisper. Her face is filled with regret, but I don't know which part she's thinking about. Which acts she regrets. I suspect it's all the moments I wouldn't change, even if my life depended on it. They flash in the back of my mind, each one slicing me.

She bites her lip, maybe fighting saying something she'll also regret, maybe just to avoid talking until she mutters, "It was a good game tonight."

"I miss you." I ignore her small talk and lay my heart out there for her to reject. I'm already exposed to the elements; I might as well be naked in every way. She's the only person who has ever seen me vulnerable. Well, along with Charles and Benson, but they're like parents so they don't count. "I'm a fucking idiot."

"I know." Her expression changes for a second, possibly a twitch, but she doesn't say anything. She waves and turns. "I have to go."

"Wait." I jog over and spin her around. "Wait." I say it softer the second time. "Don't go." I step in closer, brushing her hair away from her face. "Stay with me."

She lifts her gaze that hardens when her eyes meet mine. "Why?"

"Because I need you." I drop to my knees, in the snow. "Forgive me. I'm crazy about you and I fucked up."

Her lips toy with a smile but her eyes are flooded with emotions. She blinks, losing some of them down her cheeks. "Try not to get too drunk, Beast. You have a game in two days." She pulls out of my hands and turns away, leaving me there to freeze to death.

It's not the snow and the cold that will be the death of me.

It's my own stupidity.

Chapter One
Beer-soaked boobies

Sami

Oxford Circus, London
January 1, 2012
5:03 am

Walking past Banana Republic, I look at the blouse on the mannequin and then down at the beer-soaked dress I'm wearing, wishing I could say someone else dumped the pitcher on my chest.

I also wish I had the balls to just smash the window, take her clothes, and leave mine on her. A new outfit might offer a new perspective or even a new opportunity for an otherwise wasted night—wasted life.

Even with the night long gone and the morning here, cold and damp as usual, I don't feel any newness in the New Year.

I suspect it'll be the same crap year I just had, only this one I'm graduating. That is one bonus, a little more freedom from my parents.

I shiver as I stroll, hating that London and New York share the same wintery weather, and I can't say I like either version. Wrapping my arms around myself to stay warm, I want to regret staying in London the extra week but I can't. The South of France might have been a better spot to party with far better weather, but London taught me something I didn't know. An important life lesson: boyfriends are bullshit. Love is bullshit. People pretending to be in love is the biggest bullshit.

I'm glad I'm free of Drew, that moron. I can't believe I dated him for three months. It's my new record. Actually, the part I can't believe is that I made it past the first week. His being a Londoner likely helped. We didn't see much of each other.

My feet are killing me, so I pull off my Louboutin boots and slip on the Tieks I have in my purse. Luckily, I brought my hobo bag instead of a traditional New Year's clutch. I stuff the boots into the bag and sigh as the teal ballet flats bring me back to life. Pins and needles join the sensation of blood rushing back into my feet.

I look ridiculous in flats with my short midnight-colored cocktail dress, but the boots had run out of blocks left in them four streets back. The ballet flats can go all night, or all day rather.

As I continue down the dark street I glimpse my haggard reflection in a shadowy window and jump. I stop to stare at the mess I am and contemplate calling a car. But by the time the driver gets out of bed, in the car, and here, I could be home in bed.

I drum my nails against my lip, staring at my absurd ensemble in the glass, trying to recall when I saw a cab last.

Normally, Oxford Circus is flooded with them, but in the wee hours of the morning there's no one here.

The street gets chillier—no, creepier—as I do a full circle and see nothing and no one around me.

I'm alone, in London, in the dark. Like in one of those stupid movies Nat made me watch where the world ends and God forgot to tell the star of the show. She's alone in the city with her dog and zombies.

Being alone creeps me out more than anything, stuck with only the sound of my own voice and the empty echo of the wind.

I turn and rush past the shops, searching for the tube. There's one around here somewhere. I map it on my phone, walking faster as I turn the corners, past the rounded edges of the old gray buildings.

While I've been to London more times than I can count, I've only ridden the tube a handful of times. But it's five in the morning, and I'm still a bit drunk and not in the mood to wait, and it's doubtful I will happen upon a cab.

I hurry to the entrance to the underground, slightly smiling at the red circle with the blue stripe but losing the happy expression when I see it's not open. My shoulders slump as my plan crashes. It's exactly the end of the miserable night I should have seen coming.

I want to lift my head to the night sky and ask exactly what I did to deserve this, but I think I know the answer so I just stare at the closed doors.

"Shit. Is it closed?"

I jump, turning to find a guy close to my age with an American accent. "Yeah." I say, trying to slow my breaths from the shock of meeting a stranger in the dark.

"Well, that sucks." He looks partied out, wearing a rumpled midnight-blue suit that almost matches my dress. His silvery white dress shirt is loose around his neck and the tie is gone, ripped off no doubt, evident in the way his stiff collar is sitting to one side. The lipstick on his cheek, noticeable in the faint glow of the streetlights, is smeared and too pink for his tanned skin tone, so I have to assume a lady friend tore off his tie and wrinkled his suit.

Dry humping will do that every time.

His eyes trail my dress and then his suit. "We look like we planned our outfits."

"Yeah." I bite my lip, recognizing him from somewhere and hoping it isn't some nasty one-night stand. I hate the awkwardness of "I've seen you naked and not at your finest, but now we're at a café with other people so let's pretend we've never met."

"Well, this is bullshit," he mutters but I'm stuck staring at his clothes. His calfskin wingtip dress shoes with their burnt reddish hue are exactly the shoes I would have picked for that suit. But he doesn't seem like the metro type who would know haute couture from a sale at Bloomingdale's.

Did the lipstick dress him? Did she force the suit and tie?

"Well, shit. For a city known for its cabs, I haven't seen a black cab in an hour."

"Are you for real?" I tilt my head.

"What?" He gives me a lazy grin, the kind that normally ends with my skirt up around my waist.

"You can't say black cab. That's racist." I scoff at him. "And most of the cabbies here are white."

"Seriously?" He laughs. "This your first time here?"

"No."

"Whatever." He jerks his head to the right. "I'm headed this way. You wanna walk and see if we can't find a cab? It might not be safe for you to walk alone."

"No. I'll call a car." I lift my phone and groan, "Never mind. My phone's dying at this very moment, because why not?" I sneer as the swirling image hits the screen and it goes dark. "Shit."

"Mine died hours ago. Not that I would recall the number to my car. I don't even know my own phone number." He yawns. "Look, it's like fifty degrees out. I'm freezing. Let's just walk. You shouldn't be out at this time of night anyway. Where are you going?"

"Hyde Park."

"Me too." He sounds tired. "Come on." He takes his jacket off and puts it around my shoulders, offering me his arm.

"Thanks." He's a gentleman. I should be leery of the stranger-danger thing, but he's American, and I can't help but trust one polite American over the possibility of meeting a group of random guys in an alley while I have no cell phone.

"No prob." He takes in a deep inhale and smiles. "I love London at night. There's no traffic."

"I've never seen London this early."

"Or late." He's chipper for the hour.

"No."

We walk past the old buildings while he natters on about random things, and I focus on not noticing how sexy he is. The lipstick is like garlic to a vampire for me so it's easy to avoid flirting, but I can't help but appreciate the work of art he is.

The dim lights are just bright enough to note his perfect suit body. Not only is he big and tall, but the pants are clearly tailored to show it off. The way his ass sort of lifts the pants draws my gaze. He doesn't have a big ass but he's got a fit one—perky maybe.

In the dress shirt, his shoulders and arms are massive, stretching the material just slightly. It's a good look, apart from the lipstick on his cheek and shirt showing he's already had a ride tonight. He's actually got other girl on him, at this moment, which for me is up there with cologne I don't like.

But who am I to criticize?

At least he hasn't got half a brewery on him.

"So where are you from?" He lifts a hand, halting me. "Wait—let me guess. I think I'm good at this. I noticed a bit of a New York accent there, only the refined side of the city. You're an Upper East Side, Hamptons brat, aren't you? A debutante or something like that." His eyes dazzle and I love the fact he has no idea who I am.

"Something like that."

"I'm kind of from Kentucky, but I've been living in the North longer than I ever lived in the South."

"Cool."

He's stupid hot. How is it when I've had the worst night ever, the beer-soaked clothes prove it, I run into the hottest guy in London?

God hates me, that's why.

The way this guy talks and walks reeks of polite confidence, my kryptonite. Not just cute boys though. I like cute boys who know they're cute, even covered in kiss marks, who have enough manners and poise to say and do whatever they want while not being a dick. Not because they can't be a dick but because they choose not to be. Like a billionaire who chooses to fight crime at night. It's a fine line to be cool, confident, and forward without being a bossy jerk.

"I'm—" He offers a hand.

"Let's not," I cut him off, not wanting him to know my name. All this relaxed walking and me staring will end. He'll know me straightaway. And then it'll be him staring and me feeling awkward. Not to mention, he'll see the outfit and sell the story, and I'll be in for another stint of rag magazine rehab, the only kind that counts in my world. No one cares that I've never set foot in a rehab clinic. They care that the magazines and gossip say I have.

"Not what?"

"Not introduce. Let's just let this be a random London meet up. Two lost Americans needing someone to walk with while they wait for a damned cab." I roll my eyes. "Black cab, no less."

"It's a thing." He chuckles. "The black cabs are a traditional British cab called a hackney carriage. They're custom-made even, just for the cab companies. I got the spiel from my driver. I swear, it's a thing."

"If you say so." I lift my deadened phone into the air. "I'm googling it when I get home."

"Do it." He gives me that cheeky grin again. "So what brings you to London on New Year's?"

"My dad insisted we spend Christmas as a family, and he had to be in London so we all came here. Of course. And then I met up with an old friend and my boyfriend and we ended up going to a party."

"You don't sound happy about it."

"I'm not."

"Is that why you looked lost?"

"What?" I give him a sideways glance.

"When I saw you back there, at the tube station, you looked lost but maybe more than that." Something about the way he says it makes the moment real, not small and friendly so I am real back.

"Yeah. I just don't understand how I fall for the stupid stuff guys do every time. They do little things in the beginning that make me think they're something they're not and trick me, but I fall for it every time."

"Like what?"

"Like guys who kiss the top of girls' heads, hovering there for a moment like they're breathing us in. We're suckers for that shit. And the worst part is, I see them for who they are when they date my friends. But I end up with blinders on when it comes to me. Like I forget the guys who say the right things at the right moments are the ones who have practiced it a lot. The Mr. Collinses of the world. I need to date a guy who says all the wrong things because he's clearly never tricked a girl into being in love with him."

His confused face tells me he doesn't get my Jane Austen reference, but he stays with the general topic of conversation. "Is that how your New Year's fell apart? A guy who says all the right things?"

"Yeah. It's like a magic trick and I fell for it again. Anyway, what brought you here?" I don't want to talk about my New Year's Eve, at all.

"Hockey."

"Weird. Is hockey a big thing in England? Do they even have ice here? I thought it was all soccer and rugby."

"Hockey's bigger than you think." He grins. "I mean it's not huge—it's not like it is in Canada or something, but they have a couple teams that are all right."

"And you play?" The question is laden in disbelief. He said driver a minute ago and now he plays hockey? The driver, the beautiful suit, and the shoe ensemble would all suggest otherwise. But his body does scream athlete, especially the way his arms stretch his sleeves even when he's relaxed.

"Yeah." I like the way he smiles when he says it.

"Are you any good?"

He looks as though he might answer but then he laughs. "I thought we weren't getting to know each other. Just a random passing."

That makes me grin back. "You're right."

"Can I at least ask why you're soaked in beer?" He raises one of his eyebrows.

"How do you know it's beer?" His question makes me uneasy. He might have been there and followed me.

"You reek of it. I could smell it across the road when I crossed for the tube. I thought it was either a homeless person or a brewery."

"Oh." I laugh. "It was for five hundred dollars." I press my lips together, totally ashamed.

"I have to hear this story."

"I was partying and my boyfriend turned into a complete ass face so I left and ended up at a pub, the Prince of Wales, over by Kensington Palace. Anyway, there was an impromptu wet tee shirt contest." I cut the story there. "I won." I almost smile but the memory of pulling down my strapless dress and pouring beer on my bare boobs to win isn't something I want to share. I still can't believe I did it. I don't even know why I did.

No, that's not true.

I do know why and the look on his face still makes it worthwhile.

"That's hilarious. Your handbag costs over five grand, but you soaked your boobs in beer for five hundred bucks. Didn't see that coming. Not in a blue dress anyway. Shouldn't it be white?"

"I guess." I laugh with him. "I didn't see it happening either. It was a spur of the drunken moment. It was a stupid end to a bullshit night at the end of a week of bullshit nights at the end of a bullshit year."

"Well, I hope this is part of the perfect start of a new year." He says it in a way that suggests he might be hitting on me.

"Do you know where we are?" I don't want him to hit on me. I mean I do, but not right this moment. I am covered in beer and sweat and God knows what else.

He lifts his gaze from me to the buildings around us. "No."

"Great." I shiver as a black car comes around the corner.

"A black cab!" he shouts like an excited little kid and rushes forward, lifting his hand and whistling loud.

The cab stops in the middle of the road as he hurries to it. He gets the door and grins at the cabbie. "You need to tell her this is called a black cab and I'm not a racist."

I climb in to find a well-dressed English gentleman and a spacious backseat.

"I cannot say whether you're a racist, but you're quite right about the name of the car, sir. Black cab. Now where to?" The cabbie has a thick accent, the kind that Jon Snow has in *Game of Thrones*.

"One Hyde Park," I fight the urge to ask him to say, "You know nothing, Jon Snow."

"I'm not going to say I told you so. Because the man said it for me."

"Whatever." I get comfortable in the chair, excited to be sitting in warmth.

We drive past the Marble Arch and turn toward my apartment and I feel the strangest sensation. We've laughed and joked and I told him something I've never said aloud before. And I don't even know who he is, but I swear we've met before.

I turn to suggest we exchange names now that the night is over and we probably will never see each other again, but by the look in his eyes, he's beaten me to it.

"I have to, I'm sorry," he says as he frowns and raises his hands to my cheeks, lifting my face gently with only his fingertips, but he doesn't move in. He stays here, close in proximity but not enough. Our breath dances in front of our faces for a heartbeat before he finally bends forward slightly, brushing a trace of a kiss on me.

He parts my lips with his, slipping his tongue against mine. His hands slide down my arms and pull me into him, into the kiss and the passion that was slowly building and has now burst.

My hands lift to his hair, hauling him down to me, smothering me with him. He wraps around me as his hands roam my back.

The cab stops, jerking us both forward, and he pulls back, taking all the warmth and magic with him.

It takes a second for me to get my breath or open my eyes.

When I do he grins and winks. "Nice not meeting you, Deb." He gets out of the car and walks down the road like none of this ever happened.

I lift my gaze to the driver. "What do I owe you?"

"The gentleman already paid." He winks too. "That's some kiss huh, miss?"

My cheeks flush and I climb out of the car. "Some kiss." I watch him walk down the road, hoping he'll look back. But he doesn't. He turns the corner and he's gone.

Deb?

Why did he think my name was Deb?

A strange sadness aches inside me as I walk up to the apartment, but it's replaced with something else, delight.

I press the elevator and nod at the steel doors. "Perfect start to a new year."

The hint of his kiss still on my mouth, mixed with the ache of knowing I won't ever see him again, is the perfect aftertaste for the theme of the entire trip.

Especially as my phone goes nuts and the picture of me with the pitcher of beer pouring over my boobs flashes in Messenger.

Get your copy of Puck Buddies!!

Tara Brown

Tara Brown

I write, therefor I am—I think.

I grew up in a really small town.
I think being from a small town gives a person a little advantage when it comes to the imagination. You need one or you go mad from boredom...
I am happily married with two girls.
I feel like according to my age I am meant to be responsible and adult-like, but it isn't going well at all. I would still head off to Hogwarts tomorrow and I suspect there isn't a single wardrobe I haven't crept into, hoping to find the door to Narnia.
Thankfully, I am an international bestseller so I have wormed my way into the "Quirky" or Eccentric" category.
Thank God for that.

I am represented by Natalie Lakosil from the Bradford Literary Agency and published traditionally with Montlake Romance.

Made in the USA
Columbia, SC
08 November 2017